DREAMER

L. E. DELANO

Swoon
READS

Swoon Reads | NEW YORK

A Swoon Reads Book
An imprint of Feiwel and Friends and Macmillan Publishing Group, LLC
175 Fifth Avenue, New York, NY 10010

Dreamer. Copyright © 2018 by L. E. DeLano.
Excerpt from Traveler copyright © 2017 by L. E. DeLano.

Our books may be purchased in bulk for promotional, educational,
or business use. Please contact your local bookseller or the Macmillan
Corporate and Premium Sales Department at (800) 221-7945 ext. 5442
or by e-mail at MacmillanSpecialMarkets@macmillan.com.

Library of Congress Control Number: 2017944695

ISBN 978-1-250-10042-9 (trade paperback) / ISBN 978-1-250-10043-6 (ebook)

First edition, 2018

1 3 5 7 9 10 8 6 4 2

swoonreads.com

This one is dedicated to my readers.
I couldn't have written this book without your
excellent feedback and your unflagging support.
I owe you, every one of you. Thanks so much!

Prologue

HE RAN FOR THE TREES AS HARD AS HE COULD, PANTING with the effort as he pushed his screaming muscles into overdrive. He could hear his pursuers, but he didn't waste time with a backward glance.

A shot ricocheted off a nearby tree, and he dodged right, then left, zigzagging as he ran. Not much farther now—but they were gaining on him. He could hear the barking of dogs, which meant they had a full squad in pursuit.

It was going to be close. He sucked in air like a starving man, feeling the burn in his legs and chest as he swung his arms harder, propelling himself forward.

"There he is!" he heard one shout. "There! In the trees!"

"Stop him before he makes the edge!" another called.

"Yes, sir!" A chorus of voices this time.

Another shot hit a large boulder, sending shards of blasted rock into his shin as he passed by. He stumbled a bit but kept on going, feeling the sharp sting of the rock as it dug into his flesh, the trickle of blood as it ran down his leg. He knew he had to be close.

Suddenly, a break in the trees. He heard them shouting to one another as he moved out of the protection of the trunks and boughs, into the open. He didn't pause to gather himself, he just kept on running right off the edge, feeling his stomach lurch as the world dropped out from beneath him.

The fall down to the water took far longer than he expected, and he hit with tremendous force. In the fuzzy aftermath, he reasoned that the fall was probably a good thing—he'd be harder to shoot from far away. He kicked his legs and pushed hard for the surface, lungs feeling like they were exploding after the oxygen starvation brought on by his frantic run.

His head broke the water and he risked a glance up. He'd been right—a full squad of soldiers was assembled on the ridge, and he heard the whiz of a bullet striking the water a few yards away. He dove under again, swimming for the cliff wall, spying a small overhang where he could shelter for a moment and catch his breath.

He surfaced out of sight, panting and treading water, taking measure of his surroundings. They'd be expecting him to run for home, most likely. Or find his way up the far slope of the cliff. He pushed closer to the lip of the overhang, noting only one soldier now—presumably to stand watch—and pulled himself back under. If he could follow the riverbank down three miles to the tributary—that would take him to the freight depot. From there, a train. It was a solid plan.

He pushed out from under the overhang on the far side, ducking under and swimming as far as he could, surfaced for an instant, and went under again. He kept it up, scoping out a spot close to the trees on the opposite side. A swift glance showed no one watching, and he burst from the water, slapping at it as he waded quickly toward the bank. Once there, he gave one more look around before he squatted down. He dug quickly into the dirt at the water's edge, forming a small pool of still water. He shifted his body so that his shadow didn't cloud it over, letting the sun shine on it in full force.

"Sorry, mate," he said to his reflection. "Didn't mean to leave it this way, but I really do have somewhere else to be."

And with a jaunty salute, he touched his fingers to the reflection, and he was through.

1

Needless Jeopardy

I'M STARING AT THE BARREL OF A GUN. IT'S BLACK AND there are grooves on the handle. A finger is on the trigger and I feel my whole body begin to shake.

I know what guns do, and it hasn't been long enough since I've seen one pointed at another person. My hands curl into fists as I feel the helpless rage rush through me. I need to do something. I glance left, then right, then back at the gun. There's still time—I can run for help, if I can just get to the door before I'm seen.

If I was anywhere but where I was, I would have made it.

I step back into the aisle of the convenience store, behind a display of sunglasses, and as I pass a display for beef jerky, the edge of my hoodie catches on one of the hooks and the whole thing tilts over with a screech of metal. The man whirls instantly, turning the gun on me, and I freeze, putting my hands up, still staring at that gun.

Crap.

Here's where I get yelled at.

"Shall we go on?" Mario asks sharply as he gestures to the scene appearing on the whiteboard behind him—a replay of my last assignment.

For the last six weeks these assignments have been my life. I've been out every day shifting into other realities, making corrections and living other versions of my life. I was grateful for the distraction at first, and it's always interesting to see who I could have been if fate had sent things another way, but lately it's been dragging me down, making all these little changes in somebody else's world.

We're sent to the other realities because we're too invested in our own. We'd want to check up on the changes we made, or put our own spin on them based on our familiarity with the world we're in. But I've learned that it's not always so easy to stay out of someone else's business—especially when someone else is still you. There are so many variables.

Mario keeps track of all that—that's what Dreamers do. They guide Travelers as they make the tiny changes in other realities that end up rippling into bigger changes somewhere down the line. We meet up here, in this white classroom with its vivid red door—which is not really reality but a construct I go to when I dream. Here I get my assignments, and here I get debriefed. Or yelled at.

"I remembered to ask the guy at the counter for directions," I say, wincing.

Mario gives me a stony look. "Let's rewind and see how we got here, shall we?"

He passes a hand in front of the whiteboard and the scene devolves, coalescing into a shot of the convenience store and me walking in. I spot my target right away and head straight to the counter, asking him for directions to Stilton Street. He draws me a map on the back of a napkin, I thank the counter guy for his help, and then—I break protocol.

The magazines here all have holographic covers, and it throws me. I'm fascinated by the 3-D effect, and I pause instead of moving on.

I take my time looking at each one before I turn to leave, but I'm interrupted by the front door slamming open so hard it nearly shatters the glass. A man with a gun in his hand heads straight for the counter as I stare, wide-eyed.

"Open the register," he says, pointing the gun right in the clerk's face.

I realize this isn't the best place to be right now, so I start slowly backing down the aisle—and then accidentally snag on the beef jerky display, which rocks and then topples to the ground.

The robber pivots, leveling the gun on me.

Suddenly, the counter guy springs into action. He leaps over the counter and slams into the robber, throwing him to the ground. The gun goes off, hitting the soda machine, which lets out a loud hiss. Another clerk runs out from the back, shrieks, and then presses the alarm button, setting off a claxon that can surely be heard on the street. I leap back as the two men struggle before me.

Then I notice the gun—it must've fallen from the robber's hand when he hit the ground. I start to reach for it, and then I stop myself. Then I reach for it again, and I'm hyperventilating.

I've never held a gun in my life.

But *this* me has.

I pick up the gun—it's a semiautomatic handgun—a Taurus

PT 111. Somehow, I know that. I quickly use my thumb to press in on the magazine release. I toss the magazine into a trash can nearby, and I slide the gun across the floor under the displays, as far away as I can.

A moment later, sirens cut the air, and the robber is on his feet, looking around frantically for his gun. He locks eyes with me, and for a moment, I wonder if he's going to come after me, but I suppose he decides he's better off running. He's out the door in a flash.

"You okay?" I ask the clerk. He gives me a nod, holding a napkin to his bleeding mouth, and I head for the door. "His gun is under the candy display, over there," I say. "I'm going to go get some air."

I can hear him calling after me as I run for the door, and I keep on running, slowing down a few blocks away and putting my fingers to the window of an empty storefront in order to transfer myself back to my reality.

My mother had been more than a little shocked to see me shaking and panting as I stood in front of the microwave with my hand on the door, but I imagine my counterpart was equally surprised to be waiting for popcorn one minute and hyped up on adrenaline and dripping sweat in the next.

"So . . . ," Mario says, turning away from the dimming scene on the whiteboard. "How do you think that went?"

I wince. "You mean my nearly getting killed?"

He stares at me stonily. "You were supposed to get in there and then get out. Leave the store, head to the laundromat next door, transfer back from the bathroom."

"It all came out okay," I defend myself weakly. Honestly,

seeing it all happen again is making my palms sweat. I know I'm in the dreamscape, but I wonder if I'll wake up with sweaty palms.

"You didn't complete the assignment," he says. "If you'd gone into the laundromat, a young mother who was there would have seen you and remembered to call her brother's ex-girlfriend because she owns that same shirt. There were big ripples on this one. Big."

"Good to know you're so concerned about me," I grumble.

"You had a job to do and only did part of it," he snaps. "And if you'd left right after you did what you were supposed to do, you wouldn't have been looking down the barrel of a gun."

"You could have told me what was going to happen!"

"It wasn't even a probability at the time I briefed you," Mario said. "There were too many variables that still hadn't fallen into place. Free will changes the way the future unfolds, and that's part of why you're sent to make corrections in the first place."

I straighten my shoulders. "I handled it."

"You shouldn't have had to." Mario runs his hand through his hair so hard that it would have yanked out strands if he were human. "Let's salvage something from this," he finally says, leaning back against his teacher's desk. "How did you know what to do with the gun?"

"I—the other Jessa, I mean—she knew about guns. My mom is dating a cop in her reality. He takes me out shooting sometimes."

"Exactly. So you searched through your applicable memories and drew on the knowledge that was necessary to work through the situation."

"I—yeah, I guess so."

"Not every job is going to go smoothly. The trick is to keep your wits about you—which is something you did manage to do. I'd still prefer you not take any chances—at least until we get Rudy and Eversor rounded up."

"It's been weeks without a sign of either one of them," I remind him. "Eversor hasn't tried to finish killing me, and Rudy is stripped of his Dreamer powers somewhere."

"Somewhere in the vast, undefined boundaries of the dreamscape," he reminds me. "He'll have to show himself sooner or later—and knowing how bent he was on his cause, my guess is sooner."

"That's what you said last week. And the week before." I don't even try to hide my irritation. "You've had me traveling out practically every day, and there's been no sign of him, or of Eversor."

"We were close last week," he defends himself. "You just missed her in that reality with the archaeological dig."

"You think. You don't *know*."

"I don't know what she's up to yet," he concedes. "But we've got them on the run, and that's half the battle."

"Maybe they've given up. They can't beat us."

He makes a slashing motion with his hand in refusal. "We can't afford to think that way. That may be just what they want—to lull us into dropping our guard. We have to stay vigilant—and *careful*."

"What do you think they could do that we wouldn't see coming?" I ask in exasperation.

"That's a good question," Mario snaps back. "And a rather frightening one, don't you think?" He turns back to the whiteboard, drumming his fingers against his chin as he studies it.

"I've got another assignment," he says. "It's short. Shouldn't take you more than fifteen minutes. I'll send you somewhere you've been before, so there won't be any surprises."

The scene comes to life behind him.

"Is that . . . Philadelphia?" I tilt my head, remembering the train station.

"Yes. You'll come through here at eight thirty," Mario tells me. "Buy a pack of Juicy Fruit gum. Then head down to platform four, get on the eight forty-five train. Take a seat at first, close to the door. You'll see a teenage girl with red hair—offer her a stick of gum. Once she gets off the train, stand up, grab one of the metal poles, and transfer back when you see yourself in it. It'll be good practice—using a bended reflection."

Mario has been adamant that I keep my skills sharp. He's right, of course. I need to stay in practice. And considering I haven't had much practice to begin with, I suppose I can't afford to slack off. I don't want to be cornered somewhere just because I'm not practiced enough to get myself out of there.

I shudder at the memory of how I nearly came to an end once just because I couldn't travel through water in dim light. That's not going to happen again. I even sleep with my compact mirror under my pillow now.

"Let's keep it simple," he tells me. "I've pushed you into all this far too quickly, and without the benefit of a mentor these last weeks."

That sentence hangs in the air between us, and the pain starts squeezing my belly, radiating up into my chest. Finn was my mentor. And Finn is gone.

"Fine." My voice is high and tight. I stride to the door and reach for the knob.

"I'm sorry, Jessa," Mario says quietly from behind me.

I step through without looking back and wake in my bed in the dark of my room, rubbing my chest as though I can make the pain go away. It doesn't work.

2

Escape

"JESSA KICKED HERSELF IN THE FACE!"

My brother is exuberant, bursting with this tidbit as I slide into my place at the dinner table. My mother's eyebrows go up and she shoots me a look.

"I didn't kick my face," I explain. "It was just a high kick."

"You could break your nose!" he countered. "You could have a bloody nose!"

"I don't, Danny," I say, turning to show him. "Look."

"Was it bloody before?" he asks. "When you kicked it?"

I try not to roll my eyes. Danny means well, and he certainly can't help it when his autism makes him dwell on something. But it does get tiring sometimes.

"Danny, enough. I'm fine, okay?"

"You shouldn't kick your face, Jessa," he admonishes again.

"So I'm guessing rehearsal went well today?" Mom asks as she passes me a bowl of green beans.

"It was all right. Saturday is dress rehearsal—costumes and on the stage."

"I can't wait to see it. You've been so secretive about it all, not letting me watch. You're not doing a striptease or anything, are you?" she quips.

"At a retirement home?"

"Just making sure."

"Don't kick anybody," Danny warns.

"I'll do my best," I promise, stretching my legs out in front of me and reaching down to rub my knee. My muscles feel a little sore; maybe I—or should I say, "she"—did overdo the kicks a little.

Six weeks ago, I traveled through a mirror and discovered yet another of the many selves I inhabit, in a multitude of alternate realities. This particular Jessa is a dancer, and in her reality, our mother is dead. I'm helping her out by swapping places two nights a week so she can perform for Mom. So, a week after my first transfer with her, I started taking dance.

I know it's been a real challenge for her, whipping my non-dancer body into shape in such a short period of time. Five weeks of dance classes normally wouldn't be enough to bring me up to her level of expertise, but when my body is just a vehicle being driven by a girl who's had dance classes for a couple of years, muscle memory is really the only hurdle. She put some definite memory into my muscles today.

"Sore?" Mom asks, watching me knead my calf.

"A little."

"You're really pushing yourself with this dance stuff."

"I know. I like it."

"You don't need to be so driven about it," she says. I see her eyes slide in my direction again, with that same worried look she's been wearing for more than a month now. I sigh inwardly, waiting for the other shoe to drop.

"You know, Jessa . . ."

Ugh. Here it comes.

"Maybe you should relax after the recital is over. Take some time off. I was talking to Mrs. Lampert about your schedule—"

My head snaps up. "Mrs. Lampert? When were you talking to my school counselor?"

"I e-mailed her last week and we were going back and forth—"

"Wait." I hold up a hand. "Why are you 'going back and forth' with Mrs. Lampert? I'm doing fine. My grades are good."

"This is about more than grades," Mom says. "She has some concerns, after all that's happened. And so do I."

I want to groan out loud. In the weeks that followed Finn's death—and Ms. Eversor's disappearance—all hell broke loose around here.

My former creative writing teacher, Ms. Eversor, apparently tendered her resignation at the high school the morning of our confrontation at the old Greaver mine. She left at lunchtime and never came back. That was only half of the scandal. She disappeared on the same day as another student—who happened to be male and more than a little good-looking. The last anyone heard, she had booked a flight to Mexico, probably to avoid prosecution. The speculation was that I'd lost my boyfriend to a predatory teacher. The looks I was and still am getting, the whispers, the talk that stops as soon as I come into a room (or worse, *doesn't* stop) are now finally dying down, but that doesn't make it any more bearable when it happens.

I was questioned in my mother's presence by an officer from the local police department regarding the incident, but since Finn was recorded as being just over eighteen, and the teacher had already resigned (and no one could find either one of them) the incident wasn't pursued further.

This, of course, led to a full-on sit-down talking-to from both of my parents, who could see how devastated I was over all this. They had no idea, of course, that I was being hunted by a reality-shifting teacher working on behalf of an immortal being who wants to wipe out most of the universe.

Add into all this the stress of college applications, facing the last semester of my senior year . . . and Finn's death. Let's just say it's a lot to deal with.

"I'm fine," I say tightly. "Everything is fine."

"You've been pushing yourself too hard," Mom says. "First with this dance thing and then with school. You spend all your free time up in your room studying and doing homework. It's like we never see you anymore. And when we do see you—well, you're different. Changed."

"That's because she kicked herself in the face," Danny interjects.

Mom lets out a long breath. "Now really isn't the time to have this conversation," she says.

"No, it's not," I snap. "We don't need to have it at all."

"Honey, what is *wrong* with you?" she asks. "Honestly, it's like you're a different person lately. You're so preoccupied."

It's been like this for weeks—she's always nudging, prodding me, trying to figure out why I've changed so much. I can't tell her what I've been through. I can't tell her that I'm different because I'm not always the Jessa she knows.

"I'm just stressed. I have a big assignment due," I grit out. I do have an assignment due, in creative writing.

"Well, if it's got you that wound up, you should work on it and get it out of the way. When is it due?"

"Tomorrow."

Her eyebrows go up. "Then you'd better get started."

"Yes, ma'am," I say, giving her a salute. My sarcasm goes over badly. I push away from the table and stomp up the stairs to my room.

"Jessa—"

"Don't kick yourself!" Danny calls after me.

I sink down onto my bed, wishing it could be that easy. If only I could kick myself in the head and forget all this.

I yank my messenger bag up onto the bed beside me and pull out my journal, tossing it aside. Then I reach for some loose-leaf paper and lay my binder on my lap like a desk as I stare at the blank sheets. I pick up my pen, tapping it impatiently on the edge of my binder, willing something—anything—to come to my mind.

It doesn't.

I throw the binder and papers to the floor, and then for good measure I hurl my journal at the wall. Between the chaos in my mind and the chaos downstairs, it's impossible to focus. Just impossible.

I stare at the mirror longingly. God, do I need to get away.

The traveling I did earlier today was to facilitate my newfound love of dance. That's strictly for me. And for my counterpart.

This next travel is a job, and unfortunately, I have more than an hour to kill until I need to step into another reality and become a different me.

I make a grumpy face at myself in the mirror, going over my assignment again in my mind.

I can hear Mom and Danny downstairs, and I know she's not through lecturing me. As soon as she clears the table, she'll come upstairs and I'll probably have to talk to her again.

I am in no mood for this. I need to escape, and today's assignment is exactly where I need to go. It's not really breaking the rules if I show up a little early, is it?

Part of me knows Mario might get irked, but I've been to this reality before. It's as safe as safe can be, and I really need to be there right now.

I move to the mirror over my dresser, laying my palm to the glass, concentrating on my other self.

Do me a favor, I mouth. I stare back at myself curiously at first, and then, to my surprise, I break into a wide grin and give myself a nod. I don't even pause to question my good fortune. One solid push and I am out of here.

3

Unexpected

I TAKE A MOMENT TO ADJUST TO WHAT I'M SEEING.

I am brilliant platinum bleach-blonde, and I am wearing entirely too much eyeliner. The first time I came here, I started to wipe it all off, but then I forced myself to leave it alone. I know how irked I get when the other Jessas screw with my face or my stuff while I'm gone. I still haven't grown out the bangs I got when one of the other Jessas hacked my hair off. I'm not a fan of this look, but I'm not going to screw with it.

Right now, I'm in a bathroom at what I think is a pizza place, judging by the pictures of pizza slices and Italian food framed on the walls, so I step away from the mirror and reach for the door. It opens forcefully from the other side at the same time, and before I can let out a squeak of surprise, my arm is being yanked and I am half tripping, half running along behind a familiar head of long, dark spiraled hair.

This is Olivia, and she is talking a thousand words a minute.

"They called your name! Come on! OhmyGod, Jessa, come on! You're not backing out of this! Come on!"

I let her pull me along as I chuckle at her over-the-top enthusiasm. Olivia is almost unbearably perky but not in an annoying way. She's crazy optimistic—which is very much unlike me over here.

This is only my second visit to this reality, and Olivia was an instant friend. No. More than a friend—a sister. Liv and I have been stepsisters for nearly four years, since Dad married Shanice—that's Olivia's mother. And I'm in Philadelphia, where Liv and I attend a private school.

"I don't know what you thought you were doing in there, but you are not getting out of this one! Come on!" She tugs me forward again.

"I was going to the bathroom!" I protest.

"Well, you were taking forever, and now it's time to pay the piper!"

She finally releases her death grip on my hand and gives me an enormous shove from behind as an older guy hands me a microphone. A spotlight hits me right in the face and I squint as my eyes adjust. I finally notice the crowd, and they're all staring at me.

The pieces begin to fall into place.

Oh my God. I'm singing karaoke. In front of people. A lot of people.

I don't sing.

I mean, I really, *really* don't sing.

My panicked eyes find Olivia, and she's doubled over, laughing, the traitor. I narrow my eyes back at her as the memory trickles in.

She bet me that I wouldn't score as high as her on my pre-collegiate interviews today. She was right. I didn't even come close, and I'm really perturbed about it, too.

And now I have to sing here at Martinetti's open mic karaoke night, as my loser's price.

"Liv . . . ," I mouth pleadingly.

"Sing!" she shouts back, and the crowd—many of whom go to school with us—echoes loudly behind her.

I let out a groan as the music comes blaring over the speakers.

My eyes widen and I give her a searing look.

"Oh, you did *not* do this to me . . . ," I grumble under my breath.

I am in no way, shape, or form qualified to sing "Somebody to Love" by Queen. Or anything, for that matter. But a bet is a bet, and my memories assure me that Olivia will never speak to me again if I don't honor our agreement. Dammit.

I open my mouth to sing, and nothing comes out. I swallow and try again. Something comes out this time, and I focus on the words scrolling on the video prompter in front of me. *Hey, I'm doing this! I'm singing!*

Then I look out at the crowd, most of whom are staring at me like I'm up here strangling a frog. Because that's what my voice sounds like. Like I'm strangling a frog. Oh God.

I shoot another panicked glance at Olivia, and she's smiling and shaking her head as if to say, *You're not getting out of this.*

I go back to looking at the prompter, and the irony of singing about dying a little when you wake up each morning isn't lost on me, the girl who's been murdered in more realities than I can count.

And with that thought, the tears rush to my eyes, and I blink them back furiously as I stare at a spot on the floor and try to pull myself together. My voice falters, and I'm really not sure I'm going to make it through this. My eyes swing back to Olivia again, but she's not there.

Instead, I feel her arm come around my shoulders from behind, and her hand wraps around mine on the mic as she starts to sing with me, and wow, can she wail. Her voice is amazing, and the crowd is singing along. So am I, for that matter, and I don't need my memories to tell me why I adore this girl. We end to thunderous applause as we join hands and take a bow. Then I hand the mic off and walk right out of the restaurant.

The cold hits me in the face, and a moment later, a blast of warm air as Olivia comes through the door, carrying my coat and my backpack.

"Hey," she says. "You did better than I thought you would."

"That's because I had you."

She bumps my shoulder with hers. "You've always got me. But damn, you really *can't* sing."

I roll my eyes at her. "I know. That was the whole point, right?"

"The point was to get your mind off today. You didn't do that bad, you know. Your score was still in the upper twenty-fifth percentile." She pulls me along as we head toward the train station. "Come on," she says. "We'll get coffee on the way."

As we walk and sip coffee, I use the time to catch myself up on my memories over here, because things here are more than a little different.

We've just completed three weeks of intensive testing through the school and after school as well. The school conducts practice sessions before we do the formal interview with our career actuaries, who will let us know what collegiate or technical school courses we'll be approved for. We had a set of preliminary interviews today and I lost points for being *too insubordinate and combative.*

"Dad and Shanice are going to kill me," I say matter-of-factly. "So is my mom, for that matter."

"So?" Olivia shrugs. "It's not like you can't leave it all behind anytime you want to."

I'm startled for a moment, and then I remember that Olivia knows everything. She knows I'm a Traveler. I told her more than a year ago, and so far, she's kept the secret.

"This is home, Liv. That means something. Even when I have the power to go anywhere, it still means something."

"I hear you. But things are what they are here, and it works— for most of us."

"We don't have a choice," I point out, ticking things off on my fingers. "Our aptitude and skills are tracked from preschool. We're sorted into classrooms by peer group. Once we finish our selected college and become established in our selected careers, we find a relationship actuary to determine our potential romantic interests. It's nuts!"

"That's not a requirement by law," she counters.

"It's practically unheard of to date someone who isn't actuary-selected."

"And again, you don't have to settle for that if you don't want to," Olivia says. She stops in her tracks and steps in front of me to look me dead-on. "Maybe you aren't meant to be stuck here. People like you—the system doesn't work for them. You're too—"

"Insubordinate and combative?"

"You laughed through the introductory interview," she reminds me.

I search back through my memories and I chuckle. "I couldn't help it. Mrs. Braden has ugly bug-brows. But I did answer all their questions."

"I feel like I babbled a lot." Olivia groans as she starts walking again. "And why did I wear this stupid dress? It's like wearing a corset, it's so tight."

I glance over at her and then realize with a start that I've met her before, at a grand ball in a steampunk reality, right before I went out to the garden to see . . .

I can't help but smile a little at the memory of a certain flirty pirate, even though the memory is followed up by a shaft of pain. I barely knew Olivia over there.

"You wanted to make a good impression," I remind her.

"And you wanted to buck the system," she says smartly. "Jeans? Really?"

"Maybe the system needs a good bucking."

She sighs. "Fine. I'm just saying . . . play their game until you're old enough to be on your own, and then you've got no limits. Except for singing."

"Thanks," I say awkwardly. I should probably tell her I'm not her Jessa, but that would create a whole world of trouble for my counterpart if Liv thinks she welched on a bet.

That thought snaps me back to reality. I have a job to do and

I forgot about it. I check the time and I'm relieved to see I have twenty minutes left.

"I'm not going back to the dorm," I tell her.

"What?"

"I have to catch a different train."

"Where are you going? We have a test in biology tomorrow to study for."

"I know," I say apologetically. "I won't be gone long. I just have something to do."

"Something—" she starts to protest and then her eyes go wide with realization. "*Oh.* You better be back by ten."

"I will."

She gives me an impulsive hug. "I'm sorry I put you through that tonight. I should have chosen a different song."

"It's okay." I shift uncomfortably and glance up at the clock on the platform.

"All this stuff will fall into place, Jessa," she says. "We just gotta have a little faith in the system. Who knows." She shrugs. "Maybe they'll find your soul mate someday."

"Right." I give her a nod, even though I think what she's saying is total bunk. She gives me a wave as she boards her train, and then she's gone.

I can hear the announcements for the various trains coming over the loudspeaker, and I have ten minutes until my train leaves.

I take the escalator up so I can change platforms and I wander around the newsstand for a few minutes, killing time. I'm just about to head down again when I remember with a jolt that I'm supposed to buy a pack of Juicy Fruit gum. Crap!

I dig out the money and slap the gum down on the counter, drumming my fingers as the clerk rings me up. Finally he gives me my change, I swipe the gum up, shoving it into the front pocket of my hoodie, and race for the platform. I'm almost there when the gum slips out and hits the ground.

I hesitate. Mario told me specifically to buy it, so I could offer it to the girl in the seat next to me. He wouldn't have mentioned it if it weren't an important detail. I need to get it, and I need to get that train. I start to bend down, when a hand appears, grabbing the pack of gum and holding it out to me.

"Thanks," I mumble, and as we both straighten up, I feel all the air in the universe rush into my lungs, and my heart freezes in my chest. I am immobile, my eyes locked with his.

Finn.

His hair is cut differently—a little spiky, with sideburns that travel a bit farther down his jaw. He has a bump on the bridge of his nose like it's been broken at some point in time. It doesn't look bad, but I fixate on it, because I know if I look at those green, green eyes, I'm going to make a sound no human being should make.

"Hey. . . ." He speaks, and the word wraps around me, warm and familiar, the timbre and the slight hesitation as he tries to break the ice. Oh God. The sound of it flows into me like a hot knife in my chest, and before I'm even conscious of it, I turn and run.

I make it through the doors just as they close behind me. The car is very crowded, and I reach for the metal pole to steady myself, not even remembering that's exactly what I'm supposed to do.

As the train pulls away from the platform, I see his face

through the windows, staring in at me, his eyes carrying a question, and I look away. I put a second hand on the pole, aware that I am shaking almost violently.

It takes me nearly ten minutes to be able to focus past the turmoil in my brain, the rocking of the train, the jostling of the people around me, and the curve of the pole, covered in fingerprints. I take a few deep breaths, forcing myself to focus, and then I am back.

But not in my room. This is the bathroom at Mugsy's, and I'm lost.

I throw myself down on the floor in the corner, and the tears come again, tears I've held back for weeks, sobs that rip through me and force me from my formerly peaceful little place of nothingness. I'm holding my knees and I'm rocking.

You will find him again, Mario had warned me once. But so far he's respected my grief and my wishes and limited my dreams to actual memories of Finn—and blessedly few of them. I'd been lulled and let myself believe I could just erase it all somehow by erasing him. As if I could ever erase him.

I get back to my feet, and there on the sink, directly below the mirror, is my journal, opened to a random blank page that isn't so blank anymore. She left me a message:

> *Thanks for getting me out of karaoke night.*
> *Sorry you have to walk home but Mario*
> *made me come to Mugsy's to do a correction.*
> *He's pissing me off lately.*
> *I don't think we're making any headway*
> *and I'm so done with this.*

I can feel her anger as she wrote it—not that it's a stretch, because I feel it, too. Six weeks since Finn died and we're no closer to knowing where Rudy is or Eversor is, and what's Mario's solution? Putting me in a position to come face-to-face with another Finn, without a word of warning. Dammit. I forgot to give the girl her Juicy Fruit gum. If Mario has the balls to confront me about that after what he just put me through . . .

I should head for home, but I know I can't do it. I just can't pretend I'm okay. I should have stayed where I was, taken another train back. I really need Liv. But I can probably never go back there—not now that things have been set in motion. That Jessa will find her Finn again, or he'll find her.

I rub my chest, because I swear to God, it feels like there's a knife in there right now. I can't sit here in Mugsy's all night, but the thought of walking home alone in the dark, sobbing, just adds to my misery.

I reach for my phone, punching in a number, and within seconds, the voice on the other end answers.

"St. Clair?"

"I need a friend." It rushes out and I don't care how it sounds. I need a shoulder. I need my friend.

Ben picks up on the tone of my tear-clogged voice immediately. "You at home?"

"Mugsy's." I can barely get the word out.

"I'll be right over. Hang tight."

"Thanks."

I put the phone back in my pocket and I realize my hand is

shaking. My mind plays over the scene again, the train platform, the sound of Finn's voice, the look in those green eyes as the train pulled away. . . .

I look over at my reflection in the mirror, and I wonder how much time she'll have with him.

4

Tired

MARIO IS WAITING FOR ME, AND HE DUCKS HIS HEAD IN a guilty gesture that makes me want to punch him. As it is, I stare at him soundlessly, with my hand curling into a fist.

"Jessa."

"So you're actually going to face me?"

"I'm the Dreamer who sent you there, and I'll take full responsibility for it. I'm sure you realize it wasn't an accident."

"An accident?" I let out a choked laugh. "There are no 'accidents' with you people! You plan and manipulate and arrange everything, don't you?"

"Jessa—"

"And who's going to stop you? It's no big deal, right? It's just my heart! Just my life!" I turn my back on him, too furious to continue.

"You can't avoid him forever."

"Why can't I? Who's it hurting for me to avoid him?"

Mario folds his arms across his chest. "It's hurting you," he tells me, "though you probably can't see it that way right now."

"Oh, ya think?" The sarcasm is dripping off my words, and I lean back against his desk. "I'm tired, Mario. I'm traveling too much, my mom is getting really suspicious, and now you pull *this* on me. This was supposed to be a routine job."

"You mean the job you didn't complete? Again?" he asks pointedly.

"Don't start with me." My eyes flash a warning that he completely ignores as he studies me for a moment, stroking his chin thoughtfully.

"Come on," he finally says. "I've got something to show you."

He steps over to the red door and opens it, and I follow him through and into the dreamscape. We're in someone's backyard in what looks like an average suburban neighborhood. Mario now looks like a postal worker, complete with a bagful of letters slung over his shoulder.

"The girl you were supposed to offer the gum to was going to be reminded of an old family friend who happened to always carry Juicy Fruit gum," he tells me, pointing the girl out as she walks past us. She doesn't notice us because this is just a dream Mario is using to illustrate his point. We're merely observers as he shows me the future that could have been.

"The friend is like a second mother to her," he goes on, and the scene changes in front of us. It looks like we're on a farm or something, and Mario is now in overalls and a John Deere hat.

"She's going to make a point to visit the friend next month," he tells me. "While she's there, she's going to remark about a suspicious mole on a neighbor's arm."

My forehead creases in confusion as I try to follow the chain of events. "She saves somebody from cancer?" I ask.

"No, it's not just about that," Mario says, waving a hand to change the scene again—this time to an older man sitting on a hospital bed, with a younger woman and a nurse in attendance.

"The cancer is there," Mario says, pointing. "But it's in the early stages. The neighbor will get the treatment he needs, and his daughter will drive him to his doctor appointments. The daughter will get to know the cute radiologist at the hospital, and they'll begin a relationship. The radiologist has an ex-girlfriend who'll be heartbroken to see him move on, and she'll take nearly a year to recover from it. During that time, she starts playing guitar again—just like she needs to."

"Why?"

"That's another story that leads to a half dozen others," Mario tells me, reaching for the knob on the red door that's in the center of the hospital room wall. He opens it and I follow him back through into the classroom.

"So this guy might die of cancer and his daughter will never find true love because I screwed up—is that what you're saying?" I wrap my arms around myself again, feeling twice as miserable as I did when I got here.

"I'm reminding you that one little correction can reset the course of dozens, maybe even hundreds of lives. We need you—*you* need you," he amends, "to be the absolute best you can be as a Traveler. It's critical, especially in light of current events. Working around Finn is a handicap we can't afford you to have."

"If Rudy was going to come after me, he would have done it already. I haven't encountered Eversor once—*anywhere*."

"Yet," Mario adds.

"At all! And I'm not the only one who's tired of spinning my wheels with you. The other Jessas are tired of this, too. We've been leaving notes for each other complaining about all of this—and you."

Mario looks surprised. "You're ganging up on me?"

"We talk. And we're all in agreement. We think you're wasting our time."

He sucks in a breath, as if to draw patience from it, and lets it out slowly. "We'll talk about this later," he says. "You need some time after this one. Take the weekend and we'll revisit this on Sunday night. Besides, I want to hear all about your dance recital." He gives me a fatherly smile and I curl my hand into a fist once more. I swear, I'm going to hit him right in that smiling mouth of his.

"I meant what I said," I tell him through gritted teeth. "Either send me places without him, or I'm done traveling."

Mario shakes his head. "He's wherever you are in too many places, Jessa. He's a fact of life—of *your* life. To keep you away from anywhere he might be would severely handicap your scope and definitely limit what I can do with you."

"And that's the only consideration, isn't it?" I snarl. "Can I get the job done? Can I do it even if people are trying to kill me or I'm in the middle of a tsunami or a hurricane or if I see a ghost right in front of my eyes!"

"It's not the only consideration," Mario says calmly. "We can't afford to always take the easy way around. The forecasts predict—"

"Forecasts can be wrong. Want to know how I know that? Because they don't see everything coming, do they?" I can feel

my temper nearly consuming me, and my next words are a shout.
"How about this? I quit!"

I storm over to the red door and yank it open.

"Good-bye, Mario."

The words echo in my darkened bedroom, and I punch my pillow, wishing it was a certain Dreamer's face.

5

Out of Hibernation

"YOU HUNGRY, ST. CLAIR?"

Ben's voice startles me and I look away from my reflection in the window of the bus. It's field trip day for the Spanish Club, and Ben is sitting next to me as we pull out of the school parking lot.

"Nah," I tell him. "I'll eat later."

"You sure? I've got food in my bag."

"I'm fine."

"I have Twix in there," he says.

"Seriously. I'm not hungry."

"Who are you? And what have you done with Jessa St. Clair?" he quips. "It's *Twix*. *Twiiiiiix*." He's waggling his brows and bug-eyed and it makes me laugh.

"It's seven o'clock in the morning," I point out.

"So? Twix is the breakfast of champions. Along with a fresh can of Monster." He holds the can to his lips, draining it with a loud, gusty sigh of refreshment.

I raise my brows and look at him like the crazy person he is.

"You do realize you're going to be on a bus for a couple of hours? With no bathroom?"

"Sitting next to you," he reminds me, with an overemphasized "Ha!" for punctuation.

Today we'll be visiting the Instituto Cervantes in Manhattan and tomorrow we visit the Museum of Natural History because they have a special exhibit about indigenous cultures in Mexico and Central America. We've been raising money for this all year, and we'll even have some time for sight-seeing while we're in the city.

"Whatcha got there?" he asks, nosing his nosy nose over my shoulder as I pull my notebook out of my bag.

"Nothing. It's stupid."

"What?"

I hesitate for a moment but finally relent. Ben knows everything about me—including the fact that I am a Traveler. "One of my other selves left me a poem she'd been working on."

"I should have known when you whipped out the notebook," he says. "I haven't seen you write a thing in weeks."

"I've written two papers for English lit this month and one for history," I remind him.

"You know what I mean. *Writing* writing."

I do know what he means. Once I lost Finn, it was like I lost the spark. Finn had been the center of so many of my stories for so long. My dreams—which I now recognized as memories and glimpses of my other selves—fueled so much of what I wrote about. When Finn died, the urge to write just for pleasure died with him. I even changed my schedule for next semester to remove creative writing. I'm taking a photography class instead.

"Let's see what the damage is," I say, flipping open my note-book and reading.

I Am Darkness

The darkness calls me and I am it
It is me
Part of we
Interminably
They pull us into the light
Flip the switch
Demanding our attention
Not seeing the fist
We keep in the darkness
Clenched in our pocket
Ready to strike

"Great googly moogly," Ben says, reading over my shoulder.

I close the notebook with a sound of disgust. "Yeah, I'm a little rebellious over there."

"Is that why you told Justin Taylor he looked like walking mucus in that green shirt last night at Mugsy's?"

"Who told you that?"

"He did, when I walked in. I didn't even think you knew his name, St. Clair."

I search back in my mind for the memories my other self generated while she was here. "No . . . that was her assignment."

"To tell Justin he looks bad in green?"

I shrug slightly. "Yeah, believe it or not."

"How is that reality-altering in any way?"

"Ripples. Every decision has the possibility of making ripples that influence other decisions," I explain. "He probably obsesses over my remarks and gets distracted and trips into a guy who drops his briefcase on the foot of an elderly woman who curses him out, and that will inspire him to invent a whole new line of antibacterial mouthwash that saves the world from a terrible plague."

Ben lets out an explosive laugh. "That is *wacked*."

"Tell me about it. But there's a reason for every little thing, and it all snowballs to be something really important, somewhere down the line," I say. "Or so my Dreamer assures me."

"Is the dream guy in your head every night? 'Cause that sounds . . . not fun."

"You have *no* idea."

I lean back in the seat and close my eyes.

"Hey . . . Jessa."

My head turns at the sound of my name on his lips. He only calls me by my first name when he has something heavy to say, and I brace myself for what's coming next. I've heard it too many times these last weeks.

"I know I sound like a broken record here," he says hesitantly, "but . . . I was really glad when you called me last night. Even if it was just for a ride home."

"Thanks for coming through for me."

"That's what friends do," he reminds me. "You can't hide forever, St. Clair. You need to get back to your life, and you start with little things. Like coffee. Or just hanging out with someone."

He reaches across the seat, and his hand closes over mine.

"I'm not hiding. Honest." I give him a weak smile, but he's not buying it.

"What about writing? When are you getting back to that?"

My jaw tightens and I am done talking. "When I'm ready. Okay? Get off it already."

"Sorry." He takes his hand from mine. "I just—I want to help you, and you're shutting me out. I don't know what's going on with you and all this other . . . stuff. And I want to."

"I know."

The silence hangs heavy between us, and I play with the corner of my notebook, flicking at the paper with my fingers.

"I promise I'll call you if I need you," I mumble. "Stop worrying about me, okay? It's just going to take some time."

"Take all the time you need," he says. "I'll be here to read an official proclamation when you're ready to come out and see your shadow."

"Thanks." I lean over and give him an impulsive hug. "You're the best."

"Yeah, yeah," he says, waving dismissively. "That's what they all say."

Ben has been the perfect supportive best friend in the time since I dragged him into my paranormal drama. But I know he still thinks about the week I was replaced by another me—one who loved him in a way I'm not sure I ever can.

Being a Traveler gave me a life I could never have imagined, and not all of it has been good. Maybe Ben is right. It's time for me to stop hiding and start living my life, beginning with this weekend. I'm going to be Jessa, high school student, writer, and ordinary person on an all-expenses-paid trip to the Big Apple.

It's time for me to have some fun again. I deserve it.

6

Like the Perfect
Romantic Comedy

I CATCH A GLIMPSE OF MY REFLECTION IN THE BUS window, pulling me out of my drifting thoughts. I see him again in my mind's eye—the way he looked, staring in the window on the train door as if he were trying to transfer through it to me.

He didn't know me—just as I didn't know him in that reality, until that moment. And now, thanks to Mario, things have been set in motion for that Finn and that Jessa. The price of that is another bleeding piece of my heart.

"Hey . . . you with me, St. Clair?"

I turn my face away from the glass. "Huh?"

"We're almost there. What do you want to do first?"

We'd started our day in New York at the Instituto Cervantes, taking part in their immersive language workshop for Spanish, and then we had an early dinner at a tiny Mexican food place that could barely hold us all. Now we were headed to Times Square for three hours of free time before we have to meet up with the bus for the ride over to the hotel.

"Shopping, I guess," I finally answer. "I need to get Christmas presents still."

"For who?"

I shrug. "Everybody."

"You haven't done a lick of Christmas shopping?"

"Nobody up here does 'a lick' of anything, cowboy."

"It's two weeks to Christmas!"

My eyes shift away. "I've been a little preoccupied."

I don't need to look at him to sense that I've made him uncomfortable. "Sorry," he mumbles. I feel his hand come out to lightly rub my back before he self-consciously pulls it away.

"It's okay."

"So, no Empire State Building?"

"Been there, done that," I say. "With my parents when I was seven. Danny spit a piece of candy through the holes in the fence on the observation deck, and Dad told him not to do that or we'd get in trouble with security. Danny was freaked out and spent the rest of the day sure he was getting arrested."

"I've been there, too, when we first moved here," Ben says. "No biggie if I miss it. There's a bunch of people walking over to Rockefeller Center to see the Christmas tree."

"That sounds festive."

"There's bound to be shopping around there."

"At least a lick or two."

He playfully bumps my shoulder. "C'mon. They're unloading."

We leave the bus for the streets of New York, assuring Mr. Fielding that we'll be back at the rendezvous point at nine p.m. sharp. The sounds and smells and lights of the city are all around us, drowning out the churning thoughts I have inside.

"This way," Ben says, leading me by the hand. "Did you know that Rockefeller Center was one of the largest building projects in the United States to incorporate integrated public art? Rockefeller originally bought the land to build an opera house, but the stock market crash of '29 forced him to change his plans for the complex."

"Cool." I can't help but smile a little. Ben is in his element anytime there's history attached. I find myself relaxing for the first time in a long time.

The city is ablaze with lights and Christmas decorations. It's cold, but not painfully so, and Ben is pointing out buildings and talking about sewer systems, of all things. He's more excited about what's under the streets than all the festivities on the surface.

We finally reach the plaza, and Ben stops in his tracks.

"Whoa," he says. "That is one *big* tree."

"That's kind of the point," I say.

"Did you know it's limited to one hundred and ten feet? Any bigger and they can't transport it due to the width of the streets."

"You've just subscribed to pine tree facts!" I say, in a fakey announcer voice. "Please text 'STOP' to unsubscribe!"

"Smartass," he says. "And it's usually a fir tree. Just for the record." He puts his hand on his hip and turns in a slow circle. "They really know how to do it up here, don't they?"

"It's really pretty," I agree. "And festive."

"And you're sure you'd rather be shopping than discussing the Victorian origins of the Christmas tree?"

"You can fill me in while we shop," I say. "Come on." I grab him by the collar of his coat and pull him along with me, and it's a good thing I'm leading him because his head is turned back to look at the plaza and all the buildings.

"We're going to walk right by the cathedral . . . ," he's saying, but the rest gets drowned out by the sound of carolers on the plaza, and I let the sound of it, the lights, the colors, the jostling of the crowds fill me up. It feels nice. Nicer than I've felt in a while, anyway.

We spend the next hour visiting every curio shop we can find and I score an awesome snow globe for Danny's collection, featuring a hansom cab and horses in a snowy Central Park. Eventually, we work our way back to Rockefeller Center. Skaters are circling in the rink below us, and the lights are twinkling, and Christmas music is playing, and I'm honest-to-God enjoying myself for the first time in weeks.

I catch a whiff of something laced with cinnamon from a passerby, and it smells so delicious I'm about to suggest to Ben that we follow them to figure out what they're eating, when he turns from the railing he's leaning on.

"Whatta ya say, St. Clair?" he asks. "Wanna skate?"

I glance down at the skaters circling below.

"Do you know how to skate?" I ask.

"Sure."

"*Ice* skate?"

He holds out his arms wide. "How hard can it be?"

"Famous last words," I say. "It's a lot harder than it looks. Besides, it's really crowded."

"So? That's more people to hold us up if we start to fall."

"You mean if *you* start to fall," I point out. "I know how to ice skate. And I bet they didn't teach you how to do that in New Mexico."

"Nope."

"Do they even have ice in your country? Or running water?" I tease.

"Ha. Very funny," he says. "So . . . you want to skate or not?"

"Not," I say with a grimace. "I overspent on the Christmas gifts. Don't have any extra."

"I got you covered."

"Ben . . ."

"C'mon, St. Clair . . . it's Christmas. Rockefeller Center! A giant tree might topple over on us at any moment. Let's live dangerously!"

With a reluctant smile, I let him bully me into a pair of skates.

What happens next is going to go down in the great record book of *Remember That Time When* . . . and I'm going to bring it up again and again for *years*. Ben may be six feet of solid muscle and poetry in motion on a soccer field, but on a pair of ice skates he's just plain hilarious.

He flails. He spins. At one point he manages a full-on back-flip. He makes the most ridiculous noises while waving his hands and desperately grabbing onto me for balance. We make it once around the ice and he gestures for us to pull over.

"Whoa," he pants, and he does a comical dance for a moment as he tries to let go of me and can't seem to do it. I can't help it—I laugh out loud.

He looks startled for a moment, then he breaks into a wide grin.

"If I'd've known I could hear you laugh again just by falling on my ass, I'd've done it weeks ago," he says.

"I'm sorry," I say, reaching out to steady him once more. "We can quit if you want to."

"Quit?" He says it like he's offended. "I am *so* up for this. I am fixing to kick skating's *ass*."

He pushes off the wall and his feet slide rapidly, front and back, and I push forward and slide my arm around his waist to steady him.

"Here," I say, holding his left arm with my hand while my right arm remains around his waist. "I'll show you like we showed Danny. Two short steps, then a long one. Short. Short. Loooong."

I guide him forward and we try it again. "Short. Short. Loooong. That's it—lean into it on the long ones."

"Okay, okay . . . ," he says. "I'm fixing to get it. I'm getting it! I'm—"

And he falls again. This time, I go down with him, and we land in a laughing heap, with him on top. He rises up to his elbows, still laughing, and I reach up, touching his hair.

"Snow," I say, brushing the first few flakes away. "It's starting to snow."

"Of course it is," he says. "Makes perfect sense."

"How's that?"

"It's the setup for a perfect romantic comedy," he replies good-naturedly. "Except I'm not much of a damsel in distress, and if it keeps on snowing, I'm going to freeze to the ice."

"Guess it's my turn to rescue you for a change."

I push up to my knees and he does the same. Suddenly, we're

face-to-face on the ice with the snow falling and the lights twinkling and the Christmas music playing.

"You ready for the next step?" I ask.

He stares at me with those big brown eyes, and the snow is clinging to his dark hair.

"Yeah," he says. "I'm ready."

"Good." I get up, planting my feet on the ice to brace myself, and I put a hand down to help him. He gets one skate on the ice, and, after a bit of a flail, he's up again. He keeps ahold of my hand.

"So what now, St. Clair?" he asks. "The ball's in your court."

"Now we try short-long-long," I reply, sliding my arm around him again.

He closes his eyes a moment and makes a funny half-laugh sort of sound.

"Of course," he sighs. "Let's do it."

And we fall again. Ben rolls onto his back.

"Might as well make an ice angel while I'm down here," he says, waving his arms and legs on the ice.

"I don't think that works," I say, rolling onto my stomach and raising up on my elbows to look at him. "Not that you don't have an impressive impact crater."

He looks at me in outrage. "So now I'm so heavy I cracked the ice?"

"I was referring to the force at which you impacted," I say diplomatically.

"I was fixing to make my turn but you were slowing me down," he complains, and he goes on complaining, but I'm not listening.

My hand is on the ice, and my eyes are locked with hers, and she's signing hello. But I know this Jessa. I know her too well.

I pull my hand back and struggle to my knees, feeling a little frantic.

"You okay, St. Clair?" Ben asks, getting to his knees. "Did I fall on your hand or something?"

I didn't realize I was rubbing my fingers. "I'm fine," I say.

"You froze there for a minute." He reaches out, touching my face. "You didn't hit your head, did you?"

"What? No." I push his hand away. "I'm okay. I just want to go."

He reaches out again, this time to hold me by the shoulders.

"Jessa. What's wrong?"

I shake my head. "Just a call from someone I know. In my reflection."

He glances around at the skaters who are swerving to avoid us and pulls me on my knees to the edge of the ice with him. "You were trying to travel?"

"No. I know this Jessa."

"So?"

"Let's just say she caused some issues for me last time she was here."

It takes him a moment to connect the dots.

"Oh."

"Yeah. And I'm done with all of that. I really am. I mean it, Ben."

The sympathy in his eyes at my fierce tone of voice is making my eyes well up.

"Okay," he says simply. "Let's go."

I push to my feet, offering him a hand, but he shakes it off, pulling himself up by the wall behind us. I help him off the ice, and ten minutes later, he's handing me a hot cocoa as we walk toward the rendezvous point for the bus.

"Sorry I wrecked your first time ice skating," I say apologetically.

"Yeah, like I wasn't making a wreck of myself," he laughs, bumping me with his shoulder and sloshing my cocoa in my cup.

"You know what I mean."

"Meh. It was almost time to leave anyway." He looks down at me. "You okay?"

"Yeah. It's just that I've had a lot on my mind the last couple of days."

We climb up into the bus, which is only about half full. I sink down into a seat as we wait for the others.

"Was it that last trip?" Ben asks hesitantly. "Last night?"

I look down at my cup, refusing to stare at the window, even though I'm in the seat next to it.

"I mean, I figured something was up," he says. "But I wasn't going to pry."

We're quiet for a minute, and I can hear him drinking his cocoa. This is one of the things I like about Ben. We can just be silent with each other, and it's not awkward. He's not going to push or prod me or make stupid small talk just to fill the air.

"I saw him."

The words are out of my mouth and I immediately want to call them back.

"Who?"

I don't answer him, and I hear Ben suck in a breath.

"Oh." He sits back in his seat. "Holy . . . How do you . . . ?"

"I didn't. I ran away from him. I couldn't even speak to him."

"You're sure it was him?"

"It was him." My voice is flat, emotionless.

"Is he going to be everywhere you go?"

"Not everywhere. But he was there. Mario made sure of it," I add bitterly.

"Why would he do that to you?"

"He said it was time."

"That's screwed up."

I take a drink of my cocoa, emptying the cup. "Yeah, it is. That's why I quit."

"So you're not ever traveling again?"

"Yep."

"Yep," he echoes. "Sounds like a plan."

I look up at him. "Thanks."

"For what? Falling on my ass for your amusement?"

"Not a lot of guys could get this. Y'know?" As I say the words, I realize how true they are. Ben gets it. Ben gets *me*.

My mind strays back to the other Jessa I saw in the ice—the one who's been in a relationship with Ben for over a year. Her memories wash over me, and I'm finding it hard to meet his eyes.

"Well," he says, taking my empty cup and stacking it inside his, which is empty, too. "In my country, people jump through mirrors and run into zombies all the time. This is routine stuff."

My lips twitch. "But still no running water?"

"No, *señorita. Obtenemos agua del río.*" He bumps my shoulder with his. "So you're grounded for good? In the here and now?"

I look over at him, meeting his warm, brown eyes with mine. "In the here and now," I say. "Right next to you."

7

History Repeats Itself

"DO WE LOOK LIKE TERRORISTS OR SOMETHING?" BEN complains as we wait in the packed security line. "It's the Museum of Natural History, for Pete's sake."

"There are valuable things here," I remind him, straining to see over the crowd. "And there's security everywhere now."

"I'm wishing I could pop through a mirror out of this line," he says. "That'd be a handy little trick."

"Will you keep your voice down?" I admonish him, lowering my own voice. "It wouldn't do you any good anyway. You could just be subjecting another you to the experience."

"I could go visit rebel girl," he teases. "Help her write some more bad poetry."

My eyes go wide. "You weren't together over there," I explain. "Just because it happened once doesn't mean it'll happen again."

"I know that," he says uncomfortably, and I feel like I've hurt his feelings. Crap.

"Do you really want a whirlwind romance with a girl who

spends half her paychecks on a mountain of black eyeliner and writes angsty poetry?" I tease.

He lets out a huff of a laugh. "Talk about high-maintenance."

"You have no idea."

"Guess I'll stay away from the whirlwind romances and stick with you, then." He punches my arm lightly. He says it playfully, but his eyes hold mine just a moment too long before I make myself look away.

Mr. Fielding is allowing us to go at our own pace, as long as we meet at the bus by one p.m. Once we get through security, Ben and I start winding our way through the exhibits. Being with Ben is like having my own personal museum guide—he has all kinds of insight on people and cultures. The only danger is letting him talk to someone on the staff. We'll be here all day if I so much as let him say hello.

There's an entire exhibit called "Myths and Mysteries" that examines mythology and folklore throughout the ages, and we spend half an hour listening to interactive videos of native storytellers and looking through art and preserved texts under glass. Near the end of the exhibit, we stop in front of a mosaic depicting an oracle in ancient Greece.

"The Pythia," Ben says, touching his fingers to the description plate next to the mosaic. "The original oracle at Delphi. People sought them out from all over the Mediterranean region."

"Mario says that's what they used before Travelers. Oracles and shamans. Holy people like that."

"Makes sense," Ben says. "The temple at Delphi was built over volcanic rock, and there was volcanic steam that would rise up through the floor—it supposedly gave the oracles hallucinations, sending them into a dreamlike state to make their prophecies."

"I wonder what made my ancestor try a mirror for the first time?" I ponder. "I mean, did she trip and fall into it? Did she have a dream that told her how to do it?" I realize I'm asking the wrong person—Mario would probably know. That is, if I ever see him again. He's kept away from me since I quit, but I doubt that'll hold.

"Mirrors were used a lot in rituals within various cultures," Ben says as we move on to the connecting hallway. "They used them for scrying and divination. They'd hold a mirror suspended on a thread over a basin of water, then they'd meditate as they looked at the combined reflections. They believed it made a portal to the gods."

"So she could have been seeking guidance and when she saw things start to change in her reflection, she took a chance and pushed through."

"I like your original theory," Ben says. "She got bitten by a mutant spider, tripped over a big urn filled with olive oil, it splattered on the floor, and she slid into the mirror. Boom! Greco-Roman X-Woman."

"I'd like to think my ancestor had a little more finesse," I say as I reach for the door into the next exhibit.

"Hey, I'm gonna hit the little boys' room," Ben says. "Meet you inside."

"I'll be over by the mammoths," I say.

"Good! They only have those stupid blow dryers in there," Ben replies. "I could use a mammoth. Like a big, shaggy towel, with tusks."

I shake my head, laughing at him as I push the door open and head inside. For a few minutes, I'm lost in a video presentation of a mammoth excavation from Siberian permafrost. Apparently, I'm a little too engrossed, because when I feel a tap on my shoulder, I jump a foot.

"Don't do that!" I hiss at Ben. Then I register the sound I just heard. The clanking of bracelets.

"Hello, Miss Jessa."

She's standing at the railing right next to me, and I am as still as death. Or maybe I should say, *waiting for my death*. It's sure to come any second now. She has a colorful scarf wrapped around her face and head—probably to keep Mr. Fielding from recognizing her since he's milling around here with the rest of us.

She smiles at me fondly, like it's another day in class and she's just read over one of my stories. I glance around wildly, but nobody notices my would-be murderer is staring me down. I think about calling out, but—who would believe me? No one saw her murder anyone. No one knows she tried to murder me.

"What a lucky coincidence it is to find you here. Have you and your new boyfriend been enjoying the museum? You seemed quite entranced by the oracle exhibit." She gives an odd laugh, and I really look at her. Her eyes are sunken, and her skin is ashen. She looks ill.

"What do you want?" I ask warily.

She leans on the railing. "I want to talk."

"You want to *talk*?" I manage to push the words out of my throat. "What can you possibly have to say to me?"

"You're a bright girl, Miss Jessa," she purrs. "You always were one of my best students. So very clever, to figure it all out before we were ready to move. You've set us back, but you haven't stopped us. You and that Dreamer of yours have turned the others against us, but the fools will see that convergence is the only way. The better way. With reality returned to simplicity, we can begin shaping it anew into something far better than what it is."

She's babbling, and I can see that even though she's standing still, her hands are trembling. A fine sheen of perspiration stands out on her brow, and her eyes are fever-bright.

"We've had this conversation," I say in a hard voice. "You're not just erasing billions of lives so you can start over. What you're doing is murder. Mass murder."

"Is there anything you wouldn't do?" she asks. "For love?"

I stare at her in silence as the pieces fall together. "You're in love with Rudy," I say as it begins to dawn on me. "But . . . he's not . . . mortal."

"Does that make my love for him any less? Or his for me a thing of dreams only? And when this is all over, he will be restored and we will be truly together, as we should have been."

"You are completely deranged."

Her eyes go cold as she gives me this warning:

"Be careful who you love, Miss Jessa. For I am making it my personal mission to see that you lose them—all of them—before I finally come for you."

She turns on her heel and walks briskly through the crowd gathered at the other end of the room, then out the far door. I pry my fingers from the railing. I'm shaking hard and I feel lightheaded, like I'm going to pass out.

Oh my God, she could have killed me. She could have killed Ben, if he'd walked up while she was here.

Ben.

Where is Ben?

Be careful who you love. . . .

Her words echo in my head as I run for the door, pushing my way through the crowd of students and visitors, out into the hall, glancing each way, but I don't see Eversor or Ben. I run up to the bathroom door, and it opens.

"Is there anyone else in there?" I ask the man who just exited. "A guy my age? Dark hair?"

"Nobody in there but me." He shrugs.

I nod my thanks as I race forward again, tearing down the stairs, pushing people out of my way. Fear is giving my feet wings, but I stumble, catch myself, and I'm up again. My head is swiveling on my neck as I look for any sign of him.

"Excuse me!" I'm shouting before I even reach the information desk. I know I look like a crazy person, panting and slamming my hand down on the counter. "Someone's missing—from our group."

"Did you tell your teacher?" The security guard doesn't even look up from the computer he's sitting at.

"No—I—there wasn't time," I splutter. "Please—he's my age, tall, dark hair—"

The guard glances up. "So your teacher or sponsor hasn't been informed? Have them do a head count and then they can *personally* speak with security."

"You don't understand—he could be in trouble!"

"Talk to your teacher and—"

"Please! Please, we don't have time!" I beg. "He's about six feet, dark hair, brown eyes, and he's wearing . . . uh . . ." My mind frantically searches to remember what Ben is wearing.

"A brown leather jacket?" the guard asks.

"Yes!" My eyes widen. "You've seen him?"

"He's coming in the door right behind you," the man says dryly. I whirl around, and to my relief, he's right.

"Jessa!" Ben rushes forward just as I throw my arms around him. "You're shaking," he says, pulling back from me. "Are you okay? Why weren't you on the bus?"

"What?"

"Some kid outside the bathroom told me you got sick and you were going to wait on the bus. But I just checked and it's all locked up. Are you okay?"

"What kid?" I asked.

"I didn't know him. He said a teacher asked him to give me the message."

"Oh God," I say, leaning my head into his chest. I'm still panting, and I can't seem to let him go. "It wasn't a teacher. I mean, it was. It was Eversor."

His arms tighten around me in an instant, and he lifts his head to look around. "She's here?"

I nod, and my head rubs against his chest as he strokes my back soothingly. "She came up and talked to me like we were old friends. And then she told me she was going to kill the people I loved if I didn't stay out of her way."

Ben's hand on my back goes still. "The bike courier," he says.

"I was walking back from where they parked the bus and a bike courier rode up on the sidewalk at the corner. He nearly knocked me into traffic."

"Just now?"

He nods. "If I hadn't stepped back to check out the Solomonic columns on one of the buildings right at that moment, he would have hit me. Instead he just ran over my foot."

"Causality," I mumble.

"Come again?"

"Causality. Eversor doesn't know you're crazy about history and architecture. Her correction didn't work because she didn't anticipate you stopping to look at the building."

"She didn't hurt you?"

"She could have killed you," I whisper.

"But you're okay?" he asks again, giving me a squeeze.

I lift my head to look at him. "Okay? How can I be okay? She's trying to kill the people I care about!"

Something softens in his eyes, and he hugs me tight again. "But she didn't hurt you. That's what matters."

"You matter, too. A lot."

I'm still shaking, despite the warm strength of his arms around me. She got so close. How can we stay ahead of her when she's got a Dreamer who can forecast our moves before we make them?

How can I keep the people I care about safe?

8

A Definite Maybe

WE HAVE A LONG RIDE HOME ON THE BUS. I'M NUMB AND
exhausted, and before I know it, I drift off into a dreamless sleep.

My eyes snap open as the bus slows for a stoplight. I'm so
warm and comfortable, I don't want to move.

I stretch, and it only takes a moment to realize I've been asleep
in Ben's arms. My head is against his chest, and I can hear his
steady heartbeat under my ear. His hand is idly smoothing my
hair as it trails down my back, and the other arm is around me to
keep me from sliding off the seat. I should move.

Instead, I slowly raise my head up, and I meet Ben's eyes,
gleaming in the dim light passing through the bus window.

"Hi there," he murmurs. "Comfortable?"

"Mmmm," I answer sleepily. "You're a lot cushier than the bus
seat."

"Well, I am on the Twix Breakfast Diet."

I bring my hand up to push my hair off my face as I laugh,

and his hand bumps into mine just as he was about to do the same thing. He twines his fingers with mine instead.

"You've been out for a while. Look—we're in town already." He yawns. "At least we got some rest." He leans over, lowering his voice. "Any luck with your Dreamer guy?"

"No. He wasn't there tonight."

"Can't you summon him or something?"

I shake my head. "It doesn't work that way."

Ben makes a face. "I still don't like that she got so close to you."

"To *us*," I remind him.

"Us." He repeats the word and then he goes silent, pulling absently on the strings of his hoodie as we pull into the school parking lot.

In less than five minutes, we're off the bus and after a short ride in Ben's truck we pull up to my house. Before I can reach for the handle on the truck door to get out, he stops me.

"Wait."

"What?"

"I'm fixing to say something, so just hear me out, okay?"

"O . . . kay . . . ," I answer warily.

"This trip was fun. Up until the psycho crazy woman, I mean."

I smile. "Yeah, it was. Up until then."

"It wouldn't have been nearly as much fun with anybody else."

Where is he going with this?

"Thanks," I say.

"And . . . well . . . did you ever think that maybe a whirlwind romance is only good for ripping people to pieces?"

"Is this about the other me?"

"I'm not talking about her. I'm talking about *you*. I've been thinking about this . . . about you . . . this whole weekend." He takes a fortifying breath and goes on. "It's hard to get over someone when you feel like you got cheated out of them to begin with. When you didn't have enough time together. I get that."

My eyes soften. "Ben . . . I just . . ." I shake my head because I really don't know how to put this into words, what I'm feeling. What I'm trying not to feel.

"All I'm saying is maybe you need somebody to help you pick up the pieces in a slow and methodical way," he says, "instead of a whirlwind. Somebody who may not be as exciting until you watch him fall on his ass a few dozen times."

He gives me a lopsided grin, and I can't help but smile back a little.

"Maybe," I hedge.

"Maybe?" He raises his brows in a hopeful manner.

"I'll think about it. Promise."

"You do that. And while you're at it, maybe think about this."

He leans in, and he hesitates a moment before his lips meet mine. I have time to pull away, to turn my head, to say *wait* . . . but I don't. I feel my eyes closing, and his mouth is warm, gentle, and slow on mine. I feel his fingers lightly cupping my face, and he pulls back before he brushes his lips against mine once, twice more.

I am stunned, but to be honest, it's not in a bad way. He feels warm and safe, and he's a surprisingly good kisser. But the emotions are swirling all around me right now, and part of me is screaming that this is too soon. Or maybe not such a good idea— for Ben, I mean.

"That bad, huh?"

"No . . . ," I answer. "Not bad. Not bad at all. I just—"

He puts out a finger, mashing my lips shut.

"Let's leave it at 'not bad.' The rest we'll figure out as we go. Deal?"

I nod. "Deal."

Something just changed between us, and I am suddenly desperate to get away.

"I gotta go," I say, not meeting his eyes. I open the door and hop down, reaching into the back to retrieve my duffel bag.

"See ya," I say, working hard to keep my voice normal.

"See ya." His eyes hold mine, and he looks like he wants to say something more from the way his jaw tightens, but I guess he thinks better of it. I shut the truck door, giving him a wave as I head up the sidewalk to my front door. I'm relieved to see that I'm all alone—Mom and Danny are still at work, so that gives me some time alone with my thoughts.

I need to think. After everything that happened today, I don't know if I can risk dragging someone else who I care about into this giant mess I call my life right now.

He's already in the mess, says a voice inside my head. *And isn't it nice not to have to face it alone?*

But am I ready for this?

For Ben?

What if it doesn't work out? I'll break his heart. I can't hurt him like that, especially when there's every chance it'll end up just that way.

Not necessarily, says that voice again. *You know what I mean.*

And I do. Ben and I could be together. We are together. Just not here. I wish I had an hour over there to just give him a trial run—set a year down the road—and get another taste of what a healthy relationship could feel like. Right now, I don't know that I'm capable of recognizing one, not after all that's happened.

For some reason, that really doesn't sound like a bad idea. And I need to talk to another me, anyway. Somebody's got to get ahold of Mario. Might as well be her, right?

I'm not going to analyze this one iota further. I touch my hand to the glass, picturing her—me—and my bedroom over there. It seems like it's taking forever to get through.

I take it back. This was a bad idea. A really bad idea. I start to pull my fingers from the glass when she answers.

I can't tell where she is, and all I can see is her face—probably in a compact mirror, like I carry. I wonder if she's going to get angry at me for even suggesting this. Oh God. This is stupid. This is so, so stupid.

She must see the emotions warring across my face because her forehead creases with concern.

What? she signs.

Can you give Mario a message if you see him tonight? I sign in return. *Tell him I saw Eversor and I need to talk to him.*

Can't you tell him yourself? she signs back.

I told him I quit. He may be ignoring me for a while.

Her eyes widen, but she reluctantly nods.

Hey, what did you need? Last night? I ask.

A smile touches her lips. *I wanted to tell you that Danny was asking about you. He seems to know when I switch out, and he likes you.*

I smile back. *My Danny likes you, too.*

Her eyes shift down, and she flushes slightly, as if she's embarrassed. *Sorry about last time,* she signs. *I didn't think.*

About that . . . I take a deep breath. I didn't call her just to get through to Mario. I might as well get it all out there. She watches silently as I sign my request.

I see her eyes shift away, then back again.

Tomorrow morning, she signs back. *For an hour. Ten o'clock.* Her eyes shift away again and return. *Be careful.*

I promise, I sign back. *Thanks.*

She smiles. *I owe you one,* she signs.

I flop down on my bed. This is stupid. A really, really stupid idea. But I'm going to do it anyway. Somehow, despite the whirlwind in my mind, I manage to drift off to sleep.

9

Danny's Dream

I AM ALL ALONE IN THE CLASSROOM, BUT IT'S A RELIEF
to be there. Dreaming myself here can only mean one thing, and
the door opens a moment later, letting in a very harried-looking
middle-aged woman in dress slacks and a long gray cardigan.
She makes a clucking noise with her mouth and then pats her
pockets.

"Where did I put my glasses . . . ?" she mutters, turning in a
complete circle. I clear my throat and she gives a startled glance
over her shoulder.

"Oh! Jessa!"

She turns around and transforms into Mario in the same
instant. He straightens his shirt and gives me a smile.

"Sorry. I was out and about. Forgot to change."

"It's fine," I say, waving off his apology. "Where have you
been? I've got news. Eversor found me."

He looks startled, then he grabs a chair, straddling it and gesturing for me to sit with him.

"Where? And when?"

"At the museum today," I say, easing myself down into the chair. "She said it was a 'lucky coincidence.'" I give a humorless laugh. "Some luck."

"I told you not to get complacent," Mario reminds me sharply. "It was just a matter of time."

"She says they're still trying to start the convergence. She didn't try to kill me—she just warned me to stay out of their way."

"Just because she didn't try to kill you doesn't mean she's given up," Mario warns. "She couldn't have done it right there and made it look like an accident. Too many ripples."

"She tried to hurt Ben. It was supposed to be an accident, but he diverted at the last minute."

Mario lets out a huff of air. "No, *that's* luck. And this time, it saved his life."

"How do I keep my family and Ben out of this?" I ask him. "We need to keep them safe."

"Jessa, nobody's safe!" he splutters. "Not in your reality, not in any reality! Eversor and Rudy have shifted gears and are now actively working toward convergence. They're not just intent on eliminating you until they figure it out. The incident with Ben was a definite warning—you can't 'get in their way' unless they're actually onto something."

He taps his chin thoughtfully, then pushes up out of his chair. "Come on," he says. "I need you to take a trip with me."

He's got me curious. "A trip? In the dreamscape? Is this about a job?"

"No. Intelligence gathering. Follow me."

He reaches for the door, and I walk through, closing it behind me.

We're inside the Ardenville Public Library, and my brother is driving what appears to be a lawn tractor around the main floor. He pulls up at the desk.

"Hi, Jessa." He waves and then he turns to look at Mario, who has moved behind the desk and once again looks like a middle-age woman with frosted blond hair.

"Do you have more books, Angela?" Danny asks.

"Sure I do, hon," Mario says, reaching under the counter and handing him a stack of books. "These go to children's."

"I'm on it," Danny says. "Bye, Jessa!"

"Are we . . . ?" I turn slowly, taking it all in. "Are we in Danny's dream?"

Mario nods. "He's got some interesting dreams. He gave me some great insights as he was falling asleep and his memories crossed over."

"So you don't automatically see all our thoughts?" I ask. "I assumed you did."

"No, no, no," he says, making a waving motion with his hands. "I'm not omnipotent, you know. I operate here in the dream-scape. I can see shadows of what happens out there in the real world as things start falling together, make assumptions about the stream of events that made them happen, and even follow that stream to predict where they might go. It depends on where I've got my focus. I don't always get to know it all in real time." He runs a hand through his perfectly frosted hair. "Believe me; it would be so much easier if I did."

"I'm not sure I like you invading my brother's dreams," I say.

"I'm not invading. Just observing. Danny's got a fascinating perspective. You of all people should know that."

"Why? Because he has autism?"

He nods. "That's part of it, I'm sure. But Danny is a font of information for me, especially where you're concerned. Most people have really heavy or important thoughts on their mind as they're nodding off, and I get a glimpse of them when they're in that in-between state of consciousness, but Danny concentrates on the little stuff."

"Danny's life *is* the little stuff."

"Ah, but the little stuff is where the big stuff hides," Mario says. "My life is studying the little stuff. So you can see where a mind like Danny's can be so very important in the process."

I hadn't considered that. When I was younger, I used to wonder why he ended up with autism. What made it happen? And why him? It's interesting to know how useful a thing it is.

"Why is he riding a lawn tractor?"

"He's always wanted one, but your mother never bought one," Mario replies. "So it shows up occasionally. I was hoping he'd be at home, but we'll work with what we've got."

I start to scan the room, really looking at it, and I realize it's not . . . normal. The books seem to have much sharper edges; shadows between them highlight the differences in sizes, thicknesses, covers . . . it's so extreme it's fascinating. And the colors! So much bolder and stronger than I've ever seen them before. Almost like they're colors on a spectrum I've never visited.

"This is cool," I say, looking around.

"Reality is defined by the dreamer in the dreamscape," Mario says. "In this case, Danny. This is how Danny perceives the world around him. We're looking through his filter, so to speak."

My eyes widen as the sound of the tractor cuts off. I can now hear the rumble of the heating system, the shuffle of books and papers, the clack of fingers on computer keyboards, and I'm drawn into the rhythm of it.

"So what are you hoping to find?" I ask.

"I don't know exactly what we're looking for," Mario says. "Danny tends to focus on details that go right by the rest of us. You never know what you'll find. So I suggest we both just go with it."

"Go with it?"

Mario gives me an encouraging smile and waves me off, toward the children's section. I walk around from behind the counter, trying hard to keep from tripping as the edges of the floor tiles are standing out, dark and intersecting in fascinating ways in front of me. I finally find Danny in the corner of the children's section, seated on a mat with a group of kids. One of the library aides is reading a story, but the words are muted—I'm too absorbed in other things.

I sit down on the mat next to Danny, fixated on the way the light hits the window through a tree outside. I can see it in prisms, the ebb and flow of the scattered patterns as the wind lifts the branches. It's like a moving kaleidoscope on the floor mat, and my fingers reach out to trace it, just as Danny does beside me. Sometimes the light hits my fingers, and I can see every line of my knuckle—some are straight, some are curvy. I wonder why that is? I count them, one by one, then I count them again.

I listen for the wind and hear the hum of the heater panel nearby. I can feel its vibration in the floor. I put my hand down to feel it just as Danny does, and the story drones on in the background, a wall of words that have melody but not a lot of meaning at the moment, not with everything else that's going on.

It's amazing to me that there's a whole bright, vibrating world around us that they all seem to be ignoring. I wonder how much of the world has gone by me that I've never really noticed before. We all assume that Danny's in this little bubble sometimes, and the truth is, he's seeing more of the world than any of us.

"I'm glad you're here, Jessa," Danny whispers.

I look at him, and I feel like I'm really seeing him. "I'm glad, too," I say.

"Want a ride on my tractor?"

"Sure. Can you give me a lift back to the front?"

We get to our feet and the reader and the kids don't even seem to notice as we fire up the lawn tractor and drive in a slow circle past them and through the open door. I hop off when Danny rolls to a stop by the counter.

"I'm going to go through periodicals now," he says to Mario.

"Good idea," Mario replies, reaching for a stack of newspapers. "These came in today. You can put them in their drawers."

"Who still reads paper newspapers?" I ask.

"Lots of people!" Danny replies, taking the stack. "This one's about museums. I told Angela that you went to a museum." He puts the paper down on the counter for me to see.

"Jessa." Mario leans in over my shoulder. "Look."

The article is on the lower corner of the front page of the newspaper geared toward museum curators, and it's about an attempted theft a few weeks ago at the Museo Nacional de Antropología in Mexico City—their natural history museum. Because of it, many museums around the world have upped their security measures in response.

"Yeah, I know about the security," I say. "When Ben and I went to the Museum of Natural History in New York, they practically strip-searched us."

Mario makes a face. "I need to know what the target of the theft was. And I can't find out from this paper."

"Why not?"

"It's just a short blurb—the rest of the story is on page four." Mario opens the paper, and the inner pages are completely blank.

"What's wrong with it?" I ask.

"We're seeing things that Danny has pulled from memory or imagination. If he didn't see the entire article, we won't find it here."

Mario hands the paper back to Danny, who climbs on his tractor and takes off at race-car speed.

"What's so important about a theft from a museum?" I ask.

"Just a hunch. Especially since the museum is in Mexico . . ."

"And before I saw her in New York, Eversor supposedly booked a flight to Mexico," I say, connecting the dots. "Does this have something to do with whatever she and Rudy are planning?"

"Possibly. It's hard to know what it was the thief was after. Can you find that out for me?"

"Ten seconds on a Google search," I assure him. "No prob."

"Good. Let's go."

He walks back to the red door, which is standing in place of the office door that's usually behind the counter. I follow him over, and we're back through and into the classroom.

"Hey—" I say, stopping short as Mario nearly runs into me. "New York."

"What about it?"

"Eversor said she found me at the museum by luck. Does that mean she was there already?"

"Possibly," he agrees. "Were there any special exhibits at the museum that day?"

I think back. "Um . . . lots of whales. And a whole display on ancient libraries that Ben was going nuts over. Egyptians, Aztecs, Vikings . . ." I tick them off on my fingers. "Wait—they had an exhibit about oracles and mythology. Could that be it?"

"Perhaps. I need to think about this awhile," he says, rubbing his chin. "In the meantime, keep your eyes open. Just in case."

"I will."

He walks me over to the red door. "Oh, and good luck at your recital. Not that you'll need it." He gives me a smile.

"My first dance performance. It's going to be interesting."

"You're doing a very nice thing."

I shrug. "No biggie. She'd do the same for me."

"Well, get some rest so you're fully charged. I'll keep sifting through everything we've learned here. Whatever we're missing— we'll find it."

"Maybe I could ask Ben to help," I offer. "I mean, he knows about me already. He might remember something about the museum that I forgot."

Mario hesitates just briefly. "I suppose it's worth asking. But it's probably better for you to limit your time with him—at least until we find Eversor. He got lucky this time."

"I'm not so sure that'll fly with him."

"I see." He gives me a searching look, and he doesn't seem very happy. "You know the stakes, Jessa."

"I do. But now we have some direction. It's a start."

"So you're back on board? No more talk of quitting?"

"I'm back on board. And Eversor's not getting anywhere near the people I love."

He gives me a genuine smile. "Atta girl. We've got her running, and now we know in what direction."

I give him a reluctant nod and step through the door. My eyes pop open to see the ceiling above my bed.

He's right. I'm not doing Ben any favors here, but I also know that he won't walk away from me. Not while I'm in danger. And I can watch his back a lot easier if it's leaned back on the couch next to mine. Eversor is determined to hurt the people I care about, and that means my family and Ben.

My mind plays back over my visit to Danny's dream, and I turn and walk to my door, opening it as quietly as I can before stepping across the hallway and into Danny's room. He has one muted night-light shaped like the genie from *Aladdin*, and it casts a bluish glow over everything in the room. I can hear his breathing, slow and even.

When we were really young, we used to share a bed, and I fell asleep to the sound of Danny's breathing every night. Mom and Dad always gave us separate rooms, but we didn't want to sleep by ourselves. I don't remember when I outgrew it exactly—probably when I got into my preteens. Danny would still invite me for a long time after but he adapted to the change eventually.

I sit down quietly on the edge of his bed, but I guess not as quietly as I thought.

"Jessa?" His voice is groggy.

"Sorry, Danny. Didn't mean to bug you." I start to get back up.

"Did you have a bad dream?" he asks.

"No. I had a good dream. I just wanted to say hi," I finish lamely. That line would only work on Danny. Anybody else would think I was nuts.

"You can sleep here, if you want," he says, shifting over to make room. "I don't mind."

"Thanks."

I lie down next to him and pull the edge of the comforter over me.

"Danny?"

"Huh?"

"You're a good brother."

He reaches out, patting my head. "Thanks! You're a good sister. G'night, Jessa."

And I fall asleep to the sound of his breathing, watching the patterns of blue light as they play across the walls.

10

The Visitor

YOU CALL THAT SYRUP? BEN SIGNS TO ME, STARING down at my plate of pancakes. I've just returned from the restroom at the diner—it's a name I don't recognize—and he's making fun of my breakfast.

The pancakes soaked it up, I remind him as I take my seat, then I raise a hand to stop him. *Don't you dare put more on there!* I sign.

He stops the syrup in mid-flow, causing some to drizzle down the side of the dispenser. Then he scoops it up with his finger and stuffs his finger in his mouth.

I make a face at him. *Where are your manners?* I sign.

I'm not signing with sticky fingers, he tells me.

Such a gentleman, I sign back.

Here we are. He took me out to breakfast this morning, and we'll be spending some of our day together. Right now it's food, then he has to work until six at the movie theater, and then we'll hang out at my house. We may get a little alone time in my room later, but with both Mom and Danny home we have to be careful.

I feel my cheeks heating up as the memories slide in, warming me and making me feel a little flustered. Ben gives me a quizzical look as I drop my fork.

Do you need some syrup for your fingers? he signs. *Might keep the fork in your hand.*

Do you have a syrup fetish or something?

He raises and lowers his brows in a way that makes me laugh out loud. Then I cover my mouth because I know that was probably very loud just from the vibration of it. He pries my hand off my lips, pulling it across the table, and drops a kiss on my fingertips as I laugh again, softer this time.

I'm suddenly hit with a memory of Ben all dolled up in a top hat at a steampunk ball, bending over to kiss my hand before we danced. I barely knew that Ben over there. He wasn't a romantic interest, not with pirate Finn in the picture.

My hand tightens as a shaft of pain hits my chest. Why do I let my mind wander like that? That's not what I'm here for.

I feel Ben squeeze my hand. *Hey,* he signs. *You're a million miles away.*

Sorry. Just thinking.

Well, stop that. I'm trying to get the syrup off your fingers. He stuffs the tips of my fingers in his mouth and I pull them away, laughing again.

You are such a goof.

I'm a lovable goof.

You are. Very. The words are through my fingers before I can even fully frame them in my mind. My hands could sign *I love you* in my sleep, it comes so naturally over here.

We finish our pancakes, talking some more about school, about taking Danny to a holiday fair tomorrow, about what Ben's going to buy his mom for Christmas. Before I know it, the time has sped by with us just being . . . us. Free and easy and practically finishing each other's sentences.

I can't deny how nice it feels. Not painful. Not tumultuous. There was nothing whirlwind about the way we got together over here. We took our time, and it paid off. Maybe Ben is right. Slow and steady is the safer—and smarter—course.

I have to wash my hands, I sign, glancing up at the clock again.

What? Didn't I do a good-enough job? he signs back, reaching for my fingers again. I shake my head as I stand.

Oh no, you're not using me to fulfill your freaky fetish.

He still has my fingers, so it's easy enough for him to pull me down to him. I feel a little guilty, but it would look too awkward if I pulled back now.

The kiss is short, sweet, and somewhat sticky.

And I think to myself as I press my sticky hands to the mirror glass that a girl could do a lot worse than having someone who makes you laugh.

Thanks, I sign. *That helped. I think.*

She points down to my dresser, and we make the transfer. A moment later, I'm staring down at the note she left me.

Don't rush. But don't make him wait too long, either.
He deserves to be happy.

He does. And maybe . . . with time, we can both get
what we deserve.

He's taking you to rehearsal at 1 p.m.

Despite my pancakes on the other side, this body hasn't eaten breakfast yet and I'm starving. It looks like I spent my time here lying in bed and texting Ben. I can remember now how hard it was for her to keep it friendly. She just couldn't resist giving me a little nudge by finally agreeing to let him watch my rehearsal. He had no idea she was me, of course. I can't help but wonder what he'd think if he knew that. After all, he dated her for a week.

I help myself to some toast and absently flip through channels until Ben shows up, and when he rings the bell, I feel . . . okay, I feel weird. Not butterflies or anything. I'm calm but willing to be more, if that makes sense. We're spending time together. We'll take it from there.

"Ready to rock?" he asks as he picks up my dance bag for me. "I still can't believe you're gonna let me watch."

"It's not me you're watching," I remind him. "If it was, you would have never agreed to sit through a whole rehearsal."

"Wanna bet?" He grins widely as we climb into the truck. "After the spectacle I made of myself on the ice? You think I wouldn't kill to see you traipsing around in a leotard?"

"I'm a little more graceful than you were."

"A little."

"Hey, I've got a job for you. From Mario."

"Dreamsicle guy?"

I roll my eyes. "You can do better than that."

"Working on it," he says. "What do you need?"

"We need to find out about a recent attempted theft at a history museum in Mexico City. Mario thinks it may have been Eversor. Find out whatever you can, okay?"

"That's it?"

"So far. I just figured since your dad's a history professor . . ."

"I might be able to dig a little deeper for you," he finishes. *"No problemo."*

"I'm going to need you to speak English here," I snark. "This is America, not your home country."

"Muérdeme me," he replies.

I stick my tongue out at him and we laugh. And he keeps me laughing, all the way there. We say a quick good-bye before I make my transfer, and when I return three hours later, my muscles are sore and he's gushing with praise.

"Holy guacamole!" he says. "You can really move! I mean, I know the music is hokey, but you were such a standout!"

"I have an unfair advantage," I say sheepishly. "She's been dancing for a while."

"That can't be *all* her," Ben says emphatically. "You have to have some latent talent in there that she's channeling through. Come *on.* You were ridiculously good."

I can't keep the smile off my lips as I help pack the props away. My—her—memories are seeping in now.

Ben didn't complain a bit as we ran the numbers two times each, stopping to figure out where our props went and testing the sound system levels—which delayed us more. He even made a run to McDonald's for a load of fries, which we all devoured as they fixed the colored gels on the lights. The other me summed it up perfectly in the note she left me:

Ben is a hero.
Tell him that from me.

Lauren, my dance teacher, gives me a nudge as I hand her my props.

"So Mr. French Fries is with you?" she asks.

"Sort of." I look over at Ben and he raises his Coke in salute. "It's complicated," I finally add.

"He doesn't look complicated to me," she says, closing the lid on the prop box. "See ya tomorrow."

"Yeah, see ya."

It is complicated. But then, maybe I'm the only one who's making it that way.

I stuff my face with what's left of the cold fries as he drives me home, laughing out loud as he puts on his best dance moves while we're stopped at a red light.

"Two o'clock at the auditorium at Haven House tomorrow," I remind him.

"Wouldn't miss it," he says. We stare at each other a moment, until it's nearly awkward. "Tomorrow, St. Clair."

"See ya tomorrow," I say, and when he leans in and kisses me, I feel a weird—but good—sensation someplace in the middle of my chest.

"Better that time?" he asks.

"Yeah."

"Good. I was fixing to get a complex about the whole thing." Time to get real. I owe him some honesty. "I like you, Ben."

"Well, I should hope so. I just kissed you."

"I mean—" I struggle to find the right words. "I don't know if this will work out. I mean, I'm willing to try. I just don't want to hurt you. Ever. And I can't promise—"

"No promises," he says, mashing my lips with his finger to shush me. "It's okay, St. Clair. I don't know where this is going, either. This is for sure fixing to be the craziest ride I've ever taken."

"For sure," I agree. "Anytime you want off, I totally understand."

"You're not getting rid of me that easy. Besides, I can't go back to my country. You can't imagine the living conditions. . . ."

I laugh, and he leans in to kiss me again. "See ya tomorrow."

"See ya," I say, and I turn to wave before I walk into my house. My brother is in the living room, and he doesn't seem to hear me come through the door.

"Danny, where's Mom?"

He doesn't look away from the movie he's watching, and he answers me around a mouthful of popcorn.

"She's at the store. We don't have Go-Gurts."

"Okay, well . . . tell her I'm back when she comes home."

He doesn't answer me.

"Danny?"

"Uh-huh," he replies, clearly engrossed in his movie. "She's going to get the SpongeBob ones."

"Okay, but let her know I'm home. I'll be up in my room."

He doesn't answer me again, so I give up. She'll figure it out eventually. I drop my sweaty leotard and tights off in the laundry room, pour myself a glass of iced tea, and plod up the stairs to my room, with Ben's words playing over and over in my mind.

Maybe you need somebody to help you pick up the pieces, he'd said.

I had a whirlwind romance and it left me in pieces. I'm in too many pieces. And they're scattered so badly, I don't know that I can find them to even give them to Ben if I wanted to. But I recognize what it took for him to make the offer, especially after all I've put him through. He's stuck by me, even though my life has taken a serious turn for the crazy.

I open the door to my bedroom, dropping my dance bag on the floor.

He's still Ben, and he's still here. The thought makes me feel . . . good. Better than I've felt in a long while. I'm moving forward, and that's a good thing. Ben is a slow and peaceful river that flowed into my life, and I'm finally brave enough to take the plunge and see where it carries me. Peacefully.

I flip the light on, and a bare second later, that peace is shattered when reality slams into me like a freight train powered by two little words:

"Hello, love."

11

Assigned

I AM FROZEN IN THE DOORWAY. I AM FINDING IT VERY, very hard to believe my eyes, but there is most definitely a pirate in front of me. He's lounging on my bed as though he owns the place, one booted foot crossed over the other. His black shirt is tucked into his black leather pants, and his green eyes are staring at me just as intently as I'm staring at him.

Finally, I find my voice.

"How did you get in here?" I manage to choke out. I clench my fists and force myself to stay and not run, even though running is exactly what I want to do. I want to run and keep on running from him.

He swings his feet off the side of the bed, and he sets his elbows down on his knees.

"Your brother was kind enough to let me in," Finn says. "That's the easy answer."

"There's a harder answer?"

He takes in a breath. "Mario thought it was time."

"Time for what?"

He's not making any sense. If Mario wanted me to run into Finn again, he could have sent me to any one of hundreds of realities—even back to that train platform to finish what I'd started with that Jessa. Why send a Finn to find me?

Why send *this* Finn to find me?

"It's time for you to have a protector close at hand," he answers. "And I'm the man for the job."

I look at him warily. "You've got your own Jessa to protect."

The awful knowledge shows plainly on his face. He says nothing, but his jaw tightens and he looks away.

"I'm sorry," I whisper, reaching back behind me to close the door.

He's still looking away, and I have a moment to study him, my eyes playing over every beloved feature, from the angular jaw to the line of his brow, the way his bottom lip is slightly fuller than the top, the way his dark hair falls to the right just so over those forest-green eyes. He's got a slight scruff of a beard, unlike the Finn I lost, but still . . . that face is that face. Finn is Finn, or so he always assured me. And this Finn is still as captivating as ever—maybe more so with the rawness of my loss.

And his loss is no less painful. He wears it on his face, in his eyes, probably in his bones, like I do. I sit down beside him.

"How?" I ask.

His lips purse, as if he can't form the words, and I feel bad for asking. Finally, he gets it out.

"The night of the ball, shortly after you and I said good-bye. You went into the ladies' salon to get your corset laces adjusted,

84

and someone knocked over a gas lamp near the door. It ignited the carpet and wallpaper. Twenty-three people perished in the blaze."

My stomach flips at the realization of how close I came to dying without knowing it, and then flips again when I realize that I sent my other self to her death. If I hadn't been so picky about that corset—if I hadn't been the target of a deranged Traveler to begin with—his Jessa would be alive and well.

I bury my face in my hands. "Oh God. I'm sorry. I'm so sorry."

"You couldn't have known," he says.

I shake my head. "I knew there was someone trying to kill me. I should have told you."

"I knew it as well. Why do you think I was at the ball that night? I should have never let you out of my sight."

"And I shouldn't have even been there that night," I say, pushing to my feet. I'm pacing, I'm so upset. "I should never have traveled. I wasn't even on a job!"

"I knew that, too, love. You were there because I was irresistible."

He gives me an attempt at a smile, but it still doesn't hide the pain in his eyes. "And now Mario tells me that you've lost me, just as I've lost you. Perhaps it's a good thing for us to find each other again."

I pull my arms in across my body as if they'll shield me somehow. "No. I don't know what Mario was thinking. You shouldn't be here. I've got enough going on—"

"Which is exactly why you need me," he interrupts. "Rudy will surely make his move soon. He can't hide forever."

"He's a Dreamer," I remind him. "He can absolutely hide forever. He can wait until I'm dead and come after my descendants five generations from now."

"Not when he feels things are already out of hand," Finn points out. "He sees the convergence as the only way to control a universe of realities that have grown and expanded out of control—at least, that's what Mario has told me."

"How long have you been talking to him?" I ask. "Mario?"

"Since shortly after the night you perished," he said. "I had to know which of you was gone—if you'd made your transfer before or after the fire. Rudy, as you know, was nowhere to be found, but a few nights later, Mario was waiting for me in the dreamscape. He told me what had happened with Rudy and let me know you'd made it back safely."

"Eversor must have set up the gas lamp in your reality and then transferred through to plant the handbag your Jessa tripped over on the roof in my reality," I say as I sit down next to him again. "She must've thought she was covering her bases, and that she'd end up getting me either way."

"Eversor—that's the Traveler?"

"She's Rudy's right hand. She killed . . . you. Here, I mean."

"I'm sorry, love."

His hand comes out to close over mine, and I am swamped with the warm familiarity of it to the point of feeling like I'm choking. I pull my hand away and rub my palms on my knees.

"Anyway, she's surfaced again. And now she's targeting people around me. So you're better off steering clear."

He grabs me by the shoulder. "Wait—you saw her? Here?"

"In New York City. We ran into each other."

"That means she could be here," he says, leaping to his feet and pacing. "She had to have followed you here. Think! Where would she hide?"

"I have no idea. And I'm certainly not going to go looking for her. Not until we know exactly what she's planning to do."

"She's bloody well planning to kill you!" he fumes. "And all of us, if she gets around to it! What more do we need to know?"

"We need to know what she's up to—and I'm working on that. She's after someth—"

"What? What is she looking for?" he snaps.

I hold up a hand to shut him up. "I don't know!"

"But you must have some idea? Any link to that is a link to her, and we can *find* her!"

"I know that!" I say, jumping to my feet to get him out of my face. "Don't you think I know that? We're working on it! And we don't need you here making things difficult!"

"*Difficult?*" He's good and offended now, and I couldn't care less. "I'm supposed to be helping you—and at Mario's request."

"I don't need a bodyguard."

"I'm to continue your training," he says. "Mario says your skills have grown stronger but still need some refining."

"I don't need you here!"

We stare at each other in the awful silence, and I realize my words have struck their mark. He's looking at the ground, and a muscle in his jaw is ticking furiously.

"Look . . . I just—" I break off, shaking my head and biting down on my lip. I know what I want to say. What I want to shout, really. I take a deep breath and try again. "I can't do this. I can't . . . have you here."

His eyes widen slightly. "You think this is any easier for me to bear? Seeing you?"

I tamp down on the little flutter that comes with his words. This is Finn, but he's not my Finn. I can't let him be.

"That's just what I mean," I say. "This isn't good for either one of us. How does Mario expect us to do our jobs when we're forced into a situation like this?"

He stands up in front of me. "D'you really think I was forced to come here?" he asks. "I've been trying to find you for weeks. Mario wouldn't allow me to until he felt it was time. I think he finally realized I'd tear through the entire bloody universe if I had to in order to find you."

There goes that flutter again, somewhere in the region of my belly. *Whirlwind romances only tear you apart. . . .*

"It's not going to work—" I begin.

"Finding you means finding *her*! Eversor! And when I do, she will pay for what she's done."

"So that's all this is to you? Vengeance?"

"And it's not for you?" he snarls. "Or wasn't I important enough over here?"

My open hand flies out and connects with his jaw, hard enough to turn his head.

"Get. Out," I say furiously.

"I'm not going anywhere, love."

"My room. My house. Get out!"

He stares at me and his eyes go from blazing to thoughtful.

He reaches out, touching a strand of my hair in an entirely too familiar way.

"I suppose you need some time," he says quietly. "I can't give you much, but I'll respect your need for it all the same."

Why is my throat so tight? I manage a stilted good-bye, and then, with a nod, he's out the door, down the stairs, and gone.

12

Under the Surface

I COULD TELL I WAS IN FOR IT JUST BY THE WAY MY MOM was gnawing her lip. She always does that right before we're about to have a heavy conversation. Like I need this on top of everything else. I sit down at the dinner table and wait for it.

"Jessa . . . ," she starts, and she slides the bowl of broccoli across the table to me before she reaches for the rice that Danny just finished helping himself to.

"What's up?" I say lightly.

"Danny told me your friend Flynn is back?"

"*Finn*," I correct her, and then I glare at Danny. "And yeah, he's back."

"Well . . . ?" She gives me a very pointed look.

"Well what?" I really don't have the patience for this.

I start stuffing chicken into my mouth, determined to get through this dinner as quickly as possible. I swear, this is a setup. Mom suddenly decided a few weeks ago that we should have more sit-down family dinners instead of eating in the living room, and now two nights a week I'm part of a captive audience. I think she was secretly hoping something would come up so she could give me the third degree over it.

"Mom says Finn is a criminal," Danny blurts out. "Did he rob a bank?"

"*What? Mom!*"

My mother gives Danny a glare of her own. "Danny, I said no such thing. I said that Finn had been *involved* with a criminal."

"He wasn't involved with a criminal," I say through gritted teeth. "He left for another reason."

"Did he say why? Because the school seemed to have no idea why he dropped out. And the police were unable to find or contact his parents."

"He's eighteen, Mom," I remind her. "The police dropped the case. Why can't you?"

"Because he's visiting my daughter," she says stonily.

"He just wanted to say hi," I mumble. "And no one could find his parents because there was a family emergency, all right? He had to leave, and now he's back. Despite what everyone thinks, there's nothing more to the story than that."

She looks like she wants to say more, but instead she's cutting her chicken into minuscule bite-size pieces with a thoroughness that borders on manic. Danny is dipping his broccoli into a big glob of ketchup.

"Is that why he's changed?" Danny asks. "'Cause of the emergency?"

I look at him warily, and once again I'm flummoxed by the way he seems to see right through the Traveler thing.

"He's just had some different experiences." My eyes dart to

my mother, who's still cutting chicken. "Since he's been gone, I mean."

"So is he back for good?" Mom looks up from her chicken, and she's clearly not happy with this thought.

"I don't know," I say. "Things at home for him are . . . sort of unstable."

Mom's eyes show her concern. "Is everything okay? Does he need help? Police intervention?"

"No, it's not like that. It's just that things are kind of up in the air for him, and they may be for a while. He only came by to say hi."

I shovel in the last mouthful of my chicken, wash it down with a gulp of iced tea, and then stand up.

"May I be excused? I have homework to work on."

Mom eyes me for a moment before she sighs. "Go ahead."

I run for my room and hesitate in the doorway after I switch the light on. It's empty. I close the door and then sink down onto the bed. My brain is in such a state of turmoil right now, it's hard to think. I yank my messenger bag up from the floor, getting out the snow globe I bought for Danny so I can wrap it later and setting it aside, and my fingers brush the edge of my journal. I pull it out, laying it on the bed in front of me, and I just stare at it.

My fingers itch to slide the pen from where it's clipped to the cover, open it up to a crisp, white page, and work out everything that's inside me with swirls of ink across the paper, but I still can't do it. I don't think I can, anyway.

I open it up to the angsty poem the other me wrote, and I can't help the half smile that touches my lips as I read it again. I mean, it's not all bad. If she reworked it, took out some of the drama, and fleshed out the ideas behind what she was really trying to say, maybe it could be salvaged.

The fact is, I have another creative writing assignment due, and I've got to put something down on paper. I've held my own for weeks by turning in old stories and poems I wrote back in middle school, but I've run out of stuff. I have to turn in my piece by Monday on the theme "Beginnings," for the January issue of *The Articulator*, which is stupid because come January, I won't be in creative writing anymore.

I feel a weird pang at that thought, but I know it's for the best. I've lost it. Whatever it was that made me write—drove me to write—it's gone now.

Maybe I could turn the poem in and title it "The Inner Turmoil." Our new teacher, Miss Hawthorne, would probably eat it right up. She's fresh out of college and used to work as a sub until she had to stand in for Ms. Eversor. She has a degree in political science and has no idea what she's doing, so she thinks everything anyone does is "just great."

And it's not really cheating to turn this in. I wrote it, didn't I?

I pull my laptop out of my bag so I can transcribe the poem, but a tap at the door interrupts me.

"Jessa?"

Ugh. What does she want now?

"What?"

"I've got your laundry."

"Okay," I call out. "Come on in."

Mom opens the door, balancing the laundry basket against her hip, and then she walks over to set it down on the bed.

"I don't know what you got on the bottom of this shirt," she says, handing me my stack from the basket. "Looks like mustard?"

"Yeah." I take the stack and pull the shirt off the top to look at it. "Ben dropped his pretzel on me."

"How was the trip?" she asks. "You didn't tell me about it."

"Nothing much to tell. Spoke some Spanish, saw some dinosaur bones. . . ." I shrug, and then I pick up the snow globe. "Check out Danny's present."

Mom takes it from my hand and gives it a shake. "Oh, he'll love this."

"I hope so. It cost me enough."

She sits down on the bed next to me and holds the globe out for me to take.

"Hey," she says. "I wanted to say I'm sorry. I'm not trying to talk bad about—"

"Don't call him Flynn," I interrupt, holding up a finger.

She rolls her eyes. "*Finn*. If you say we've all misunderstood the situation, then I'll believe you. Just make sure you aren't misplacing your trust, okay?"

"You just said you believed me, but you think I'm being lied to," I say. "Make up your mind."

"I'm not talking about his reasons for going away. I'm talking about your heart." She sets the snow globe down on the bed, and her hand comes up to tuck my hair behind my ear. "Jessa, you fell hard for that boy, and when he left . . ." She stops for a moment and takes a breath. "Why do you think I started family dinners again? You've been so lost, honey—it's been hard to watch. I've just been trying to connect."

I don't know what to say, so I trace the designs on my bedspread with my finger.

"He may have had a legitimate reason for being gone and not contacting you all that time, but there's obviously more that went on with you. I don't need to know what." She raises her hand when she sees me start to interrupt. "I mean, I *want* to know what, but it's your choice not to talk about it, and I respect that. Just . . . be careful, okay? I know what it's like to have it all pulled out from under you."

That's the closest my mom has ever come to talking about her divorce with me. I give her a nod.

"Thanks. I'm okay, though. Really."

"It also hasn't escaped my notice that Ben's been stopping by. . . ."

"Mom." I give her a look.

She gets to her feet and grabs the basket. "All right, all right—enough interfering. I'm just doing the mom thing and reminding you of all the people who've been here for you. As opposed to those who have *not*."

"Duly noted."

She heads for the door and gives me one more hesitant smile over her shoulder before she pulls it closed behind her. I stare down at the poem again and realize that the other me might be onto something, after all. I've lived in darkness for the last six weeks, and now people are trying to coax me out of it before I'm ready. I hadn't realized how closely they were all watching me.

The thought sinks in, and I find my eyes drifting to my window. The blinds are closed, but something trails down my spine—an inkling—and I walk over to it. My fingers slip between the louvres, pushing them apart enough for me to see out into the backyard.

And there he is.

He's standing just under the old oak in the far corner of the yard, half in the shadows. He must have been looking up at my window because he starts forward when he sees me watching. I pull my hand out and the blind closes again.

Is he going to stay out there all night?

He has no counterpart here. And last time Rudy had someone—I realize now it was probably Eversor—set Finn up with a room and money and a phone. He has none of that now, unless Mario made arrangements somehow. Knowing Finn, it wouldn't matter. He'll sleep in the backyard in the freezing December cold just to keep an eye on me. Too bad Mom didn't buy the lawn tractor like Danny wanted—at least then Finn might have had a shed to sleep in.

I start to reach for the blinds again, but I clench my hand into a fist, refusing to open them and look. I know I'll see him out there, hoping to see me. I open the blinds a hairbreadth. Just enough to look out.

He's in the middle of the backyard now, just standing. His hands are shoved down in his pockets.

I drop the blind and dive for my bed, punching the pillow down, determined to keep the tears at bay.

13

Betrayed

MARIO DOESN'T NOTICE ME WHEN I ENTER THE classroom, and I don't say a word, choosing instead to stare at him for a minute while I figure out whether or not I'm going to hit him or yell at him.

I'll probably hit him. I seem to be on a roll with that one. He's slumped down sideways at his desk, rubbing a tired hand over his face.

"Rotten day?" I ask sarcastically.

He takes the hand off his face and straightens in his chair. "We're down a Dreamer, remember? There's a lot going on. And don't forget I've got two Travelers now."

"I'm aware of that."

I cross my arms over my chest and stare him down. He pushes back from the desk and gets to his feet.

"Jessa, I'm sure you're upset. . . ."

"By what? The uninvited pirate I found in my bedroom today?"

"*I* invited him. He had to have help to get to your reality," he says with a put-upon sigh. "Not that I had much choice. He's a very determined guy."

"Why, Mario?"

"Things are getting . . . complicated. Eversor is on the move again, and it won't be long before you're back in her crosshairs. You need someone to train you hands-on—I can only do so much from here—and you need an extra set of eyes watching your back."

"You know what I mean. Why *him?*"

"I thought you'd feel more comfortable with someone you know and trust," he says. "I know you've dreamed about him since you last saw each other."

I feel myself flush a dull red, which is silly considering this place is all in my mind.

"Don't be embarrassed," Mario says kindly. "He's dreamed about you, too."

"Of course he dreams about his Jessa—"

"Not just his Jessa," Mario replies. "You specifically. And as such, I thought the two of you could help each other."

"All we have in common is that we're two people who barely know each other and we both travel."

"You know each other pretty well, whether you want to admit it or not. And you've both lost someone," he adds quietly. "You understand each other and the issues at stake in ways no one else could. That makes you a good team. And for what it's worth—you can be a big help to him."

"How do you figure that?"

"He's here for one reason only, or so he thinks. Vengeance. He wants Eversor."

"So do I." My voice is cold and hard and I mean every one of those three words.

"You know her on sight. He doesn't. But you do know *him*."

"What's that supposed to mean?"

Mario leans back against his desk. "It means he needs to shift his focus. That kind of single-mindedness isn't going to serve our purposes."

"You mean *your* purposes," I say. "Getting Eversor suits me and Finn just fine. And don't we need to stop her before she kills us all?"

"I've got enough going on without a pirate with a thirst for blood getting in the way and making rash choices without super-vision."

"So he's my bodyguard and I'm his babysitter," I say bitterly.

"It's not like that."

"Yes, it is."

He lets out a sigh. "I'm not going to fight about this, Jessa. What's done is done. Finn is here, and he's staying for as long as it takes."

I start to object again and he holds up a hand.

"And before you go quitting again, I'll remind you that you're not the only one involved anymore. Eversor is going to eliminate anyone she perceives as a threat or an obstacle. You're not doing anyone any good hiding in your room."

"I'm not hiding," I retort. "I'm going after her. I just don't want him to get in my way."

"So don't let him. He'll fall in line soon enough."

I make a huffing sound. I'm not even going to dignify that with a response.

"Get some sleep, Jessa," Mario says as he walks me to the door. "We could both use some rest."

I pause with my hand on the doorknob. "Hey—about you-know-who. He's sleeping in my backyard. In the cold. Can't you set him up with something?"

"I did. Come next semester, he's reenrolled in school—they think he was pulled for homeschooling, by the way. He's also got his room back at the YMCA. My guess is that he doesn't want to be that far from you."

"Great."

"He's worried about you, Jessa. He can't help but hover."

He's worried about losing his one sure link to Eversor, I think. This isn't about me. Not for him. Not anymore.

And it's better that way.

14

Motivations

I OPEN THE BACK DOOR, ZIPPING UP MY HOODIE BEFORE I step outside. At first, I don't see him, and I walk a little farther out.

"'Bout time," he chides, falling into step beside me. "It's nearly noon."

"Sorry. I slept late."

"Did you sleep well, at least?"

I give him a disgruntled look. "I slept."

"And now you've come out to see how I've fared overnight."

"I came out to tell you not to do this again. Mario says you've got a room. Use it."

"Not bloody likely, love."

"Stop calling me that."

He raises an eyebrow in response. "I haven't spoken with Mario since the night before my arrival. Any news on our missing friends?" he asks.

"Still no sign of Rudy. And Eversor hasn't resurfaced since the museum on Friday."

"Jessa!" Danny's voice calls me from the doorway. "Oh, hi, Finn!"

Finn takes a breath and wipes the dark look off his face to smile at my brother. "Hello, Danny. Good to see you again."

"Want to watch me play Minecraft?"

"Later, perhaps. I need to speak with your sister first."

"Okay. Jessa, Mom says come and eat something."

"I will," I say over my shoulder. "Ask Mom if he can have lunch with us."

I glance over at Finn, and he looks surprised. "You *are* hungry, aren't you?" I ask.

"Very," he says. "But I'd assumed I was persona non grata in your household."

"Who told you that?"

"Danny. He seems to think your mother isn't impressed."

"It'll be fine. Come on, it's freezing out here." I motion him to follow me, and we head inside. Mom is sliding the last of a pile of grilled cheese sandwiches onto a platter as Danny grabs two and runs off to the family room.

"There's tomato soup in the pot," she says, pointing to the stove with her spatula. "Hello, Finn." She gives him a forced smile and I sigh with relief when she gets his name right.

"Hello," he says, smiling back. "Thank you for your kind invitation. It smells delicious."

She looks at him oddly and I realize why: She's never heard his Irish lilt before.

"Ha!" I pin on a bright smile and give a little laugh. "My mom isn't used to hearing your accent. Last time you were here, you were practicing for that play, remember? You were using your American accent?"

"Right." He gives a nod and a smile. "I gave it up. Apparently, I'm terribly unbelievable."

Mom's eyebrows go up. "Well, you fooled me," she says. "And it's only grilled cheese and tomato soup. Nothing fancy."

"Your hospitality is welcome all the same," he says, reaching for a plate and helping himself to a sandwich.

I dip out a couple of mugs of soup, and my mother leans in and lowers her voice. "Is he coming to the performance?"

"I don't know," I answer quietly.

She gives Finn a furtive glance. "Didn't you invite Ben?"

Uuuuuuugh. I almost smack my own forehead until I remember I have a ladle in my hand.

"Something wrong?" Finn asks, picking up on my body language.

"Nothing. Just nerves."

He looks at me curiously and I explain. "I started dance classes a little over a month ago. The studio always does a holiday performance for the retirement home where my mom and Danny work. Today will be my first performance with them."

"Splendid." He looks intrigued. "What sort of dance is it?"

"It's a jazz number." I feel my cheeks redden. "It's kind of silly. Sparkly red tuxedo jackets and giant candy canes."

"It sounds brilliant. I look forward to it."

"Hey, don't you need to be getting ready?" Mom asks. "Dancers have to report by one, don't they?"

"That's right. I'd better go pack my bag." I grab my mug of

soup, passing one over to Finn. Then I scoop up a sandwich onto a plate and motion with my chin for him to follow me up to my room.

Once we're behind closed doors, I set my food down on the dresser and rummage through my closet for my dance bag.

"You were saying something about Eversor?" Finn asks around a mouthful of grilled cheese.

"Huh?" I peek my head back out of the closet, with my red leotard in my hand.

"When we were speaking before," he prompts. "You were about to tell me something about her."

"Oh . . . uh . . ." My voice is muffled as I root around for my dance shoes. "Mario thinks she may be trying to steal something."

"What?"

"I don't know, and he won't say till he's sure," I say, emerging from the closet. "Didn't Mario tell you everything that's been going on?"

He makes a face and reaches for his mug of soup. "We're not exactly on speaking terms."

"Since when?" I mean, Mario sent him here, after all.

"Since I threw a padlock at his head."

"A *padlock*?"

"I don't know how he fashions your meeting room, love, but mine looks like the captain's cabin of my ship. He shows me my instructional scenes through my porthole. I have a large trunk at the foot of my bed, and the lock was within reach."

"You threw it at his head?" I snort. "I mean, it's not like you can hurt him."

"I let my temper get the better of me. But I suppose it finally made him realize how very determined I was to find my way to you. He'd pulled me into the dreamscape to address my excessive traveling, you see."

He gives me a pointed look, and I wet my lips nervously. "You were looking that hard for me?" I ask.

"Yes."

"But you already knew I wasn't your Jessa."

"So I was told. I suppose I had to see for myself."

"Well, now you know."

"I wanted to know that you were safe as well," he says quietly. "And here you are."

"And here *you* are."

We stare at each other a moment. The pause that stretches between us goes on entirely too long, and I'm startled by the sound of my mother's voice.

"Jessa! Leaving in fifteen!"

"Okay! Be right down!" I call back before taking a breath and addressing Finn. "Listen . . . it would be better if you wait here. I mean, not 'in my bedroom' here, but also not going with me to the performance."

He's drinking his soup while I'm stammering through my request, and he's got one eyebrow up and it's really irking me.

"Not a chance," he replies, setting the mug down.

"It's not going to be me dancing anyway," I say. "I mean, it's me, but it's a different me. She's the dancer."

He's smirking now. "That's cheating, love."

"It's not cheating. And stop calling me that," I huff, pulling my tights out of my drawer and shoving them into my dance bag. "She lost my mom in her reality, and she always wished that Mom had seen her dance. So I'm kind of helping her out."

"Really?" He breaks into a genuine grin. "We've more in common with every passing moment. Remind me to tell you how I became a magician."

"A magician?"

"It's quite the tale, I assure you."

I shake my head to clear it. "I mean it, Finn. I need you to stay here. There will be kids from my school there—and there's a rumor going around that you took off with Eversor."

He makes a face. "Then this will be the perfect opportunity for me to disabuse them of that notion."

He is not going to make this easy.

"Ben will be there," I finally grit out. "He's a . . . friend. And I need to talk to him first so you're not a surprise."

He sits up straighter, and all his teasing humor is gone. "Ben? Who the devil is Ben?"

"I told you—he's a friend. He was with me when you—when you died. Here. He knows about us."

"Us?" His eyebrows go up.

"Travelers."

"So what's the problem then? If he's a friend?"

The way he said that last word makes it decidedly uncomfortable.

"He's *my* friend. Not yours."

"I see." He says it quietly, way too quietly.

"So . . . you need to hang back. I don't need you there."

"And you, *love*"—he stresses the word on purpose—"need to

learn not to give orders. As I recall, only one of us has an officer's rank. I'll be going, and that's an end to it."

"You can't order me around!" I huff. "If we're going to work together, you need to back the hell off. I'm not your Jessa. I'm not going to let you walk all over me."

"I'm here to do a job," he shoots back. "Until it's done—you won't be rid of me."

I open my mouth to tell him no, and then I close it again. Why waste my breath? He's clearly not going to leave my side.

"Fine." I reach for my phone.

"What are you doing?"

"I'm texting Ben to tell him I'm transferring over now so there's no point in him even coming." I finish the message and push my dance shoes and makeup into my bag and zip it shut. "Leaving now is a better idea, anyway. This way she gets more time with Mom."

I start to put my hand to the mirror over my dresser, and I give him an unfriendly glance over my shoulder.

"You coming?"

"Do I have a counterpart over there?"

"Not that I've met. I'll have to pull you through."

He's smiling in a smug way that makes me grit my teeth.

"Wouldn't miss it for the world," he says.

15

The Gloves Come Off

"SHE'S LOOKING AT YOU AGAIN," I SAY, GIVING FINN A nudge.

"She's been staring at me for nearly ten minutes," Finn says under his breath. "How many ways can you squeeze a peach? She'll bruise the lot of them."

We're standing in the grocery store in Arizona running errands until the recital is over—but this is an Arizona unlike ours, and this grocery store is beyond anything I've ever seen before.

Coupons hang from decorative hooks on the walls and displays, and some even dangle in clusters from the ceiling on colorful wires, all while the dozen or more TV screens around the store blare out ads for various products. Even the glass doors on the beverage cases have ads that interact with you. I'm fascinated by it all, flashing around me, screaming their catchphrases and playing their jingles.

I'm meandering down the aisle, thoroughly intrigued by the strange and unusual products I'm seeing on the revolving store shelves. Therapeutic tar and strawberry face gel? Sticky-Wicky Chips? And what the hell is Candied Rage Fruit? You never know what you're going to find when you enter an alternate reality, I guess.

"What do you think she wants?" Finn asks.

"How would I know?" I shrug. "Why don't you ask her?"

He stares at the woman warily, and I have to admit he's not being paranoid. The woman is watching his every move.

"I don't have a good feeling about this," he says. "We don't know if she has an ulterior motive."

I realize I've been so busy looking at all the crap in this stupid store, the thought didn't even occur to me.

"I'm going to go talk to her," I say, but before I can start forward, he puts his arm out to stop me.

"I'll go," he says.

I lower my voice again to a furious whisper. "If she's being duped by Eversor into setting us up—"

"—then I'll find out," he finishes. "I'm the one she's staring at. I'll go."

He wanders over to the display of blueberries beside the peaches, then leaps back in surprise as a giant stuffed berry on top of the stand comes to animatronic life, singing to him about the wonders of antioxidants. Sheesh. This place is unreal.

I hear him say hello to the woman and make some small talk about the weather, and then my hand claps over my mouth as I hear the dirty old broad proposition him in *very* descriptive terms. He shuts her down as diplomatically as possible, and I turn and walk for the cover of the nearest aisle so he can't see me laughing.

"Amused, are you?" he grumbles as he falls into step next to me.

"Oh, come on, you have to admit it was funny."

Finn gives me a death glare. "She was fifty if she was a day. And she was moments away from grabbing my arse."

"She was a cougar," I say with a smirk. "And she thought you were cute."

"Well, let's reverse that, shall we?" He glowers. "If some middle-age man with a bad hairpiece was chatting you up in the market, trying to get you to accompany him to his home to do his domestic chores without a shirt on, would it still be funny?"

I hadn't thought of it that way. "No, it wouldn't. You're right."

"'Course I'm right," he says. "And do I look like I'm a lawn boy? I don't even have a lawn!"

"You didn't have to come along," I remind him. "There isn't even a you in this reality."

"And what about you?" he asks grumpily. "Are you aligned with the mysterious 'Ben' here?"

"I haven't seen Ben Hastings in this reality at all. I'm not in Ardenville, remember?"

"Hastings?" Finn looks surprised. "Lovely."

"You know Ben?"

"I've run into him a time or two."

"Good or bad?"

"Mostly indifferent," he replies as we start loading stuff onto the conveyor belt at the checkout stand. "He's a bit of a fop, if you like that type. How long until we can return?"

I ignore his remarks and glance at my phone. "They're at the end of the finale—I'm in that, too. Once that's done, I need to give her at least five or ten more minutes so Mom can come backstage and congratulate her."

"Pity I won't see you dance."

"It's pretty impressive—for me," I tell him. "I have a solo in the middle of the number. Lots of kicks and a triple turn with a giant candy cane in my hand."

"It sounds quite thrilling."

"A real showstopper," I say as I pay the clerk and he grabs the bags. We head for the doors and out into the parking lot.

"Speaking of shows . . . ," I say. "You told me to ask about you being a magician."

"Ah, yes. I did." He nods.

"We've got some time to kill. Might as well enlighten me."

"There's not much more to it than your own ballerina story," he says, raising his voice a bit to be heard over the sound of the advertisements playing over the loudspeaker in the parking lot and the noise of the video screens over the cart returns shouting out the weekly sales.

"I have a younger brother in some of my alternate lives," he tells me. "In one particular version of my life, he's injured and uses a wheelchair. In the early days after his accident, he didn't get out as much. I used to teach him magic tricks."

"So you became a magician in order to do that?"

"I borrowed the knowledge from another of my selves," he says with a smile. "I cheated."

"I think we established that it's not cheating. It's shared knowledge."

"You have to admit, it all comes in quite handy at times."

I glance at the time once more as we reach the car and start loading our bags in. "Not too much longer. They're just about done now."

"Hey, handsome!" a voice calls from behind us. "Little help?"

We turn in unison, and it's the older lady again. Her grocery bag hangs in tatters and peaches are rolling all over the parking lot.

"Are you kidding me?" I huff under my breath.

Finn rolls his eyes and hands me his bag. "I suppose I should do the chivalrous thing and help her."

"Watch your arse," I goad, and he gives me a dark look before stalking over to her. I follow behind.

"Nice selection of man candy at this store," the woman calls out to me with a wink. "Am I right, honey?" She gestures to her fallen bag, and I bring my hand up, pretending I have an itch on my nose so Finn can't see that I'm trying not to laugh. He glowers at me anyway, and when he bends over to pick up the fruit, she's definitely enjoying the view.

I can't help it, a laugh squeaks through, but a heartbeat later I am stone-cold serious as I see a car round the corner at the end of the aisle behind Finn—and I hear the engine gun. There's no time to call a warning. I reach out and grab his arm, spinning him and yanking him back hard as the speeding car whizzes by. We both slam down onto the asphalt of the parking lot. The car screeches around the corner at the end of the row and keeps on going, but not before I get a clear look at the driver.

My palms are scraped, and my right knee feels like I ripped it up, as well. I flip over as fast as I can to see Finn, lying on the ground not far from me, his body contorted and writhing. I scramble over to him, keeping an eye on the car as it leaves the parking lot.

"Oh my God!" the woman says, rushing over to us. "She

could have killed you! I didn't get the license plate. She was going so fast!"

Finn grips my arm, and he's still not breathing right. "Jess—Jessa! H-help me up."

I look at him frantically because his breathing is so labored, and he's clutching his shoulder. I don't see blood anywhere, and he's rolled to his knees.

"I'm all right," he says. "Let's just get out of here."

I glance at Finn again, alarmed by how flushed he is. I wrap my arm around him and he manages to stumble to his feet with a grimace as the woman admonishes him for moving. He throws himself into the passenger seat of my car as I climb in and shut my own door. Then I throw the car in reverse, driving out of the lot as fast as I safely can. I pull off once we reach a side street.

"Are you okay?" I pant. "Tell me you're okay!"

"Was that her?" he thunders.

I nod. "Yes. It was her."

"Dammit!" He punches the door, and then he groans and grabs at his upper arm.

"You're hurt!"

He waves me off. "The mirror on her vehicle clipped my shoulder. I'll have one hell of a bruise, and I got the wind knocked out of me, but I'm all right."

"Hang on," I say, putting the car in gear. "I'll get us out of here. We'll go back to the store and get some ice for your shoulder. We can wait there until we're sure she's good and gone."

"Are you mad?" His hand shoots out, grabbing mine. "We have to catch her! Which way did her conveyance go?"

"We're not going after her!" I say adamantly. "She's trying to kill you!"

"We don't have time for this!" he snaps. "If you're not going to chase her then get out and I'll bloody well drive!"

"I am not losing you again!"

He stares at me in silence, tense and very, very angry.

"I didn't even see where she drove off to," I lie. "So calm down and let's get you taken care of."

I take my foot off the brake and ease out onto the road, determined to ignore the trembling of my fingertips, the pain in my body, and the sound of Finn grumbling under his breath. My eyes scan the road, trying to tune out the blaring, blazing billboards on either side. It looks like Eversor is long gone, but I'm not taking any chances.

I return to the store, being careful to park around back so we won't be recognized from the road. Finn waits in the car while I run inside. He glowers at me when I take the keys out of the ignition, but I wouldn't put it past him to drive off and leave me, as pissed as he is. I return with a bag of frozen peas.

"Can you move it?" I ask, laying the bag of peas across his shoulder. He winces and reaches up to adjust it.

"I'll get by."

"We should have a doctor look at it."

"It's fine." His jaw is ticking furiously, and he won't look at me. I glance down at the dashboard clock.

"Let me leave my other self a note so I know to be on the lookout—just in case Eversor comes back," I say, fishing a pen out of my purse and scrawling a quick note on the back of the cash register receipt. I leave it on the dashboard and then I angle the rearview mirror so I can see into it.

"You ready?"

He glowers at me again and gives a nod as he shifts over next to me. He's smushed into me so we can both see the mirror, and I can feel that every muscle in his body is stiff and rigid. I place my fingers against the mirror, and a few moments later, she responds.

In the space of a heartbeat, we're through to the dressing room at the retirement home, and I'm clutching a big wad of tissues in my hand—which is a really good thing because I immediately burst into tears as the aftermath of both realities washes over me.

Here, I had finished my final curtain call and run around to the back, where my mom met me in the middle of the hallway. She had thrown her arms around me with a "Wow! Jessa! You're amazing!"

She'd gushed over me for a good long time, and I knew I was about to cry so I'd just hugged her and hugged her. Mom had finally had to awkwardly pry me off her and remind me that I needed to get out of my costume. Then I'd made my way to the now-empty dressing room and, according to the tearstained note I'd left myself, I doubted I'd ever been this happy.

Well, at least that went all right. I feel guilty because I had to leave her a note explaining why she's covered in scrapes and bruises.

I can see my reflection in the mirror in front of me. I'm riding a crazy mix of elation and fear. Everything's a jumble. I see Finn in the mirror behind me, pacing the room and rotating his arm.

"Is your shoulder okay? We can probably get some ice for you."

"Damn!" he exclaims. "She was *that* close!"

He slams his fist angrily down onto a nearby table, and a couple of props tumble off and hit the floor.

"Hey! Watch it!"

"How did you not see her before that?" he demands. "She had to be close by. Perhaps even following us through the market!"

"I was shopping!" I shout back.

He turns away with a growl and kicks a chair, sending it skittering across the floor.

I get shakily to my feet, wanting to put some distance between us. "My mom must think I'm nuts, falling apart on her like that. I'd better get out there."

He's not even looking at me, and now I'm adding a new emotion to go with my alternating joy and terror: anger. He's acting like this is my fault.

Mario was right—Finn is only here because he wants to get Eversor. And I can lead him right to her.

I am suddenly incredibly tired. I just want to go home. I reach down and start packing up my stuff as Finn throws himself into a chair and sulks with his arms across his chest. Eventually I walk over to the door, not even bothering to look at him. He can just sit there and stew all day, for all I care.

Of course, I don't get that lucky. He stomps out after me. We make it down the hallway and turn the corner, where I run smack into somebody carrying a bouquet of flowers.

Crap.

I guess Ben decided to show up after all.

16

Sparring Match

"WHAT THE ... ?" THE FLOWERS SLIP OUT OF BEN'S fingers and fall to the floor as he stares openmouthed at Finn.

"Ben," I say, stepping between them. "We have to talk."

"He's *here*?" Ben is still staring at Finn, who has jammed his hands into his pockets and is rocking back and forth on his heels.

"Is he always this astute?" Finn asks blandly.

I give Finn a warning look, but he's staring at Ben.

"He can't be here!" Ben hisses. "Everyone thinks he's gone!"

"Well, now I've returned," Finn says amiably. "I'm sure I'll pick up right where I left off."

He gives Ben a purely taunting smile, and Ben looks like he's about to turn green and split out of his shirt. I need to defuse this situation, and fast.

"Can we take this someplace private?" I ask. "Please?"

"Fine," Ben bites out. I turn to walk back to the room we just left, but Finn takes a few steps forward and scoops up Ben's flowers.

"Here you go, love," he says as he hands them to me.

Ben takes two steps and yanks the flowers out of my hands. "I'll give her my own damn flowers!"

"Stop it! Both of you!"

I turn and walk back into the dressing room, holding the door for Ben. I put a hand to the middle of Finn's chest when he tries to go in behind him.

"Hold on," I say. "Let me talk to him alone for a minute."

Finn gives me a stony look. "Not a chance."

"Stop." Honest to God, I'm just not in the mood for this.

"Less than half an hour ago we were very nearly killed," he reminds me. "I'm not letting you out of my sight."

"You were *what?*" Ben demands from behind me. He spins me around. "Was it Eversor?"

I nod. "Not here. Over there. And she was aiming for him." I jerk a thumb over my shoulder in Finn's general direction.

"And if she tries again, I'll be waiting," he snarls.

"Of course you will," I shoot back. "You wouldn't miss it for the world!"

"And what is that supposed to mean?"

"Hey!" Ben snaps. "I'm over here, remember? And I need some explanations. Now."

I let out a sigh and motion for Finn to enter the room before I shut the door. "Stay there," I tell him.

He rolls his eyes at me as he leans his shoulder against the door, but he looks like he's going to stay put. I grab Ben by the arm and walk him back toward the far corner of the room.

"He's here to keep an eye on me while I travel," I tell him quietly. "Like a bodyguard."

"I thought you told Luigi—"

"Mario."

"*Mario.* I thought you told him you wanted to be away from him."

"Mario thought that since we knew each other already, we'd be able to work together."

"What do you mean, 'you knew each other'?" Ben's voice rises with alarm.

"Will you calm down?" I urge. "I met him in another reality. I met you, too, over there, if that makes a difference to you. Only you weren't a pirate."

"He's a *pirate?* Great."

"He's a *privateer,*" I correct.

Ben gives me an annoyed look. "That's a pirate who just happens to be on the right side of the current government."

"An important distinction," Finn says, coming up behind me. "But I'm still the man with the ship and the dashing reputation."

I let out a huff of air, and before I can answer him, Ben reaches out to take my hand.

"Hey," he says, "he's not the only one watching out for you, y'know."

"The lady doesn't need another bodyguard," Finn's voice cuts in. "You can go about your business and let us handle it from here."

"I'm not going *anywhere,*" Ben says. "And you don't even belong here."

"Yet here I am," Finn says, folding his arms across his chest.

"Come on, you guys," I growl. "We don't really have time—"

"Jessa?" My mom's voice breaks through from the other side of the door. "Is everything okay, honey?" she asks.

"Mom!" I call back. "I'll be there in a couple of minutes."

"Well, hurry up. Danny wants to treat you to ice cream."

"Two minutes," I promise her. "I'll be right out."

"I'll be waiting in the car."

"Okay."

We all listen as her footsteps fade away down the hall.

I grind my teeth together and look at both of them. "Listen, you two. I've got enough to worry about without having to play referee here. And I don't need either of you to play knight-in-shining-armor for me. Once I talk to Mario, I'll have some more answers, and we can take it from there."

Finn starts to open his mouth, and I shut that right down.

"Zip it," I bite out. "I mean it. Now let's go get some damn ice cream."

"All of us?" Ben asks carefully.

I don't even bother looking at Finn because I know just what look he has on his face.

"Come on." I stomp to the door and out.

In the last hour I've been terrified, pissed off, flooded with heart-wrenching sentiments, and right back to pissed off again. I could hop through a dozen mirrors to a dozen different lives and not feel as exhausted as I feel just bouncing between three different emotions. How the hell did I end up in this roller coaster of a life?

I don't have time to feel sorry for myself, because Danny is running up to hug me, and he pulls me along toward the door, telling me all about the recital—which probably seems odd to passersby, but as usual, Danny knows I wasn't myself today.

We get to the car and my mother gives me a wide-eyed look as she sees Finn and Ben standing behind me, pointedly ignoring each other.

"Want a ride to the ice cream place?" Ben asks.

Danny unwinds his arm from around my shoulders, and says, "Sure I do, Ben!"

Ben manages to paste on a smile and awkwardly tells me they'll meet us over there. Finn looks a little too smug as they walk off, and I swear to God, I'm ready to smack him again. I slide into the passenger seat next to my mom and slam the door as he gets in behind us.

Mom gives me another worried glance, but she's wise enough to stay the hell out of it. The ride to the ice cream place is mercifully short, and then we all spend the next twenty minutes making awkward, stilted small talk—all except Danny, of course, who's blissfully oblivious to the two pillars of simmering testosterone at the table. My mother's eyebrows are going to become a permanent part of her hairline if we don't get out of here soon.

Ben finally decides he's had enough and pushes his chair back from the table.

"Leaving so soon?" Finn asks.

Ben gives him a narrow-eyed look and asks me to walk him to his truck. He scoops up my flowers from where I laid them on the table, holding them out to me once again.

"You were amazing today," he says as we walk out to the parking lot.

"It wasn't me," I remind him.

"I'm not talking about the dancing. I saw you with your mom. You did a really nice thing."

I take the flowers, and I bury my nose in them. "Thanks again for coming. And I'm sorry about today. I should have warned you."

"Yeah, well . . . I guess you had enough to worry about, with Eversor showing up again." He smacks his forehead. "Speaking of which—I did some research on that theft in Mexico—at the museum."

"Was it her?"

"It was a woman who matches the description—and she got away. I didn't get to dig much deeper yet, but I'm fixing to go home and put my head into it."

"Thanks, Ben. I really appreciate your help. Let me know if you find out what she was after—and how it ties in with New York."

He glances through the windows into the dining room to where Finn is sitting. "I'll tell you all about it tomorrow when Captain Reflecto isn't around."

"Captain *Reflecto*? That's the best you could come up with?"

"I'm not at the top of my game," he grumbles.

"We need to keep him in the loop. He's working on this, too, Ben. Like it or not."

"How about *not*?" He sighs and reaches out and takes my free hand. "Sorry. I'm being a jerk. This can't be easy for you, either."

"You're not a jerk." I bat the tip of his nose with my flowers and a smile lights his eyes—and then slowly fades into a look of annoyance. I don't have to guess who just walked up behind me.

"Time to go, love," Finn prompts. The endearment makes me grit my teeth.

"I'll be there in a minute," I say over my shoulder, without really looking at him. I hold my breath until I hear him walk away. "Sorry," I say to Ben.

Ben takes a calming breath of his own and forces the smile back to his face. "We'll talk tomorrow," he says. "Hey, that new sci-fi movie is out. The one with the exploding space eggs. The theater runs a five-dollar movie at five tomorrow. You in?"

"You had me at exploding space eggs," I answer. And before I can get another word out, Ben leans in and kisses me, right in front of the world. And Finn. I give my flowers a self-conscious shake as we pull apart, making sure they didn't get crushed or bent.

"Later, St. Clair," he says, climbing into his truck with a satisfied grin.

Finn says not one word to me as I walk over to the car. I toy with the idea of telling him to get lost, but I can't. Even though I'm pissed at him, I still worry that Eversor isn't done for the day.

I open the back door and climb in, then he flounces down into the seat next to me, crossing his arms over his chest. Danny turns around from the front seat to address the situation.

"Is Finn mad 'cause you kicked yourself in the face?" he asks me.

17

Beginnings

"JUST HOW LONG ARE YOU GOING TO IGNORE ME?" FINN asks, steepling his fingers together and looking at me from across the table.

It's Sunday after dinner. Danny's in the other room playing on his Xbox, Mom has a late shift at the drugstore because Christmas is only a couple of weeks away, and I have an assignment due tomorrow that I can't seem to finish because I'm being irritated by a pirate.

"I'm trying to work," I say, forcing my eyes back to the blank paper in front of me.

I can hear him sigh.

"Jessa, I apologize."

I don't look up from my paper. "For what, exactly?"

"I had no idea your friend would be in such a snit over the sight of me."

I put my pen down and look at him. "Is that what you think this is about? And Ben wasn't in a snit. Nobody uses that word here. It's archaic."

"Oh, but they use words like *archaic*, do they?" he snaps back. "And how was I to know he'd behave that way?"

"I told you to stay home—or at least out of sight!"

"Perhaps it slipped my mind as I was injured and nearly killed by a maniac in a motorized conveyance! You didn't ask me how I'm feeling now, by the way," he points out.

"I've been too distracted by a sulking pirate!"

Now he looks really offended. "What I do is perfectly within the bounds of the law."

"You know what I mean."

"I suppose I do," he says grimly. "It seems to boil down to the fact that I'm not *him*. Not your Finn."

I shake my head. "That's not the issue here."

"Isn't it?" His eyes are blazing with anger. "You think my way of making a living is beneath you? I'll never live up to his sainted memory because I'm *just not him*."

"That's not fair! I'm not *her*, either!"

"Yes, you are! You're a part of her, you've lived in her skin!"

"So what?" I demand. "You want me to be some kind of replacement?"

"Why are you fighting?" Danny asks, appearing in the doorway. "You shouldn't be fighting."

Finn takes a deep breath and sits back in his chair. I pin a smile on and look up at Danny.

"We're just discussing something," I explain.

"No, you were fighting," he says. "And you're going to get in trouble for fighting, *Jessa Emeline St. Clair*."

I groan inwardly at the use of the dreaded triple name. "We're fine, Danny. Everything's okay."

"You should both say sorry," he says, "when you fight."

"He's absolutely right . . . Emeline," Finn says. I look over at him with serious irritation that only gets worse when I see his smile.

"You can go back to playing Xbox," I say to Danny. "We won't be shouting anymore."

"*I* certainly won't be," Finn says.

Danny shrugs and returns to his game, and I pull my notebook closer and give Finn a disgruntled look.

"If you don't mind," I say stiffly, "I need to finish this."

"By all means," he says a bit too formally.

"Fine."

"Fine, then. Damn." He swears softly under his breath and he rubs his hand across the back of his neck. "Jessa, I'd like to apologize for both my careless words and my anger at you earlier. I know you couldn't have seen the way our outing would play out. I was just bloody furious that she came so close, only to dance away unscathed."

"I understand the anger," I say. "I feel it, too. But I'm not going to apologize for taking care of an injured friend."

"And you consider me a friend?"

I let that hang there a minute. "I guess."

"Jessa—I need to know. You and Hastings. Are you . . . ?"

I raise my brows and give him a pointed look. "Am I . . . ?"

"Bloody hell, you know what I'm asking."

"Would it matter to you if I say yes?"

"*Is* that a yes?"

"I don't see how my life in this reality is any of your business."

"Not my business?" he splutters. "I only tore through the universe to get to you!"

"And now you're tearing into someone I care about!" I fume. "And for your information, he's working with us now. He was with me when I lost . . . when the other you died," I get out. "So he knows. And he's an absolute wiz when it comes to history."

"A wiz? Does that have a different meaning over here?"

"Oh for . . . it can also mean someone's very good at something," I explain. "Ben's dad is a history professor, and he's really well-informed on the subject. Ben also loves a good mystery. If anyone can track down what Eversor is looking for, he can."

"All right, all right," he says, holding up a hand in surrender. "If you say we need him, I'll defer to your judgment."

"Good," I say, picking up my pen again. "Then it's settled."

"You didn't answer my question about Ben." His eyes are searching mine, and I fight the urge to squirm. I make myself hold his gaze.

"We're trying it out," I finally say. "He's been there for me. I trust him. And he makes me laugh."

"Well, there's a ringing endorsement."

"It is, actually."

"Very well, then," he says quietly. "I'll do my best to work with him in a civil fashion. He can do the research while I watch your back."

"Watch it from the other room," I say, gesturing with my pen. "I need to get this done."

"Perhaps I can look through this," he says, reaching over to the end of the table and pulling our local newspaper toward him. *The Hudson River Round-up*," he reads. "Sounds riveting."

"All twelve pages of it," I snark. "You're not going to find any breaking news about psychopathic Travelers in there."

He leans back, shaking the paper open and laying it on the table in front of him. "It'll give me a feel for the area," he says. "This is a charming little town."

"You think?" I crinkle my nose at him.

"It's easy to long for unseen shores, but home can hold its beauty in the simplest of things."

I blink at him slowly. "Do you rehearse this stuff? I swear, nobody talks like you."

He gives me a cheeky grin. "Saw it embroidered on a sampler once. Still true, though."

I return to my work. The minutes roll by and I'm doing my best to stay focused, but I find myself looking up entirely too often. Worse, I'm meeting his eyes when I do it most of the time. I force myself to look back down.

I'm staring at the paper, and this is hopeless. I've tried to rework that crummy poem four different times, and it's just not falling into place. Poetry has never been my thing, but still, I should be able to write *something*.

I'm not a writer. Not anymore.

I let out a huff of air and shove my face into my hands.

"Problem?"

"Yeah. I think I broke my brain."

"I have no doubt your brain is as sharp as ever. Which area of study is this for?" he asks, gesturing at my paper.

"Creative writing. I have to write something about beginnings."

"Perhaps I can help?"

I shake my head. "I don't see how. Unless you want to write it for me."

He smiles slightly. "No, that's your forte. I'm the one with all the stories. I've been traveling—both on sea and otherwise—for quite a long time, you know."

"I wrote? I mean . . . she wrote?"

"She kept a journal, as do most young ladies of her station. I always felt she had a gift for words."

"Really?" I don't know why, but I'm pleased by that.

"Perhaps you could write something of your other lives. It seems to me you have a circumstance a writer would envy, being able to see yourself in so many ways."

You have something that any writer would kill to have, my Finn told me once. *Unlimited worlds to explore. . . .* Before I met him, that's all I did—I wrote about my other lives. Of course, I had no idea I was writing the truth back then—I thought they were all remnants of my dreams.

"That's a good idea," I say begrudgingly. "Thanks."

"I'm not entirely useless, love."

"I never said you were."

A pause hangs between us before he gives me an encouraging nod. "Back to work," he says as he gets out of his chair to refill his mug of tea.

I look down at my notebook and let my mind drift, sifting through memories, both here and elsewhere.

I touch my pen to the paper and write the word *She.*

I live so many lives, have access to so many memories while I'm in those lives. Surely there must be something.

A dancer. A deaf girl. Living in a crime zone, and in glittering opulence. Facing the actuaries. Swimming with talking dolphins. . . .

That memory brings me back to a cozy little restaurant on a dock, strange green bread, and Finn—my Finn—warm and alive as we talk about how the smallest of actions can ripple into the largest outcomes.

We are what we are, and who we are. Infinite Jessas and infinite Finns, just stumbling our way through so many of our lives, and doing the best we can. *Maybe we're more resilient than most,* he'd said.

I think of Finn as he is to me now, kicking down doors between realities until Mario gave in and let him through. I know they're different, but very much the same in the things that make them who they are. Or were.

My pen touches the paper again, striking a line through the *s* in *She*, changing it to *He*. And for the first time in what feels like a very long time, I fill myself up with the memories my Finn once shared with me.

I can't tell my stories so well right now—but maybe, maybe I can tell his.

My pen begins moving against the paper, slowly at first and then with more determination as the words begin to flow.

He was born in a time of growing darkness. A time of cold dirt and fallen logs, lifeless seas and empty skies. Each day was just like the last, waking in fear at every stray sound, finding a safe place, just for now (because safe places never stayed safe—this he'd learned long ago), and if he was lucky, something to put in his stomach.

He was walking that day to nowhere in particular. Each place was always like the last, picked over, scattered, broken glass and the same bland smell of a town or a house full of nothing to sustain him. He'd woken from a dream that morning, vivid and full of warm sun on his back, the sound of water rushing by.

And her face. He didn't know her—surely she was a construct of his dreams to keep the loneliness at bay—but she was so much a part of his nocturnal world, she felt real. As if he might truly know her, perhaps meet her someday, when he was older.

He made a scoffing sound that was almost a laugh. He couldn't be sure as he hadn't heard laughter, particularly his own, in a very long time. But it was foolish to the point of madness to entertain dreams of growing old in this place. No one grew old here. Even if he should keep going another day and another and another after that, the world was dying as fast as he was.

He trudged up the rocky hill, covered in scraggly, yellowed mounds where patches of grass once covered the ground. If he grew any hungrier today, he'd dig some of them up and eat them, grimacing at the grit of dirt in his teeth. It wasn't nourishing, but it would keep his belly from hurting.

He crested the hill and staggered back, reeling from the sight below. He even shook his head, wondering if he was seeing things that weren't really there. It happened every so often, usually when he'd gone too many days without food, but this was no hallucination.

It was a tree, and it was still green.

The oak stood alone on the bank at the bend of a small river—or perhaps a wide creek. He wasn't sure because he had no knowledge of where he'd wandered to. Maps were a bygone thing.

He stumbled down the side of the hill on legs made rubber by the excitement, running full-on into the trunk and laying his fingers against it. He stared up through the branches at the glorious green;

then, realizing his thirst, he threw himself down next to it to scoop handfuls of cool water into his mouth.

He saw no fish, which was a disappointment but not a surprise. The soil had eroded away to the point that he could see the tree's roots as they grew into the water, splitting as they branched out up and down the bank. Between the split lay a pool created by curve of the roots, and the water within was still as glass.

He lay down, pillowing his head on one of the larger roots, trailing his fingers through the water as he listened to the sound of wind rushing through the leaves above him, wondering if this was what it used to be like, in the time of his parents, when trees were lush and full and grass was everywhere, green and soft beneath your feet.

His eyes met his reflection, and within the depths of the pool he saw his life play out, as it should have been. Could have been. Running across grass, sharing meals with a family, laughing with friends, traveling by car, or train, or ship. Walking the good green earth and never feeling hungry or afraid. Growing old with her at his side.

But those were dreams for another time, and another life. He lived in the now, and this, for him, was as good as now could get.

He sighed, settling his head more comfortably on the tree root, and reached out to touch the water once more. His fingertips grazed the surface, and his eyes, within the pool, were as green as the leaves above. He saw his lips curve into a smile and then they moved, forming words.

And in the rustling of the leaves above, he thought he heard a voice whisper, "Come over. . . ."

I set my pen down with a long, cathartic exhale of air. I did it. I wrote something. And oh, does it feel like pure relief.

"Are you all right, love?" His eyes are concerned and I wave him off.

"It just feels good to be writing again. I couldn't for a long time. But I think I've finally bounced back."

"Of course you did," he says, grabbing his mug and sitting down next to me at the table. "When every mirror could be equal parts adventure or precarious situation, you don't have the luxury of not bouncing back."

"No, I guess we don't. Either of us."

He turns his mug back and forth between his hands. "D'you know why I came here?" he asks.

"You need me to lead you to Eversor."

"I'll find Eversor, love, never doubt it. And when I do, there will be a reckoning," he says firmly. "But I wasn't tearing reality apart and lobbing padlocks at a Dreamer's head just for the likes of her."

He brings his hand up to cup my face, and the look in his eyes stops the breath in my lungs.

"I was looking for you. *This* Jessa. Because I find you intriguing."

He's weaving a potent spell. I pull away out of sheer self-preservation.

"Sorry," I mumble. "I'm just . . . I don't think we should . . ."

He drops his hand. "I'm trying to jump to the middle, when we've barely begun to know each other," he says, shaking his head. "I apologize. Perhaps we should go back to the beginning. Start over."

He extends his hand. I smile as I reach out to shake it, but he turns my hand over and kisses it instead.

"Captain Finn Gallagher, at your service," he says. "And you are . . . ?"

My lips twitch with a smile. "Jessa St. Clair," I reply.

He leans in. "You forgot *Emeline*," he whispers.

"No one's ever going to let me forget it."

He breaks into a lopsided grin. "Well now, love. That's a proper beginning. Let's see where the wind takes us."

"Okay."

"And now . . . are you up for an adventure?"

18

A Night to Remember

IT'S COLD. HOLY COW, IS IT COLD.

"You're sure this is the right p-place?" I ask through chattering teeth. "I can't f-feel my face."

Finn reaches over and adjusts my scarf so that it covers my nose and mouth, then he gives my knit cap a tug and pulls it down tighter over my ears. He's wearing a fur-lined cap of his own, complete with ear flaps, along with a scarf, parka, gloves, and boots, just like me. It's dark here, snow is falling lightly, and I have no idea where we are.

"This is the place," he assures me. "Set it up with our counterparts earlier. After this afternoon's debacle, you seemed like you could use some fun."

"Freezing into a human Popsicle is all kinds of fun," I agree. "I can't imagine Eversor would look for us here."

"It's not all that bad. You'll be warm soon enough."

I turn slowly, taking in the scenery. Sparse trees dot the landscape, and we're not far from the shore of a lake, glossy and black in the darkness. Behind us is a large lodge, and even though my mind tells me I don't know this language, I can easily read the sign.

"It's a hotel," I say.

"Very good," Finn praises me. "And where are we?"

I think for a moment, searching my memories.

"Norway. We're in the eastern Finnmark region, near the Russian border. My father came here to study fjords." I think back. "Ten years ago. Hey! I speak Norwegian!"

"And I work in Kirkenes—that's our town—at the docks. But today we're visiting a nature reserve. We'll have to be back on the bus in ninety minutes." He gives the tour bus a thump, and we move away from the large side mirror we'd been looking into.

I give him a nod and slowly turn around again as we walk. "Wow!" I exclaim. "Norway!"

"We'll have to return again in a few months when the sun is shining. The Varanger fjord is quite spectacular."

I see it in my memory, and he's right. Spectacular is an understatement, and I definitely want to see it in real time. Right now, though, I'm acutely aware that I haven't eaten over here, and I'm hungry.

"Can we get inside and warm up?" I ask. "I'm starving, and if we stay out here much longer I'm going to turn into a block of ice."

"Well, we don't want that," Finn says with a grin. "I know just the place for dinner, and just the floor show we want to see. Come along, then."

I follow him up the trail to a large, raised platform with an enormous fire pit at its center, and he motions me over to it. There is a group of people standing about, drinking coffee from mugs or sitting on benches near the fire. I feel a blanket drop around my shoulders and I smile at Finn as I pull it around me.

"What's this for?"

"Wouldn't want you to catch a chill," he says. "Hold mine, will you? I'll get us some food."

My stomach rumbles again as I smell it now, and I see him waiting patiently as someone behind a table ladles two bowls full of something and sets them on a tray for him, along with two steaming mugs and several wedges of bread.

He gestures with a tilt of his head as he walks back, and I see an open spot on one of the benches near the fire. He joins me there, and I spread my blanket on my lap as he sits and then sets the tray down across our knees.

Lapskaus. The word comes to me without effort. It's a beef stew and it smells incredible. I bring the mug of coffee to my lips, nearly scalding them before I remember to blow on it and cool it off. Finn is dunking a chunk of bread into his stew.

"Good?" he asks.

"Really good!" I answer around a mouthful of my own bread. "But do we have to eat outside?"

"You don't want to miss this," he answers. We eat in silence, wolfing down our stew until someone near the edge of the platform rings a bell. A spotlight shines out toward the nearby trees.

I can feel them before I can see them, shaking the ground as they lumber out of the darkness. My bread drops from my mouth and my brain is having a hard time reconciling this particular memory, even though I know it's absolutely true:

Those are mammoths. Genuine, they-ought-to-be-extinct woolly mammoths.

"It's time for their nightly feeding," Finn says. "Watch."

I stare in awe as bales of hay are pushed off the edge of the platform, tumbling over the railing. The mammoths stomp the ground, shaking the bench beneath me, trumpeting and snuffing as they break the hay bales open and begin to feed. I feel Finn's fingers under my chin as he gently closes my gaping mouth.

"First time seeing a mammoth?" he asks.

I look at him incredulously. "I saw one on Friday morning. Just not *breathing.*"

"Would you like to feed one?" he asks.

"Feed . . . ?" My mind and mouth are just not connecting.

"Come on," he says, taking the tray off our laps and setting it on the bench next to him. He leads me by the hand to the edge of the platform, and one of the park workers who dropped the hay bales hands me a tree branch full with leaves.

"Just hold it out over the railing," Finn says, closing his hand over mine and helping me, since my arm is frozen in place. Holy cow. Mammoths! Right in front of me!

One of them raises his head, his trunk twisting in the air as he makes a snuffing sound and lumbers over.

"Easy . . . ," Finn says. "When he grabs the branch, be sure and let go."

"Right," I say, nodding a little too fast. "Right. Let go."

Part of me wonders if I'll have a hand after this, but I make myself hold the branch out farther. The mammoth plucks it from me and I let go quickly. He shoves the whole thing in his mouth, chewing and smacking noisily. Then he lowers his trunk and steps closer.

And closer. He's rubbing his head against the railing, clearly wanting more, and the park worker lets out a laugh.

"All right, Dex," he says, reaching out and patting the mammoth's shaggy head. "Wait your turn." He motions me closer. "You want to pet him?"

"Pet him?" I can't seem to stop repeating people—I think because I have no words of my own in my brain at the moment. I shuffle forward, putting my hand out, and as my fingers tangle in his shaggy coat, he raises up, blinking slowly. I scratch lightly between his eyes and he tosses his head, pushing into my hand.

"He likes it!" I laugh with delight, scratching harder, as Finn pushes another branch through the rungs of the railing to him. He slurps it down noisily, shaking his head side to side when he finishes, clearly wanting more. The park worker tosses another bale over the railing and Dex goes after it as it bounces along on the ground.

"I just pet a mammoth," I say, staring at my hand. I look up at Finn, and he's grinning at me, clearly enjoying my excitement.

I take a moment to regroup, searching back through my memories in this body. Mammoths are an endangered species, but no more uncommon than the elephant around here. I've been to the preserve here before, and other me doesn't find it nearly as exciting as I do.

I'm leaning over the railing, staring at them as they eat—there are even a few calves, fuzzy and utterly adorable. Finn taps me on the shoulder.

"Are you ready for the grand finale?" he asks.

"What could beat this?"

He reaches out, taking my hand. "Come on, I'll show you."

He pulls me back over to the bench, where he spreads one of our blankets down so we have a warmer seat.

"We need to turn our backs to the fire," he says. "If we want the best view."

I sit as he directs, making room for him on the blanket beside me as he pulls the other blanket over our shoulders. My stew has cooled off, but I don't care. The coffee is still hot, and just as we're finishing the last of our dinner, it begins.

The first wash of color streaks the sky, rolling across in a wave of brilliant green, shimmering into a yellow-orange and then streaming out to the horizon, where it fades into pinks and purples. Just as it dies out, another wave takes its place, then another, playing across the sky in colors so fierce and fiery, they take my breath away.

I let my mind wander back over the memories of this Jessa—just until they reach the edge of where Finn and I began here. I pull my mind off that thought, refusing to indulge it. This is them. Not us. We're just visiting.

So we sit together and watch the magnificent northern lights, with the mammoths snuffling in the background, and heat of the fire toasting our backs. I can feel the solid warmth of him beside me, and I just breathe and let myself be in the wonder of it all.

"Thank you for bringing me here, Finn."

He makes a slight sound and I turn my eyes away from the sky to look at him.

"What?" I ask.

"It's nothing," he says with an odd smile. "It's just—that's the first time you've called me by name since I found you."

19

Date Night

"NO. ABSOLUTELY NOT. I MEAN IT, FINN."

"I'll sit six rows behind you at the theater. I won't even come into Mugsy's."

It's Monday night, and Finn has this bizarre idea that he's coming along with me on my date tonight.

"I will not spend my evening with Ben with you creeping on me from a distance," I tell him as I shift from foot to foot. "No way."

"I don't like this."

"Really? I hadn't guessed." I pull out my phone, which is lighting up with Ben's text. "He's driving over to pick me up now, so you need to leave."

He doesn't move, so I stare him down.

"Oh, very well," he splutters. "Make sure he brings you home promptly."

"What? You're my mother now?"

"I don't like this."

"You said that. Go."

He stomps off across the backyard, and just in time. Ben pulls up out front a few minutes later, and we're off to take in the early showing of *Interstellar Spawn* at the movie theater near the mall in Manortown. It turns out to be a one-star flick, which makes it even more awesome because Ben and I are snarking on it all the way through. By the time we hit Mugsy's, we're laughing our butts off over some of the more ridiculous plot points.

"Hey, at least the atmosphere on the planet was breathable, right?" Ben says as we wait for our coffees. "Never mind that all that scientific testing they were doing—an airborne microbe that dissolves your vital organs within seconds—just zoomed right by them somehow." He makes an airplane motion with his hand, glancing it off the top of my head.

"But how were they to know they'd find the alien dinosaur eggs," I say. "You know, from the dinosaurs who live in the snow at the top of the mountain?"

"They were *alien* dinosaurs," he reminds me, grabbing our cups as I grab the plateful of cookies and muffins we selected. "They don't need a warm climate. And I loved how a three-ton dinosaur could skate across the ice and not fall through because of his sharp dinosaur hooves."

We slide into a booth and I'm still chuckling as I put sugar in my coffee.

"I'm glad we got to hang out, St. Clair," he says, taking an enormous bite of a muffin. "I was afraid he wouldn't let you off the leash."

"Ben . . ."

"I still don't see why he needs to be here," Ben says. "People are already talking about him."

My eyes snap open wide. "Who?"

"Chloe Merrick texted me to tell me that she saw him walking near your house this morning. And he's coming back next semester."

"Who told her that?"

"He did," Ben says. "She stopped to talk to him when she realized who he was."

I'll just bet she did. I realize I'm making a face and carefully smooth my features. "She is such a gossip. I swear, she talks about everybody."

"He's the juicy news," Ben snarks, wadding up the wrapper from his muffin and tossing it down on the table. "And speaking of news—"

"Wait!" I interrupt. "Me first, because you are *not* going to believe where I was last night."

"Last night?" He looks alarmed. "You traveled back out somewhere with him?"

I hold up a hand to stop him before he starts griping. "Ben. I saw a *mammoth*."

"A m-m—" he stutters slightly, his eyes widening, and I finish the word along with him, nodding enthusiastically.

"Mammoth. I saw a *mammoth*, Ben. I got to *pet* it."

"How . . . ?"

"In that reality, they never died off. To the people there it was like visiting a zoo and seeing an elephant."

"Where?" It's clear Ben is having as hard a time wrapping his head around this as I was.

"I was in Norway!" I gush. "Speaking Norwegian! And then we saw the aurora borealis, and there were little baby mammoths, and oh!" I sink back with a sigh. "It was amazing. Just plain amazing."

"I'll bet." He looks uncomfortable. "Guess a bad movie kinda pales in comparison."

I realize how I must sound, and I reach across to hold his hand. "I don't mean it like that. I'm having fun tonight."

"Me too." He looks slightly mollified, and he turns my hand over, squeezing it. "I like it when we laugh together. And just generally are together. Alone."

I take a drink of my coffee, letting that one go by. "So what's your news?"

His eyes widen. "Oh yeah! So get this: Eversor—and it *was* Eversor trying to rob the museum in Mexico—"

"You're positive?"

"I saw the security camera footage on a TV station website out of Mexico City. It's her, all right." He leans forward. "And she was after—get this—an Aztec mirror."

"A mirror? That can't be a coincidence."

"What are the odds, right? She broke into a display that held an obsidian mirror, taken from an exhibit with items from an archaeological dig in Mexico. They were able to retrieve the mirror, but she got away."

"Let me guess . . . it was like she vanished into thin air."

"Pretty much," he says. "Oh, and one other thing . . . it's likely she was under the influence of some sort of narcotic. They said she was babbling and half out of her mind with hallucinations."

"That would explain why she looked so sick," I ponder. "She's lost thirty pounds at least since she was here. She looked like she hadn't slept in a month. If she wasn't trying to murder me, it'd be sad."

"So get this: I decided to do a little more digging into the Aztecs—hell, I was up at five thirty this morning scouring the Internet," he confesses sheepishly. Ben loves a good research project. "It turns out that the Aztec exhibit at the Museum of Natural History in New York carries items from the same archaeological dig."

"Any mirrors?"

"Not sure yet. I'm fixing to work on that some more tonight. But at least we've got something to report to your Dreamer guy."

"This is great," I say. "Ben, thank you."

"Easy-peasy," he says. "And now you owe me."

My coffee stops halfway to my mouth. "Owe you what?"

He rolls his eyes. "A copy of the movie on DVD when it comes out. I need to brush up on my ice-skating skills, and I figured I'd watch the dinosaur for pointers."

I'm laughing again—not that it's hard to do around Ben. He's always good for that.

"And I want the director's cut," he goes on. "If they have one."

"Why, it's practically an *ahhhrt* film," I say in a really snooty voice.

"Come on, St. Clair," he says, swiping up the empty plate and his cup. "Let's blow this taco stand. It's a school night and I don't want your mom yelling at me."

"She would never," I say, following him out. "She adores you."

"I'm adorable," he agrees as we climb into the truck.

Ben blasts the vents and they throw icy air right in my face, making me shriek. He laughs unrepentantly as we drive to my house, and, like usual in his truck, it's barely—just barely—getting warm as we pull up in front of the house.

He reaches across the seat to take my hand. "I had fun tonight," he says.

"Me too. Nobody brings the snark like we do," I admit. "That's what's so great about us."

He squeezes my hand. "There's a lot that's great about us, St. Clair. I just don't want you to forget that."

And a heartbeat later, his body is turning and his other arm is around me. His mouth comes down on mine, warm and more familiar now as our lips move together. I slide my hands up around his neck and let myself relax into him.

"Getting better?" he asks when we pull apart.

"I think you've got it down now. And for the record, I've never complained."

"No, I guess you haven't."

"Thanks again for tonight. It's nice to have some normal for a change."

"Normal can be a good thing," he tells me. "I know what you're dealing with, and I am fully prepared to be your personal safe haven. Your port in the storm."

I pull away, reaching for my purse, and he gives a nervous little laugh.

"That was a nautical reference," he says. "Maybe not the best idea for comparison."

I let out a huff of air. "Maybe not."

"I'm here, St. Clair. I'm not going anywhere. I'm just reminding you that I've been here, while he's been sailing around in his own little worlds."

I can't help my frown. "He's had a lot to deal with. He's lost someone, too."

"And now you're just the easy substitute, right?"

I suck in my breath, and he knows he's pushed it too far. "Sorry. It just—I don't think he's healthy for you to be around. And I know that's biased, but it's how I feel."

"I know it is. And I'm being careful, I promise. Good night, Ben." I open the door and hop out.

"St. Clair—I'm sorry," he says, and for a moment, we just stand there looking at each other until I finally nod.

"See ya tomorrow," I mumble.

I walk to the door, and then I shut it behind me and let out an exaggerated breath.

"Rough evening?"

My eyes find him, sitting in the front room. Danny is playing Minecraft, and he's so engrossed I doubt he even knows Finn and I are here. But we know it.

"I'm going upstairs," I say, feeling the color rise to my face. "I know it's early but I'm really tired."

Finn isn't even looking at the game. He's looking at me, and it's unnerving. Finally, he stands up.

"Danny, I'm retiring for the evening, all right?"

"Okay, Finn," Danny says, still focused on his game. "See you tomorrow?"

"I have no doubt," Finn says, and still, his eyes are on me. He walks over to the door and I step aside so he can pass me. His eyes are searching my face like he's reading every ounce of whatever this is that's making me feel so off-balance around him.

"Sweet dreams, love," he finally says, and the door closes behind him. I push my hands through my hair, and I can still smell Ben's cologne on them, from where my hands were on his neck.

What the hell is wrong with me?

20

A Little Girl Time

THE PROBLEM WITH GUYS IS THAT I KNOW NOTHING about them. I mean, I've had boyfriends before—a week or two here and there, never anybody longer than that. Most of the time we're just texting and not really hanging out. Ben was the first guy I ever really wanted to hang with, and he sort of snuck up on me.

Then again, Finn is the master of the surprise entrance. And hanging with him is getting to me. I have to admit it. He's witty and smart and that accent just does something funny to me inside. I don't feel as comfortable around him as I do around Ben, and I don't mean that in a bad way.

I don't look at Ben and wonder if he's going to reach out and touch me. But I do that with Finn—and I mean all the time. And I hate that I do it, too.

Nights like this remind me that I am in serious need of some female friends to hang out with. I've never made much of an effort in that area—and not because I'm excluding females. I'm just such an introvert that I spend all my time with my journal. Or hanging with Danny and Mom. Ben is the first person I've really hung with since middle school.

Right now, I need a female perspective, and I don't have one. I suppose I could talk to my mom, but that's awkward because . . . she's my mom. The last thing I want to do is talk about my love life with my mom. Besides, I know who she'd probably root for. I need somebody unbiased.

I can hear Danny watching a movie in the living room now, and I walk over toward my door, contemplating going down there instead of hiding in my bedroom the rest of the night.

Maybe the actuaries had it right, I think. *Take all the choice out of your hands and pick the most suitable guy for you based on tons of data and established criteria.* The geek in me sees the logic in it. No muss, no fuss, no wondering.

"Right," I say, looking at myself in the mirror on the wall of my bedroom. "I don't suppose you feel like coming over and figuring out my love life for me?"

I don't look amused. But as I pay closer attention, the scene behind me starts to shift, and I'm looking at a different bedroom. One with a visitor. A visitor I can use.

I put my hand to the glass.

"Do you mind?" I ask. I really need a buddy. One who's not a guy.

She gives me a tiny shrug, as if to say, *knock yourself out,* then she puts her hand to the glass, and I'm through.

"So then Ashlynn said that Mackenzie told Mr. Hunter to get stuffed, if you can believe that," Olivia says as she swipes her toes with polish. "The girl finally grows a backbone and now she's just making waves. He told the whole class he'd be taking off points for any lapses in critical reasoning—and you know how the man lives for his critical reasoning."

She leans forward, shaking her dark, curly hair carefully out of the way and pushing her face—which is slathered with a face mask—toward me.

"Scratch my nose, will you? My nails are still wet."

I give her nose a dutiful but gentle scratch. "So listen, Liv . . . I, um . . . I'm here for a favor."

She looks at me in confusion. "What do you mean?"

"I mean—I just transferred over. I'm not your Jessa."

"Oh?" Her eyes pop open wide. "Oh! Wow. That was fast! When was this decided?"

"Just now. She's helping me out."

She points a wet nail at me. "Are you the circus girl? Or are you from the house by the rock quarry?"

I look at her in confusion. "Neither. I live in Upstate New York. I'm nothing special."

"Except you can step through mirrors and shift into alternate realities just like everybody else, right?" she scoffs. "Don't be so humble. You got it going on."

"Thanks. Wait—I'm in the circus?"

"Haven't met her yet, but I've heard about her," Olivia says, settling back and taking another swipe at her nail with the brush. "Trapeze artist—your whole family performs. Crazy stuff."

I make a mental note to check that out sometime. "And the rock quarry?"

She waves her hand to dry it. "You don't even want to know. That one, I've met, and if you think we've got it bad here . . ." She trails off, and ends with a low whistle. "The quarry is owned by the state, and you have to give them more than half of your profits. You don't even get to go to school over there. You just work hammering rock all day. Jess says she's got biceps as big as my thighs over in that reality."

I blink owlishly. "Well. That's something."

"Uh-huh," she says, putting the cap back on the polish and bringing her bare foot up onto the bed.

"I can do your toes if you want," I offer.

"Are you kidding? You can't stay inside the lines and you know it."

I smile at the knowledge that I really am the same in some ways, wherever I go. I never paint my nails because I suck at it.

"What is it you need, Ms. New York?" she asks, shaking the polish once more before unscrewing the cap and starting on her big toe.

"It's a hypothetical situation," I say to her as I sit carefully on the other end of the bed. "What if you've got two guys—both in your peer group, I mean—who are good matches for you, but in two really different ways?"

"That's a question for an actuary," she says, dabbing at her toes. "I mean, it's not like there's only one fish in the sea, right? It's like you're charting your own course through this ocean of fish, and you know some will try to attack you and some will make you sick and some will be just fine and keep you fed, but part of you wants the tastiest, most beautifully colored one. Know what I mean?"

I stuff my fist under my chin. "You had to make a nautical analogy."

"I'm just sayin' that options can be a confusing thing for most of us. Not everyone is a born rebel like you. That's why we leave it to the professionals over here. Oh God, get my nose again. The left side this time."

"My left, or your left?"

"Mine. Watch the face mask."

"Why do you even use this stuff?" I ask as I scratch again. Olivia has this amazing, glowing caramel skin that perfectly complements her big brown eyes. "You don't need to work to look gorgeous."

"I make gorgeous look like it's not work," she agrees. "And it starts with an avocado-and-Dead-Sea-salt mask. One more scratch, please."

I scratch again, and Olivia lets out a sigh. "Better. Now, as your stand-in actuary, the way I see it, you need to take your time with this. If you don't have the benefit of an *actual* actuary—"

"I don't. And I wouldn't use one anyway."

"Rebels. All of y'all." She shakes her head and then points at my compact mirror, which is lying on the bed next to her.

"Open," she says. I open it up and hold it out as she leans in to look at herself. "That's a zit, isn't it? On my nose."

"Might be a bug bite, the way you were scratching." I shrug. "It's hard to tell."

"Great," she says, checking her fingernails again. "Anyway. Love is not something to be trifled with. If it's real, you'll feel it."

"That's just it," I complain. "I mean, with one, I think I feel—"

She holds up a hand. "You either feel it or you don't. If you only think you feel it, you are *so* obviously not there. But that's not to say you'll never get there with time. Hypothetically." She smirks.

Just like Liv, calling me on my own nonsense. "Thanks," I say, getting up from the bed.

"Did that answer your question?"

"Not really. But it helped. I really just needed an ear."

"You can borrow my ear anytime," Olivia says, smiling. "You know I'm just an expert on love. Even though I can't even say his damn name."

"Who?"

She gives me a disgruntled look. "*Shoulders*. We were talking about him earlier today. You were trying to get his name out of me, but until he makes a move I am keeping my big mouth shut. I don't need any group gossip wrecking this for me."

"Now you know why I have to jump reality to find a friend," I say with a grimace. "People love to gossip, don't they?"

"Do you have a reality where that doesn't happen?"

"Probably not. Human nature, I guess."

"I guess."

Olivia leans off the bed, almost falling as she reaches gingerly for a shopping bag on the floor. "Hey, I got a ridiculous high school horror movie. It has singing zombies. We could watch it together. It's somewhere in here. . . ."

She gets up and walks duck-footed across the room to preserve her pedicure and carefully picks up another bag by the door.

"Liv," I say, "you are exactly my kind of friend. But I'd better get back. Enjoy your movie."

"Oh, I will," she assures me, then she looks up from her bag. "Hey, what am I like over there? With you?"

"I don't know," I tell her. "My dad didn't remarry, so I've never met you."

"Would I fit in with your other friends?"

I shrug.

"You *do* have other friends, right?"

"I've got a friend. Or two."

She rolls her eyes. "Let me guess. We were just talking about them."

The look of chagrin on my face is confirmation enough. She shakes her head and makes a *tsk*ing sound. "You need to get out more."

"So I've been told. It's just not easy for me. I'm a writer. I'm a lot more comfortable having conversations with people I made up."

"You're talking to me, aren't you?"

"It's just—I've been through a lot lately. I lost somebody and . . ." I take a breath. "It's just not easy. That's all."

She walks awkwardly over and puts an arm around my shoulders. "Listen. When I lost my dad, I wanted to curl up in a hole somewhere. I wanted to sit in bed all day with the covers over my head and the lights out. I didn't want to go to school, or hang out, or even have to talk to anybody. When you get a hole like that ripped in your life, the last thing you want to do is stuff it with all that other junk."

I nod. "That's it exactly."

"I know how it is. But the thing is, life doesn't work that way. It keeps moving forward, and you're going to have to start moving with it. Sitting home alone and living your life through other people—even if the other people are all you—is no way to find your own life. You can't hide forever."

"Maybe I could break rocks for a living," I say with a half smile. "Nice and peaceful with nobody to bother me."

"With arms the size of legs, I guarantee no one will bother you," she points out.

"Thanks, Liv." I give her a hug. "You're just what I needed."

"And now you've got avocado on the side of your face," she says. "Have a nice trip!"

I turn back to the mirror to let my other self know I'm done, and I'm still thinking about Olivia's words when I get back to my side. I start to turn away, but I realize I have a pen in my hand. My journal stands on the dresser in front of me, and my other self has decided to chime in with her thoughts.

I don't know Ben well and I don't know Finn at all, but I can feel what you're feeling, and this is incredibly confusing for you. I don't have anything to compare it to from my life, but here's my advice, for what it's worth to you:

It's not about who you love more, or who you can see yourself with, or who you can't live without, because they both meet all that criteria. So I think the question is, if you don't end up with one of them, which one would make you ask "What if?"

I think that's the saddest question anyone could ever have in their life. It's a question that can reduce you and all you could be or want to be. So ask it.

Those are my thoughts, for whatever they mean to you. And I think you know that answer already.

J

Girlfriends are a good thing to have, I think. Especially when one of them is yourself.

21

Friends with Connections

THE CLASSROOM SHIMMERS TO LIFE AROUND ME, AND Mario is sitting at his desk, looking through a stack of papers.

"Isn't that a little old-fashioned?" I ask. "Can't you just materialize an iPad or something?"

He looks up from the papers, and his face is a mask of irritation. "I can do it any way that works for me," he reminds me. "I'm in charge."

"Sorry," I say sheepishly.

He waves a hand and gets up from behind the desk. "Didn't mean to bite your head off. Things are just really hectic at the moment."

"Still no Rudy?"

He grimaces. "We're working on it."

"You do that. I'll just keep dodging Eversor. She tried to kill Finn on Sunday."

"*What?*"

"I've been waiting for you to call me in," I say, more than a little irked by the lack of focus.

"How did I miss that?" he asks, running his hand through his hair. "Hold on, let me pull Finn in."

The words are barely out of his mouth and I sense Finn instantly, sitting in the chair next to me.

"Hi," I say.

Finn glances around. "Where the devil are we?"

"It's a classroom. Like in school," I tell him. "Mario wants a debrief about Eversor."

"Jessa's told you that she tried to run us down?"

"She was aiming for you," I say. "I think it's important to her that I suffer before she goes after me—she blames me and Mario for the way the Dreamers have turned on Rudy."

"Vengeance is a powerful motivator," Finn agrees.

"How did she know where you'd be?" Mario asks, staring at the blank whiteboard and tapping his fingers on the desk in frustration. "Rudy can't catch any echoes from either of you—I have you both on lockdown."

I look at him in confusion. "Meaning . . . ?"

"As a Dreamer—even a Dreamer on the run in the dreamscape—he can pull images and echoes of memory from a subconscious mind," Mario explains. "That's how we get our information, and with that, we can form our forecasts.

"But in Rudy's case, he can't get into either of your minds because I have them under constant surveillance—the same with your family, Jessa. I don't want him having any clues as to what your day-to-day plans are. So for Eversor to know you were traveling means she's watching you somehow—either physically or via Rudy getting clues from someone else."

"I've been having dance classes more often these last weeks, gearing up for the performance," I say. "If Rudy got inside my dance teacher's head . . ."

"You did show a surprising aptitude in a very short period of time," Finn adds. "He could have easily determined you were cheating if he's monitoring someone in your dance group."

"It's not cheating," I reaffirm.

"And I'm not a pirate," he replies with a bland smile.

"He's got eyes on you, so we've got to be careful," Mario says. "I don't mind you traveling—just clear your destinations with me first, so I know where you are. You need the practice, and we need to keep you moving to throw Eversor and Rudy off your scent, so to speak. Just don't forget you've still got a target on your back."

"Got it. Look over my shoulder everywhere," I reply glumly.

Mario turns away from the board. "Did you manage to dig any further into the incident at the museum in Mexico City?"

I nod. "Ben did. We're pretty sure it was Eversor, even though they didn't have her name. It was an Aztec mirror. It was from an archaeological dig somewhere."

"A mirror?" He looks alarmed.

"And there was an Aztec display at the museum in New York City the day we went as well," I continue. "Ben was looking into the specific items they had in the display, but I haven't circled back with him yet."

"Hmm." Mario puts his papers down. "Well, let's get him in here, then." He strides over to the door.

"Wait—you're going to go get Ben? You can do that?"

"He'll be dreaming, but yes, I can do that. It's not standard procedure, but we're not operating in standard mode around here right now."

He knocks sharply on the red door three times, and it opens, revealing a mildly interested-looking Ben in his soccer uniform on the other side. He's even holding a soccer ball. He looks past Mario to me.

"'Sup, St. Clair?" he asks, walking into the room and closing the door behind him. "Has class started yet?"

"This isn't a normal class," I explain. "You're in the dreamscape with me—and Mario."

Ben's eyes go wide. "I'm dreaming?"

"Yeah," I reply, watching him closely to make sure he's not going to freak out. I don't need to worry—he's just rolling with it.

"And you're Mario?" Ben asks, holding out a hand to Mario. "Nice to meet you."

"A pleasure," Mario says, giving his hand a quick shake. "I'm afraid I don't have time for chitchat. We've got a lot to cover. You know Finn, of course."

Ben's enthusiasm suddenly disappears.

"Does he have to be here?" he asks, glaring at Finn.

I can't help but wonder the same thing. I know we're all working toward a common goal, but putting these two in a room together—even an imaginary one—is not a stellar idea. I could easily debrief Finn in the morning.

As if sensing my thoughts, Finn rises up out of his chair, dragging it over to sit even closer to me. It makes a horrible screech on the floor. Ben narrows his eyes and Mario gives him a stony look as they both pull desks into a semicircle with us and sit.

"Jessa said Eversor was after an Aztec mirror," Mario begins, turning to Ben. "Were there mirrors in the other exhibit, as well?"

"Yes. And get this—from the same archaeological dig at the pyramid of Tenochtitlán in Mexico."

"I was afraid of that."

"Does this have something to do with the convergence?"

Mario nods. "Yes. If my hunch is right, these aren't just normal mirrors. These mirrors belonged to a Traveler, and a powerful one, at that."

"Why would it matter whose mirror it was?" I ask.

Mario gets out of his chair and heads over to the whiteboard again. "Across the centuries since Travelers came into play, there have been a handful who were exceptionally strong," he says to me. "It's common practice for a well-seasoned Traveler to carry their own mirror. I'm sure you've discovered how handy that can be."

He directs our attention to the whiteboard, and the image of a chipped, blackened shard of what looks like polished tile.

"This is an Aztec mirror," he says.

"They could see themselves in that?" I tilt my head from side to side, but it just looks like black to me.

"It's made of obsidian," Ben chimes in. "Most of them were back then. Mirror glass was unheard of in that region until the Europeans landed."

"When it's highly polished, it works," Mario says. "This particular mirror belonged to a man named Tizoc. He was an Aztec ruler and one of our strongest Travelers in that era. If it was one of his personal mirrors, this would have been his conduit for countless transfers—and it would still carry a lingering echo of his power. It becomes imbued with it."

"And what would happen if Eversor got her hands on it?" Finn asks.

"She might be able to trigger the convergence," Mario says. "There's not much to it—all it would take is a powerful Traveler and the ability to sustain a dual state of consciousness between a reality and the dreamscape."

"You mean, half awake?" I ask. "How do you sustain that?"

"Rum?" Finn asks.

Mario smiles. "Inebriation would only get you unconscious in the long run. Most likely, she'll look for a drug. Something that can bring on hallucinations that would keep her in a dream state while conscious. But it would be a very tricky and unstable thing unless the Traveler was quite gifted."

"Ben said the oracles at Delphi used to inhale hallucinogenic smoke," I remember.

"And according to what I read in the police reports from Mexico City, she was hallucinating when they apprehended her," Ben supplies.

"She's taking drugs?" Finn asks.

"They'd have to be powerful to keep her in a hallucinogenic state," Mario muses.

"Like an animal tranquilizer?" Finn presses. "Would that do it?"

"That would knock her out," I say. "And where would she get animal tranquilizers?"

"I was only wondering because your local newspaper reported

a robbery at a veterinary office," Finn explains. "The cash inside was left untouched, but the culprit took some sort of tranquilizer that has value on the street."

"I heard about that. They took ketamine," Ben says. "It's hallucinogenic. I mean *really* hallucinogenic. If she's hooked on that stuff . . ."

I get a chill down my spine as I remember how Eversor looked when I saw her at the museum, the bones sharp beneath her skin, the sunken eyes and lank hair. She'd always been so full of life and so put together—now I know why she looked so ill.

Mario doesn't like the sound of that. "Once she's in the 'between' state, she transfers through a conduit—like the mirror—directly to the dreamscape. Being in both places at once would create a rip in the reality stream, triggering the convergence."

"Is she strong enough to do that?" I ask.

"That's where the mirror comes in," Mario replies. "She's not. But with the extra power of that mirror, it may be possible. We need to be one step ahead somehow and keep her from getting the weapon she needs."

"That's why she was at the museum in New York," I say. "But she didn't get what she was after."

"I would imagine they have some serious security protocols in place," Ben says. "She'll have to find something else."

"And with countless Travelers throughout history, and countless artifacts scattered about, how do you propose we stop her?" Finn asks incredulously. "It's bloody impossible."

"Not impossible," Mario says, drumming his fingers on the desk as he thinks. "But difficult. At least we know who she's focusing on."

"You said there were other strong Travelers," I point out.

Mario shakes his head. "The others on that list would have been too far back for something as fragile as a mirror to survive. And some didn't use mirrors. Like . . . Narcissus."

"*Narcissus?*" I ask, wide-eyed. "As in the Greek demigod Narcissus?"

"He was Greek," Mario says. "But hardly a demigod. And contrary to legend, he wasn't always staring into reflecting pools because he was full of himself."

"How would we find anything belonging to Narcissus?" Ben asks.

"You won't," Mario says. "It's been millennia. I can't imagine anything of his would have survived. Likewise for Viatrix, your ancestor," he says to me. "Tizoc is the only Traveler within the recent past who might qualify, and he lived nearly five hundred years ago."

"Well, I can't just jet off around the world looking for Aztec mirrors," I say, shaking my head. "I'm only seventeen. I don't even have a passport."

"You won't need to," Ben says, leaning back in his chair with a satisfied smile. "I think I may have already solved our problem. It turns out there's a local connection to the digs that went on at Tenochtitlán: an archaeologist by the name of Eli Greaver."

"As in the Greaver family?" I ask. "Founders of Ardenville?"

"Those are the ones. He's the brother who traveled the world."

"Greaver." Finn has an odd look on his face. "Interesting."

"Why?" I ask. "You don't even know the Greavers of Ardenville in your world."

"No, I don't," he says. "But my great-grandmother hailed from Greaverville, which stands where Ardenville is in my reality."

"That family has a bloodline that goes back to sixteenth-century England," Ben says. "They owned most of this area."

"My great-grandmother was an unwed mother," Finn shared. "It was quite the scandal. She immigrated to Ireland to start a new life, and here I am."

"Wait—*Clara Gallagher?*" I ask.

Finn looks surprised. "Yes, that was her."

Now it's Ben's turn to be surprised. "She was the girl in your ghost story! The one who threw herself off the bridge because she was carrying the mayor's child."

"Who would have been my grandfather," Finn fills in.

"And that explains why you were never here," I murmur.

"Cause and effect," Mario says. "Some choices have larger repercussions than others." He turns to Ben. "So Eli Greaver may have had an Aztec mirror in his possession?"

"More than one," Ben answers. He crosses his arms and gives us a smug look. "And now they're on their way here."

I look at him in confusion. "What? How?"

"My dad," he says, and he's obviously patting himself on the back for thinking of this. "There are four Aztec mirrors in a small collection of Central American art at a private museum in Chicago that came from the estate of Eli Greaver. My dad sits on the board at the Lower Hudson River Museum over in Manortown. He requested them for a special Greaver exhibit and they agreed to a six-month loan. I told him I needed them for a history project. He set it all up, and they'll call us when they come in."

"Wow, Ben. Thanks." I look at him with serious admiration. "It pays to have friends with connections."

"Guess I don't need to jump through mirrors to stop a bad guy. Or girl." Ben gives Finn a taunting smile along with that dig, and Finn responds with a glare of his own.

"What are the chances one of these mirrors actually belonged to this Tizoc?" Finn asks.

"Fairly good," Mario answers. "Tizoc built the pyramid of Tenochtitlán."

"So we get the mirrors before Eversor puts two and two together and goes after them herself," I say. "But she'll just try again, won't she? It's not going to stop her."

"No, but it'll slow her down," Mario answers. "With most of the remaining mirrors under heavy guard, she's going to be stalled—hopefully long enough for us to get a fix on Rudy."

"And you're all so very busy with that," Finn said sarcastically. "Weeks and weeks of nothing!"

"Finn!" I admonish.

"I want answers," Finn growls. "I want to know why none of these omnipotent beings can seem to find the lone dissenter in their ranks. I want you out of harm's way and I want to know every bit of what they know about all this."

"We're all frustrated, Finn," Mario says, pushing his hand through his hair. "But every piece of information we can gather will help us get closer to finding the answers we all need."

"I don't think an immortal dream god needs to answer to you," Ben says.

"You're not even qualified to be here," Finn shoots back. "Why don't you go back to dreamland?"

"Stop it," I snap at them. "You both have skills we need here."

"Damn right you need me," Ben says. "I'm the one watching your back."

"And what, exactly, is that supposed to mean?" Finn asks, staring him down.

"It means that Eversor's come within a few feet of killing her twice now. And I don't see anything you've done to prevent that."

"And if memory serves," Finn growls, "Eversor got closest to her on your watch—and where were you at the time? Did all that history get you too excited to *do your job?*"

"You were probably checking yourself out in the mirror while Jessa was getting run over!"

"Knock it off!" Mario says in exasperation.

"I'll knock it off," Ben snarls, pushing up out of his chair. "I'm fixing to knock his damn head off his shoulders!"

He takes a swing that Finn ducks, and then Finn is out of his chair and diving for Ben, slamming him into the red door.

"Stop this!" I yell. "Stop it, both of you!"

Ben tosses him off and swings again. Finn gets it full in the face and jabs back, catching Ben above the eye. He winds up to swing on him again, but Ben grabs his arm, yanking him off-balance, and then shoves him back. I get out of my desk to move between them and suddenly . . . we're all in the middle of a forest, overlooking a mountain lake. Ben and Finn are grappling on a dock over the water.

I turn to look at Mario, who is watching the two of them through narrowed eyes, with his arms folded across his chest. He gives me a disgruntled look and then I hear a loud splash, followed by a bevy of curse words as Mario dissolves the dock beneath them.

He strides over to the water's edge as Finn and Ben surface and wade out, slogging through the icy water.

"Are you two finished?" Mario asks. "Or should I send you in for another dunk?"

"Where the hell are we?" Finn asks, wringing out the bottom of his shirt.

"Alaska. I can keep you here all night, too," Mario threatens. "You do *not* want to piss off your Dreamer."

"He started it," Ben says, rubbing his arms to try to warm up.

"I need you two to get a grip, and not on each other," Mario tells them angrily. "I've got a lot of work to do, and so does Jessa. Neither of us has time for babysitting!"

"He's right," I tell them. "We need to work together, at least until this is all behind us."

"Fine," Ben says, shooting Finn an unfriendly look.

"Fine." Finn shrugs, though his eyes are still narrowed at Ben.

"Fine," I repeat, glaring at the two of them.

"Oy vey," Mario says.

22

A Series of Unlikely Events

You're working tonight, right?

Ben texts.

Yeah,
in half an hour

What about after?

if you want to come over
we can all talk

I'll pass
I guess alone time
is not an option

I stare at the phone and make a face at Ben's text. Then I look up and realize Finn is watching me make a face. Ugh.

> I gotta get ready
> I'll call you later

> K

Finn turns back to his vantage point near the window.

"I don't know what you think you'll see out there," I grumble. "It's not like Eversor's going to stand in the backyard with an assault rifle."

"I have a gut feeling about her," he retorts. "And don't snap at me just because your dear Ben is behaving badly."

"He's just not comfortable around you. I think that's understandable."

"He's been bloody unreasonable from the moment he met me." He looks back out into the yard again. "I don't think you should go to work."

"I'll be in a crowded supermarket with Christmas shoppers all around me," I remind him. "It's five days to Christmas, and they asked me to pick up an extra shift. I can use the hours since I had to miss last weekend for the field trip, and a three-hour shift isn't going to kill me." I glance down at my phone again. "Speaking of which, if you're going to walk with me, we'd better get going."

Finn is totally annoying when we get to the store, hanging outside the employee entrance to the back room as Mr. Kellar, my manager, gives me my promo materials.

"I know we normally put you over by the bakery," Kellar says, "but we had a customer spill a gallon of cooking oil over there just a little while ago and it's still slippery, so we had to section it off. We've got you back in the corner by the deli."

"The corner?"

"Right at the end of the cases—that alcove where we usually put the extra condiment stand. It's all set up—you'll see it."

"Got it." I tie my apron in the back, pick up my cooler full of frozen pizza puffs, and head out to the floor. Finn falls into step right behind me, and of course, just my luck—Mr. Kellar walks out right behind him.

"I have to work now," I tell Finn as I pull out and step behind the giant cardboard facade they set up around my wooden display table. "Go find someplace else to be."

He folds his arms, leaning against the edge of the deli case across from me.

"Finn, I mean it," I say. "My boss is watching." I risk a glance over at Kellar, and he's definitely not liking me having a fan club.

Finn gives me a resigned look and slowly, very slowly starts to circle the floor near produce, looking over at me as I finish my setup. I start heating up the toaster oven, and I look for my food service gloves, frowning when I can't find them. They must have run out again. A glance at my display confirms it—there's an extra-large pump bottle of hand sanitizer right on the table. Great. That stuff dries out my hands so badly and I'm going to have to use it after every batch. The customers start coming as soon as the first batch is done, and I'm barely keeping up with demand.

"Will you find someplace else to hang," I hiss at Finn as he walks over for the fourth time in an hour. "You're going to get me in trouble!"

"Jessa—"

"I mean it, Finn. Go next door to the sandwich shop and get me a soda or something."

"You can buy a soda here," he says.

"Not a fountain soda with ice, I can't," I explain. "Come on, please? Go now while there's a lull in the crowd."

He makes a face and gives me a disgruntled nod. "I'll be back in five minutes," he warns. "Five minutes."

"And I'll be fired in six," I mumble under my breath as I reach under my stand for the roll of paper towels. Someone left something sticky on the plastic tablecloth they have over my display table. I rise back up to put the towel roll on the display table, and suddenly Ben is there.

"Jessa," he says, in a low, urgent voice. "I need to talk to you. I waited for him to leave so we could speak without him."

"Are you nuts?" I exclaim furiously. "I am *working* here." Honestly, between him and Finn, it'll be a Christmas miracle if I have a job after today.

"You have to listen to me!" he says, and his voice is getting more urgent. "This whole thing with Eversor—the way she showed up the same day as him, and then again when you were traveling . . . he's going to kill you! Didn't you tell me that's how it works? He kills you everywhere he goes?"

"What?" I look at him like he's crazy, and that's because he is. "I never said that about him! Finn's here to protect me."

"Then where is he?" Ben asks, splaying his arms wide. "Why isn't he here? I'm here!"

He punctuates that final sentence by slamming his fist down

on my table, and I watch the next several seconds as though they were in slow motion.

First, the hand sanitizer falls over, and for some reason, the top isn't screwed on tightly. It splashes out, splattering all over the back and top of the toaster oven, the paper towels, and the edge of my cardboard facade. It leaves a large, dripping pool on the tablecloth that runs down over the side and into the garbage can, which is full of discarded napkins and paper plates.

And then it all goes up in flames.

A spark from the toaster oven ignites the alcohol in the sanitizer, and in a split second, I'm standing behind an enormous torch—in an alcove with walls around me. I throw myself to the floor, but the table is solid, full of shelves underneath, and backed into the alcove like I am, the table is mostly blocking my only way out. I hear Ben shouting my name, people are screaming, fire alarms blaring. The sprinklers come on overhead, but they're not dousing most of this area—I'm too far back. I grope blindly for a way out, shielding my face with my arm as the heat becomes searing.

I can hear Ben as he screams my name at the top of his lungs, and then a second later he's gone, knocked to the floor, and a shopping cart is blocking my way. I push at it, only to find another behind it, wedging it in. I'm looking through them and all I can see are Ben's legs. He's lying prone and he's not moving.

The flames have spread to the large display of potato chips on the other side of me, and I'm coughing so hard at the smell of burning plastic, I can barely suck in air. I look up through tear-stung eyes as I hear a voice ringing out over the mayhem around me.

"Jessa!" Finn is shouting like a madman, throwing carts out of his way, pushing against all the people who are determined to trample him on their way out. And then through the smoke and flames, I see his head turn, watch his body freeze in place as he sees her in the crowd at the same time I do.

Eversor.

His lips frame the words and I see his muscles tighten as he prepares to run her down. She's running now, along with the others, and I know he's going to turn and go, and Ben and I are going to die.

I fall completely prone now, turning my lips to the floor, coughing and retching as I gasp for clean air. I hear Ben groan and I see his foot in my peripheral vision as it moves, pulling away. A few more seconds pass and my eyes close to block out the smoke.

"Finn . . ." I can feel my lips move against the floor, and a second later, what's left of the table crashes to the ground. My arm is jerked hard and I shriek as I feel the flames lick my skin. I open my tear-stung eyes in protest. Finn has me, and his hand is against the glass of the deli case.

"Hold on, Jessa!" he shouts, but it's too late. I can't breathe anymore. I let the darkness take me.

23

Returned

"JESSA . . . JESSA, PLEASE. PLEASE, LOVE. PLEASE. OPEN
your eyes. Please, love. . . ."

I can hear Finn's voice like it's coming through a tunnel, and
as it grows clearer, I'm suddenly seized with a fit of coughing, pulling the bitter taste of smoke through my mouth and nose as I hack
and wretch.

"That's it," he murmurs. "That's it, love. Get it all out. Deep
breaths."

I suck in a lungful of air, and that sets off another round of
coughing, not as hard now but still burning my raw throat.

"Water . . . ," I manage to croak, and a moment later, a cup is
pressed to my lips. I drink deeply, giving another shuddering
cough or two, and I feel him gently wiping the grime from my
eyes with a wet cloth.

I inhale two more times, swearing to myself that I'll never
take air for granted again, and then I open my eyes.

"Ben . . . ?"

"He's all right. Someone helped him to safety."

"You're sure?"

He nods and lets out a big whoosh of air before he wraps his arms around me tight.

"I thought I'd lost you," he says, rocking me back and forth, and I realize we're on the floor. Well, he's on the floor and I'm on his lap. And we're not the only thing rocking.

I glance around at the dimly lit cabin of his ship in alarm.

"You brought me *here?*"

"Aye. I had to get you away to somewhere that you wouldn't have a counterpart. This was the first place that came to mind."

I scramble to sit up. "But it's against the rules," I remind him. "I *died* here. I can't be back."

"You can't return on your own, that's true enough," he says. "But you can be sent by a Dreamer or pulled through by another Traveler—and so I did."

"We have to go back!" I say, looking around wildly. I'm not sure what I expected, but it feels like I've just broken a major law of the universe here. I mean, I'm technically a ghost.

"Relax," he says. "You're out of sight, and so long as we remain that way, no one here will even know you visited."

"Good. Now let's go."

He shakes his head. "We need to wait for a little while. Let's be sure Eversor has realized you're safely away."

"Are you kidding?" I look at him incredulously. "Ben will be crazy thinking I died in there!"

"The firemen were on their way," Finn says. "Ben was conscious, and one of them was helping him out when we transferred. No one could see us through the smoke, but I could hear them. They'll put the fire out and realize soon enough that no one's been left inside. They'll likely think you got lost in the crowd, and Ben will certainly know I got you out of there."

He hands me the cup of water again and I take another drink as he lights a gas lamp, brightening up the cabin. The adrenaline is finally ebbing from my bloodstream, and I am conscious now that the side of my wrist hurts—a lot.

I turn my hand over, looking at the bright red patch of skin on my lower arm.

"Let's have a look," Finn says, cradling my hand carefully. "It's not bad—but it will likely blister. Hold on."

He rummages through a trunk that he pulls from under the bed, pulling out a small jar of ointment. He gives it a sniff, then, with gentle fingers, he spreads the soothing salve on my reddened skin.

I hiss slightly, and then I let out a sigh. "That feels nice," I say.

"The peppermint oil in it will soothe your burn, while the coconut oil and aloe will help it heal," he says, reading the label. "I got this from a barge carrying unregulated homeopathic medicines."

"Pirated goods?"

"Legally seized unregulated merchandise," he corrects. "'Course, I helped myself to a few cases of interesting things."

"Of course you did." I smirk. "Do you think we should bandage it?"

"Not unless the skin breaks," he says. "We'll keep an eye on it." He turns my hand over, kissing the back gently. "There now. Better?"

I nod. "What about you?"

He flips his wrist over to show me the singed cuff of his shirt. "No skin, just material. Although I did fancy this shirt." He lets out a sigh.

"You saved my life." The words come out in a whisper as I realize just how close this one was, and I feel myself starting to shake.

"It's all right, love," he says, pulling me in close again. "You're safe now."

"You came back for me."

He pulls away now, raising a brow as he looks at me. "'Course I came back," he says.

"But Eversor got away."

I can feel his whole body tighten with anger, and I reach up to touch his face. "Thank you."

He slides his hand around mine, pulling it from his face. "Don't thank me. I shouldn't have left you in the first place."

"This wasn't your fault."

"When I saw her in the crowd—" His jaw tightens and he works to get the next words out. "I shouldn't have hesitated. I very nearly sent you to the same death once again."

"Finn." I rest my head against his chest, rubbing my cheek back and forth. "It wasn't your fault. We're here now, and that's what matters."

"Yes," he agrees. "This is what matters." His arms tighten around me again, and for a moment there's only the sound of him and me breathing, and the gentle rocking of the ship beneath us.

"Are we in port?" I ask finally.

"Yes. I left her moored in New Devonshire and told my crew

I had to take a land journey. The ship's locked up tight. No one will bother us here."

I carefully roll off his lap to my knees and he pushes to his feet, offering me a hand.

"Easy now," he says. "You're bound to be a bit dizzy after all that."

I sway slightly, but I think it's more from the motion of the ship beneath my feet. "Not too bad," I say. "Guess I have to get my sea legs."

"Well, you're off to a good start. You've got great legs."

I let out a laugh that turns into a cough, and he's there, supporting me with his arm around me. I'm assailed by memories of our first meeting. He was so charming, so funny, and oh, the way he'd kissed me—until he realized who I wasn't.

"Are you sure you're all right?" he asks. "Let me refill your drink. Still a bit fuzzy, are you?"

"No. I was just thinking. About the first time we met."

"Ah yes," he says with a smile. "You were quite the surprise. And then you surprised me again by coming back."

"I guess I wanted to see it all again," I say, gesturing around me. "We had fun that night."

"We did," he agrees. "And it was quite the memory for me as well." He hands me my cup, watching as I take another drink.

"She thought it was funny, you know," he says. "You and me."

"Funny?"

"You—she—said it seems as though we're bound to be together, no matter where we are. She was a bit of a romantic. I suspect you are as well. But she wasn't one for dramatics."

"We definitely have that in common."

His hand touches my face, and I can feel his thumb tracing my jawline as he moves his fingers to lightly grip my jaw. He turns my head slowly left, then right.

"You're not her. I know that," he murmurs. "No matter the similarities, you are entirely and uniquely your own person."

"Thanks." I meet his eyes, and I know I should probably move away, but I can't seem to do it. "You're in a category all your own, too. You have been from the moment I met you."

"I was impressed the first time we met. By the night of the ball I was truly enchanted to have you back again."

"I wasn't expecting to see you again, either," I remind him. "You weren't supposed to be at the ball."

"I wanted a dance," he says. "I should have danced with you when I had the chance."

I smile wryly. "Instead you taught me to defend myself. That little trick saved my life, by the way, so I guess I owe you twice."

"Really? That must be quite the thrilling tale." He steps away a moment, to what looks like an old-fashioned Victrola, cranking it up. "Since we have some time to kill . . . ," he says as the sound of violins floats across the air.

"Miss St. Clair, may I have the honor of this dance?" He bows and then holds his hand out to me.

"You want to dance? Now?"

"It's not a fancy ball, but I think I can manage."

I give him a smile and drop into a ridiculous curtsy. "Why, Mr. Gallagher, I'd be delighted."

He pulls me into his arms, and he's really good at this. I'm absurdly grateful for my newfound confidence courtesy of my dancing alter ego. He's twirling and dipping and I'm keeping up, laughing at how well we move together. The song ends and another comes on, slower, and he pulls me in closer, waltzing me slowly around the cabin.

"You dance divinely," I say, putting on a cheesy accent.

"So I've been told. Though I didn't get to practice as often with you—her—as I'd have liked."

And just like that, it's like she's standing in the room with us. He feels the difference immediately.

"We probably should go—" I begin, but Finn shakes his head, cutting me off.

"Do you want to know how I did it?" he asks me softly as he continues to dance me slowly around the room.

"Did what?"

"Got through all this? Got through losing her?"

I stare up at him mutely—not really sure what I should say. He takes a breath and goes on.

"I looked in the mirror—don't laugh—and I told myself the truth."

We slow to a stop, and I ask: "What's the truth?"

"The truth is, as much as I loved you here, I knew I had to find you there."

He pulls our hands up to his lips, and I am swamped by the feelings his words are dredging up, feelings of loss and pain and regret and guilt.

"Tell me the truth, love. Please. Tell me your truth."

The tears are welling in my eyes, but I don't look away.

"The truth is I never stopped thinking about you," I say. "Even when I was with my Finn. We had such a short time together—me and him—and my time with you was even shorter." I pause to swallow, because the words, the truth within them, are clogging my throat.

"I couldn't get you out of my mind," I confess in a guilty whisper. "I don't know why."

"Don't you?" he asks, and the brightness in his eyes is warming me, warming all the parts that have been cold for so long.

I'm not sure when I finally notice the slow movement of his hand on my back, the way his fingertips trace the vertebrae in my spine, or his other hand, sliding into the hair at my nape. When I look up at him, something in his eyes changes—a shifting within us both that steals the breath from our lungs. His thumb comes out to slide along my jaw, and I feel my lips parting as his mouth comes down on mine.

The kiss deepens, turning into something wilder, stronger. My fingers twine into his hair, and the slide and dance of his tongue around mine is all I know—the taste and feel of him as his arms tighten to pull me in closer.

Our breath mingles for a moment as he lifts his head, and his lips graze mine once more.

"We're part of a plan, you and I," he murmurs. "And despite the thoroughly bizarre circumstances that brought us together, I think we have to be all right with that."

He leans in to continue where we left off, and I push against his chest. He releases me instantly, a question on his face.

I take a step away, and then another. "We should get back," I tell him. "I shouldn't have gotten carried away like that. People at home are worried about me."

And by *people*, I mean Ben. Shame brings a flood of color to my cheeks, and I need some time and space between us so I can sort out everything that's just bubbled to the surface.

"I need to get back," I finish lamely.

He masks the hurt in his eyes by turning to the mirror on the wall, next to the porthole.

"Very well," he says, holding out his hand. "Miss St. Clair, I'm at your service."

He doesn't look at me as I put my hand in his.

24

Revelation

WE TRANSFER BACK TO THE RESTROOM AT MUGSY'S, which is empty—thank God. Right now, I'm facing myself in the mirror, and I look like hell. I have black soot streaking parts of my face, and my eyes are still red from smoke irritation. I wash off as best I can with paper towels, but the smell of smoke is still clinging to my clothes. We walk over to Wickley's, where Mr. Kellar nearly hugs me with joy, he's so glad to see me.

Luckily, the fire didn't spread far and no one was hurt. The alcove was scorched black and the fire got so hot the paint melted off the wall there. The store would be reopening tomorrow. Mr. Kellar asks me to come in later in the week and give a statement to the insurance company, and he rails on me a little for not going straight to the doctor to get checked out.

No one seems to know anything about Ben, and he isn't answering when I text him. Despite Finn's assurances, we run for home, hoping Ben headed there once he realized I was gone. We rush through the door and I'm immediately engulfed by two hundred pounds of flying brother.

"Jessa!"

"Oh thank God!" My mother's voice carries from the other room as she runs up to hug me, too. "Jessa! Oh, honey, are you okay? Where were you? We've been worried sick!"

"I'm fine, Mom—is Ben okay? Did he come by? Danny, let go!" I peel myself out of Danny's arms, but Mom is still holding on.

"He's okay," she says, pushing my hair off my face. "You weren't burned? You're breathing okay?"

"I'm fine," I tell her again. "I've got a tiny burn on my arm, but Finn got me out of there in time."

She turns to look at Finn, and two seconds later he's wrapped in my mother's arms. "Thank you," she says. "Thank you so much." She pulls back and runs a hand over his hair, too. "Are you okay?" she asks. "Do you need a doctor?"

He's a little flustered, and I can't help but wonder how long it's been since he's been fussed over by a mother. Probably a very long time.

"I'm fine," he says.

"You smell like camping," Danny says to me. He takes another sniff to be sure.

"Yeah, I smell like a campfire," I agree. "But I'm okay."

"Ben's mother called me from the hospital," Mom says as she gives my burn a once-over.

"Hospital!"

"The EMTs took him there as a precaution," Mom explains. "He hit his head on the floor when some idiot pushed a shopping cart into him—but other than a big knot, he's okay. He had his mom call to find out if you were all right."

I put my hands over my face in pure relief. Ben is okay. He's really okay.

"You probably want a shower," Mom says, giving me a sniff of her own. "I'm going to run out to the drugstore for some more antibiotic ointment. We have a little bit in the upstairs cabinet—put it on for now. And Mr. Kellar from Wickley's needs you to call him."

"I talked to him already. Sorry I worried you," I say, hugging her again. "Things were a little confusing with everyone running out and all the firemen coming in. Finn got me out of there and we went down the street to Mugsy's so we wouldn't be in the way. I was shaken up," I improvise—and it's not really a lie. "I didn't think to call."

"It's okay, honey. Just as long as you're safe." She looks over at Finn. "Both of you."

"I'm going to get that shower," I say. "Finn? Are you hanging around?" I know the answer before he even answers.

"I don't mind smelling like a campfire," he says.

"I like to camp. Do you?" Danny asks.

"I do," he says. "I worked as a trail guide for a time, in the Appalachians. Did a lot of camping there."

That's a new one. "I haven't heard that story yet," I say.

"Get your shower and I'll tell you all about it," he promises, settling into the chair opposite Danny as my mom grabs her car keys.

I reach for my phone as I climb the stairs, texting Ben to tell him I'm home and I'm fine. Before I press send, I peel my shirt off, pulling the smell of smoke into the air all around me. I like camping, too, but I think if I never smell fire that close again, I'll be a much happier camper.

I spend a long time in the shower, soaking until my skin is lobster-red, and thinking. Mostly thinking.

We're a part of a plan, he said. He spoke of truth, and that is the truest truth there is. If there's one thing being a Traveler has taught me, it's that everyone is part of a plan. But Finn and I— we're just different. We belong together. But do I belong with this Finn? Am I his default? Or is he mine? Or are we forging something new?

I don't know the answer to that. All I know is I don't want to feel like a consolation prize. And I don't want him feeling that way, either. But at the same time, he's Finn, and I'm Jessa. We are what we are—and who we are—to each other. And that means I have to be honest with Ben. And hurt Ben.

I pull some pajama pants and a shirt on and decide that I've done enough thinking. After the events of today, I'm honestly feeling a little brain-numb from being so overwhelmed. I don't know how much more I can take.

And just as I'm registering the sound of voices, my bedroom door is flung open, and Ben comes charging through.

"She's taking a shower!" I hear Danny yell, and I see Finn right behind Ben, looking seriously perturbed. Danny is behind Finn looking—well, like Danny.

"Ben! You're okay!"

I throw myself into Ben's arms, and he catches me as I hug

him tight. He pulls back to look at me, and then he turns to look at Finn. The fury on his face makes every muscle in his body tighten.

"You!" he says as Finn steps into the room.

"Are you going to fight?" Danny wants to know.

"Everything's fine, Danny," I say. "Nobody's fighting."

"If Mom hears you were fighting she will ground you," he says. "She will *so* ground you."

"Thanks, Danny. We're good."

I push him back gently, then shut the door and lean against it, watching the two of them face each other.

"What are you doing here?" Ben demands. "You almost got her killed!"

"What are you talking about?" Finn asks, utterly incredulous. "I saved her life!"

Ben turns back to me. "I had to come over. I just . . . I had to make sure you were okay."

"I'm fine," I say. "Finn got me out in time. But I heard you were hurt. Are *you* okay?"

"Don't worry about me," he bites out. Then he seems to get even angrier. He turns and starts railing on Finn.

"She almost died again! That seems to happen an awful lot when you're around, don't you think?" he adds snidely.

"You were closest to her when the fire started," Finn snaps back. "So don't go blaming me!"

I step between them. "It was Eversor," I remind them. "She was there, and she set this all up."

"I barely got Jessa out of there in time," Finn said. "And I assisted you, as I recall."

"I'm sure you tried your hardest to save me," Ben says to Finn, in a voice dripping with sarcasm. "Or were you too busy looking out for the only person who matters—yourself!"

"Ben!" I can't believe he said that!

"Jessa, listen to me!" He grabs me hard by my upper arms, and I notice just how different he looks right now. His eyes have dark circles and he's practically shaking, he's so full of anger. This is so unlike the Ben I know.

"He's bad for you!" Ben snarls. "I know it. I feel it—I've had a gut instinct about him ever since he showed up again. This Finn isn't like the other one. He's not safe!" He gives me a hard shake. "Do you hear me? He's the one trying to kill you!"

"What in the bloody hell are you talking about?" Finn roars. "And get your hands off her!"

"Ben . . ." I look at him warily. "Let's go outside and talk, okay? I don't think you understand—"

"I do!" he insists. "I do understand! I'm telling you, he's going to kill us both! He's been trying to from the beginning!"

"Ben—" I speak in a low, soothing voice as I pull away from him. "You need to calm down."

"Calm down?" He puts his hands in his hair, tearing at it like a crazy person, and I start nervously edging toward Finn. "I'm done here!" he shouts. "I'm so done!" Then he turns and slams out the door and runs down the stairs. I follow right after him, putting up a warning hand to Finn to stay back.

"Ben!" I chase him down as he's getting in his truck. "We need to talk."

"But you won't listen!" he says in exasperation. "You won't listen."

He starts up the truck and makes one last plea to me.

"Jessa . . . please—every instinct I have is screaming for me to *get you away from him*. And you're not listening! It's so bad, I'm having nightmares about him!" He yanks the door shut angrily, and then he floors the gas and I jump back as he peels out.

Then I go absolutely still as the realization floods through me. Oh my God. I know where Rudy is.

25

The Unwanted Guest

ONCE I'M BACK INSIDE, I MOTION TOWARD THE DOOR with my head, and Finn comes over with a questioning look.

"Say good night, then me meet around back," I whisper.

"Good night, Danny," he calls out.

Danny gives him a wave as he loads up his next video game. "No more yelling, okay?"

"We're all done, Danny," I assure him. "Good night, Finn." I close the door behind him and I tell Danny I'm going to bed, then I sneak Finn in the back door and up the stairs while Danny blissfully plays Minecraft.

"I know how Rudy's been spying on us," I tell him as I shut the door.

"How?"

"Think about it," I say, sitting down on the bed and making room for him next to me. "Eversor has been one step ahead of us everywhere—like she's had inside information. She knew I'd be with Ben at the museum. She knew I'd be in Arizona during my recital—and so did Ben. She knew I was working at Wickley's today—and so did Ben. And he's been hostile to absolutely frothing-at-the-mouth crazy ever since you showed up."

"You think Rudy's taken up residence in Ben's dreams?"

"He can hang out in his subconscious and suggest all kinds of things. Mario told me once they could torture you that way if they need to."

"Torture?" Finn doesn't like the sound of that. "What d'you mean, torture?"

"He didn't say *he* did it," I tell him. "Just that if a Traveler tries to fly outside the rules, their Dreamer can make life difficult, since they have open access to the subconscious."

"So . . . how do we get him out?"

"We need to call in the big guns. We need Mario."

"Can you sleep?" Finn asks me.

"After the day I had today? I could sleep for a week. If I have to, I can grab the NyQuil," I say. "Like last time."

"Last time?" He looks confused.

"Oh." I drop my eyes. "Sorry. Other you. It's cold medicine—I took it last time I needed to get to sleep fast."

"Oh." Now he looks away. "I don't need medicine. You could stroke my hair."

"Stroke your hair?"

"Yes, we"—he fumbles for a moment—"I nod off more easily that way."

"Why don't we just wait a while and see if we drowse off?" I suggest. "If it takes too long, I'll break out the medicine."

He gives me a reluctant nod. "I'll just lie down over here on the floor," he says.

"You can crash here," I tell him. "Just stick to your side, okay?"

"Okay."

I ease myself down until I'm lying flat, and I'm aware of every inch of him next to me. The warmth of his body feels so familiar alongside mine, reminding me of the nights I shared with the other part of himself, separate, but not so different.

"Penny for your thoughts," he says, rolling onto his side to face me. I roll as well, and we're just about nose to nose.

"You owe me a fortune by now," I say.

"I'd pay it, and gladly. I can see the play of thoughts across your face, but in many ways you're still such a mystery. What's funny?" he asks as he sees my lips twitch into a smile.

"You think I'm a mystery, and I feel like I've known you forever. Like we're two old shoes sitting side by side in the same closet."

"I'm an old shoe?" He makes an exaggerated face. "Well, that's not very romantic, is it?"

"It's romantic," I defend myself. "It's wildly romantic. Not everyone gets the luxury of growing old together."

He bites his lip. "No, I suppose they don't."

I think about the target on my head and the people we've both lost. "Do you think . . . ," I ask hesitantly. "Maybe you and I are meant to live several lifetimes at once, instead of just one long one?"

"No." His voice is firm, and his hands come up to cup my face. "You're going to live until you're toothless and gray. I'll make sure of that."

"Toothless and gray. Now *that's* romantic."

"So you want romance, do you?" He moves himself closer.

"Finn. You need to sleep."

His voice drops to a husky murmur. "I know how we can get me good and sleepy. . . ."

"Finn." I repeat my warning, but I can't deny the fluttery feeling in my stomach that was brought on by his words—and the borrowed memories that go with them. "We've got a job to do."

"I suppose I'll defer to your sound judgment," he says with a yawn and a stretch. "But I'd like to continue this discussion sometime."

"We need to sleep," I hedge. Now isn't the time or place for this. Not with Ben's mental health on the line.

He closes his eyes with a sigh, then a moment later, he lets out another.

I open my eyes to look at him, and I put my hand up, laying it gently on his head. I slowly run my fingers through his hair, fascinated by the feel of its silkiness, concentrating on a slow, even rhythm as my hand moves, and Finn closes his eyes with a look of pure contentment on his face.

"That's lovely," he murmurs. "Just lovely."

I have a vision of him with his head in my lap; both of us on a blanket at the beach on a warm spring day, and my fingers play through his hair just like this as I listen to the waves rolling in to the shore. I don't know if that's a real memory or something my imagination has drummed up, but I know it could have happened just that way. And he would have this same smile of contentment on his face while I did it.

Finn's breathing begins to deepen, and I pull my hand back, taking this time to study his unguarded face. He's got a tiny scar on his cheek, very faint, and you'd have to be as close as I am to notice it. One of the differences in a sea of similarities between the Finns I've known.

My eyes grow heavy, even without the benefit of a shot of NyQuil, and I let them close. I yawn, and then I blink slowly as my eyes adjust to the brilliant light of the classroom.

"The poor boy is nearly mad from it," Finn is saying to Mario. Then he looks over his shoulder at me as he realizes I've arrived.

"There you are."

"Does Ben have any idea what you suspect?" Mario asks me.

"No. I didn't say a word to him."

Mario strides for the red door, and we're right behind him. "Stay out of the way," he says. "Just . . . find a corner and keep Ben busy. Whatever you do, don't interfere."

Mario jerks the door open, and we step into . . . a museum? I guess that makes sense—this is Ben, after all. The walls are lined with displays of soccer trophies and memorabilia, with shelves of books every so often that stretch out in an infinite line.

I walk carefully behind Mario and Finn, feeling guilty for being here. It's awfully personal, invading somebody's mind. I know I did this with Danny, but I'm not sure how Ben will feel about us being here.

We move farther into the bookshelves, and Mario holds up a hand.

"Listen," he whispers.

We go still, listening, and the soft sounds of voices in conversation carry through the cavernous room.

". . . absolutely right," Ben's voice comes through. "They're trying to make me feel like I'm paranoid, but I'm completely unbiased."

"Of course you are, of course you are. He's the interloper." I recognize Rudy's genteel British tones.

"That's exactly what he is. An interloper."

"And he's unnecessary now," Rudy goes on. "With the mirrors in hand, there's no reason for him to hang about, is there?"

"Nope. Hey, any more research projects like that lying around? I enjoyed that one."

"And you were very helpful," Rudy says. "But did they reward you?"

"No, I got dropped in a lake."

"And no one bothers to examine Finn's motives." Rudy *tsk-tsks*.

We pause on the other side of the shelves from where they sit. I can look through a gap in the books and see them, sitting on opposite sides of a long table. There's an entire five-gallon tub of ice cream open in front of Ben, and he's eating out of it with a spoon.

"I know all about his motives," he says angrily. "It's just like you said. He brings death everywhere he goes."

"He's obviously working with Eversor," Rudy says, with empathy just dripping from his voice. "She's playing an elaborate cat-and-mouse game with our Jessa, and it will end badly. He's been Eversor's lover, you know."

"That's right!" Ben shovels more ice cream into his mouth.

"You need to go over there again tomorrow."

"She won't listen to me," Ben says, shaking his head.

"Then you need to take action!" Rudy's voice is soft, urgent. "Or would you rather delay and find her dead? Strangled? Beaten? Stabbed, perhaps—he killed her that way already in another reality stream. How will you feel when her lifeless body greets you—"

Rudy waves his hand, and a large picture frame behind him comes to life, showing a vision of me, lying in a pool of blood, my eyes sightless and my limbs broken. The skin covering my skull has been sheared away by great force, hanging off to the side. I stare at it in horror, and I'm not the only one.

"Stop!" Ben crams his palms into his eyes. "Stop! I can't—"

"That's enough." Mario steps out from behind the shelves, and Rudy slowly gets to his feet as we step in behind him.

"Well, well, well . . . ," he coos. "We have guests."

Ben wipes his eyes and turns to look at us. Once he sees Finn, he jumps to his feet.

"What are you doing here?" he demands. "Jessa! Get away from him!"

"Ben." I step in front of Finn. "This is Rudy. The runaway Dreamer." I point at Rudy, and he stares at me with a hint of a condescending smile.

"He's been in here, feeding you misinformation," Mario says.

"No." Ben shakes his head. "He's got insight. He knows what's really going on."

"But think about how you used to feel about Finn—before," I quietly remind him. "You helped me save him, remember?"

"We *didn't* save him," he responds in a really cutting tone. "And this"—he points at Finn—"is what we're dealing with in the aftermath."

"But you knew he wouldn't hurt me," I press. "Think about it, Ben. If Finn wanted me dead, he's had plenty of chances."

"Too many!" he agrees. "And you're not even seeing his part

in it! We're the only ones who get it!" He gestures at Rudy, who is eyeing us all shrewdly.

"The game is up, Rudy," Mario says. "You know we can't allow this to happen. What you've done to Eversor—and to Ben—is a blatant misuse of your powers."

"I haven't had much to work with," Rudy scoffs. "Extreme measures were warranted. And you're a fine one to talk about misusing power. Jessa has talent that could harness the universe without resorting to all these distractions. Yet you let it lie fallow."

"I don't believe in convergence," I tell him. "There might be more reality streams than ever, but that just leaves the door open for more Travelers and more assignments. Ask us! Any one of us would be happy to sign up for more."

"Unnecessary and wasteful," Rudy says. "But it doesn't surprise me that you would take that challenge, Jessa. You have the same thirst for adventure I found in Finn. But I realized early on that he was too headstrong for what needed to be done. I began grooming my other protégé, but she doesn't have your talent."

"Are we supposed to pity you your choices?" Finn asks in a scathing tone. "You're a coward, hiding behind a weak woman."

"Don't talk to him like that," Ben warns. "He's right. He's been right about everything."

"You're strong, Jessa," Rudy says, stepping out from behind the table. "Just as your ancestor was strong. Did you never wonder why Viatrix was the only Traveler for so very long?"

"I hadn't thought about it."

"It's because this isn't the first convergence," Rudy says. "But I suppose Mario didn't divulge that."

"*What?*" I look to Mario for confirmation.

"It's happened before," Mario says quietly. "Viatrix started the convergence."

"In her defense, it was unintentional." Rudy shrugs.

"We tried to correct it, but it was too late. She was strong enough to reverse some of the damage and keep her reality intact— to preserve the origin," Mario says. "It was decades before we had enough divergent reality streams to yield us more Travelers, and we've been very structured in our corrections ever since."

"And you didn't think I needed to know that?" I ask incredulously.

"Did he tell you? She was experimenting with her abilities." Rudy waves his hand, and a montage of scenes light the picture frame behind him. There is Viatrix, struggling to keep from drowning in a stormy sea, dodging arrows and eventually getting hit in the leg, running through a burning alleyway. Finally, I see her in a shifting and tilting dreamscape, her body fading in and out as she desperately tries to keep focus and hold everything together.

"Mario was the one who encouraged all of that," Rudy goes on. "When he discovered what she was and what she could do, he had her constantly pressing the boundaries. He sent her into the unknown, put her in reckless situations. . . . Does this sound familiar?"

My eyes are locked on Mario, because yes, this does sound familiar.

"Don't listen to him, Jessa," Mario says. "It's not like that. What you and I have worked on—"

"Stop." I put up a hand. "Just let me think for a minute."

"He still bears the guilt of pushing Viatrix to do exactly what needed to be done. Now he doesn't want the convergence because he doesn't want to simplify," Rudy says. "You accuse me of wanting power, when all I want is the safety of every Traveler. Mario wants to use you for his own entertainment."

"That's not true and you know it," Mario growls. "Corrections are chosen with the utmost care and study. I wrote the damn guidelines."

"And still things get away, spin out of control. If we have fewer fires to tend, we can tend them with more care. More *consideration*."

"At the cost of millions of lives," Finn bites out. "What of them?"

"They don't belong," Rudy states flatly. "All of them created on the turn of a choice. On a whim. And like any creation, they can be remade to a better version of themselves."

"You're not a god," I tell him.

"Aren't we? Mario and I make decisions every day that begin and end lives. How is this different—other than being more efficient?"

"Wait—what do you mean, *millions of lives?*" Ben looks at me in confusion. "Jessa?"

I walk over to him. "He's going to kill me," I tell him. "The dancer you bought the french fries for. The girl who writes the bad poetry. And the girl who heard your voice for the first time."

My words have struck home, and Ben's face clearly shows it. I look at Rudy. "Mario may not always make it easy for me, but that's life. There aren't any guarantees. Isn't that what you Dreamers always say? You can't predict it perfectly. And that's what makes it so damn interesting."

"We can do great things, Jessa," Rudy encourages. His crisp, urbane demeanor cracks, and I can see the madness in his eyes. "Think of it! With me at the helm and you influencing emerging new reality streams, we could be glorious!"

"She's already glorious," Finn says. "And you're barking up the wrong tree. You've lost. Me. Her. All of it."

Rudy tenses, and I see Mario take a step forward.

"Don't try it. If you come with me peacefully—"

Mario's invitation is promptly blown to hell by an exploding bookcase, raining Technicolor papers down all around us. Light suddenly bursts out of every crack in the shelves, and the ground beneath us shakes, rattling all the items on the walls, causing pictures to fall and glass cases to vibrate.

We run for cover, diving under the table.

"What's going on?" I hear Ben ask as Rudy races by with Mario in close pursuit. I reach up, grabbing Ben's hand and tugging him down under the table with us.

"I've called for reinforcements!" Mario shouts. "Brace your-selves!"

"Listen to me!" Rudy screams as he sees me. "You can't stop this! Jessa, you cannot let this go too far! We have the chance to reset and reclaim!"

He dives behind what appears to be an old-fashioned plow as Mario pulls a wicked-looking spear from a wall display and lets it fly.

Rudy cowers behind a large display of military swords. He

picks one up, waving it threateningly, and Mario wastes no time in grabbing a sword out of the scabbard on a standing suit of armor and starting forward.

"This is nuts!" I say, looking over at Finn.

"I suppose he has to work with what he's got at hand," Finn replies.

"The standard long sword will give him extended reach," Ben tells us—and somehow he's reached up and gotten his ice cream and spoon, which he uses to point—"but the Civil War saber is much lighter. His opponent will be faster for it. It's going to come down to strategy and the potential appearance of rein-forcements."

Ben starts to move from where we're crouching under the table, and I pull him back.

"Don't go out there," I tell him, just as we hear the clang of metal on metal.

"We're not going to be able to see much under here," he tells me, raising his voice to be heard over the clanging of steel, the grunts of exertion, and then a crash as Mario is thrown across the room into a bench. He picks himself up and rushes back at Rudy again, tossing him hard into a stand of bookcases nearby. Ben lets out a yelp and dives right for them, catching a book as it falls off the shelf.

"Are you crazy!" I admonish, dragging him back under the table. "Get back here!"

"This is priceless!" he protests. "I'm not about to let these two loonies destroy my books."

"It's a dream!" I shout in exasperation. "The books aren't real!"

"Then neither am I," he counters.

"I'm not taking a chance on him permanently scrambling your brain," I tell him.

Mario is on the offense now, with Rudy backed into a corner. Rudy is pulling anything he can get his hands on off the shelves and throwing it in an effort to slow Mario down—books, vases, even a large geode that smashes to the floor right in front of Finn, spraying us all with shards of rock.

"Hey! My dad gave that to me!" Ben protests, still holding his book to his chest to protect it.

"Are you okay?" I ask Finn as he dabs at a cut on his face.

"Nicked me," he says. "They're at a standoff. They're both too strong to lose."

I'm beginning to think he's right. Mario and Rudy are grappling now, falling into tables and slamming into walls, but neither one has the upper hand.

"When opponents in battle are evenly matched, sometimes the element of surprise can make all the difference," Ben says matter-of-factly. "For instance . . ."

He crawls out a few feet to grab a fallen telescope, and then he squints a bit, judging the distance to Mario and Rudy before he gives it a strong push. It rolls end over end toward them, coming to rest right behind Rudy. Mario gives a mighty heave, throwing Rudy backward so that he hits the telescope, tripping and stumbling over it on his way to a full-out sprawl on the floor. Finn dives over the top of him, and Mario grabs Finn by the back of his shirt, hauling him off.

"Get back!" he shouts, and with a deafening roar, the red door on the wall bursts open.

We're thrown backward as hundreds of figures pour into the room, backlit by a brilliant light blazing through the doorway, surrounding Rudy in a circle that begins to tighten, pressing in.

"Listen to me!" he screams. "It has to be done! You know it! We all know it! We cannot contin—"

His voice breaks off as the circle begins to move, slowly at first, then faster and faster, until they're nothing but a blur, then a beam of light that gets brighter and more intense with every pass until we can barely look at it. A second red door appears in the wall across from us, glowing like it's lit up in neon, and with an enormous bang, it opens. Papers and books, glass and small objects fly toward the door like a vacuum explosion in a spacecraft, pulling hard and stealing the breath from our lungs.

I hear Rudy's voice like it's coming from a mountaintop somewhere, and he gives a long, sustained "Noooooooooo!" until he's sucked through, and the door slams with ear-popping force behind him before it vanishes.

"Well," Ben says. "That was intense. I guess we're done here." He crawls out from under the table, sits down in a chair, opens up a book, and goes about his business as though two godlike creatures didn't just have a war in his brain.

Mario is panting with effort but manages to let out a chuckle.

"Is he gone?" I ask, taking Finn's hand as he pulls me out from under the table. "Where did he go?"

"He's imprisoned," Mario replies. "He won't get out—not with the power of all of us keeping him in." He turns to Finn. "And what did you think you were doing? I asked you to stay out of the way."

"He's not too great at that," I say dryly.

Finn shrugs. "You needed the help."

"I had the situation in hand," Mario says sternly.

"You were getting pummeled," Finn replies. "I must say, I like to see you flustered. Makes you a bit more . . . human."

"Finn." The last thing I want is Finn pissing off a Dreamer again with his smart mouth.

"What? I'm only saying it'll do him good to lose a little omnipotence, that's all," Finn says.

Mario gives him an eye roll, then turns back to me.

"Well . . . ," he says, dusting off his hands. "That was fun. I've wanted to do that for *eons*. Rudy has always been *such* a prig."

I lean back on the table. "It's over. He's gone." I exhale, long and loud.

"It's not over yet, love," Finn cautions. "Eversor is still out there."

"She won't have his direction," Mario says. "Or his interference. She'll be tasked another Dreamer since Rudy is gone, and we'll see that she gets someone gentle. She won't be allowed on assignments anymore, either." He claps a hand on my shoulder. "I'll give you the rest of the night off."

"You're all heart," I say.

"And now I'll bid you adieu. I have some reports to make and some reality streams to see to," Mario says. "I'll see you soon."

"Do we go with you? To get out, I mean?" I ask him.

"I'll set the door once I leave. The two of you can wake Ben by coming back through."

He walks over to the red door, and with a nod, he's through. The door closes behind him, and we turn as we hear Ben call my name.

"Hey, St. Clair!" He's got a black ball—like a basketball—in his hands and he's leaning against the side of a semi-demolished bookshelf. "This ball belonged to Teddy Roosevelt," he tells us. "Did you know he had asthma? He still led an active and full life, though."

"How utterly fascinating," Finn says blandly.

"All righty, then . . . ," I say, giving Finn a pointed look. "Ben, it's time to wake up now."

He tucks the ball under his arm and looks at me curiously. "Oh, am I still dreaming?"

"Do you live in a museum?" I ask.

"Today I do," he says matter-of-factly. "And we have ice cream. Which is awesome."

"Very," I agree as Ben opens the door and we all step through.

I open my eyes and it's dead silent in my bedroom. That is, until my phone chirps with a text from Ben:

> **What the F—!!**

I throw the phone down and Finn and I erupt in laughter and more than a little relief.

26

Aftermath

I'M JUST FINISHING LOADING OUR BREAKFAST DISHES into the dishwasher when I hear the doorbell. It's Wednesday, and the first day of Christmas break. Mom and Danny are at work, leaving the day wide open for me. And Finn.

"That's Ben," I say nervously, and for a moment I wonder if I can ignore the doorbell. It's cowardly, I know, but I was just running around in his subconscious, and worse, I brought friends. He's not going to be happy about that.

"Chin up, love," Finn says. "At least he'll be speaking his own thoughts now."

"Yeah. That's what I'm afraid of."

I straighten my T-shirt—I don't know why—and I walk to the door, taking a deep breath before I open it.

"Ben." I step aside so he can come in. He looks better. Sort of. "Did you get some sleep?"

"You mean before or after you were blowing up bookcases in

my dreams?" he asks warily. "Please tell me you know what I'm talking about."

"We do." Finn comes in from the kitchen and Ben bristles instantly.

I give Finn a look—why didn't he stay in the kitchen? Then I sigh and close the door before I take Ben by the hand and lead him over to the couch.

"I can't believe what Rudy was putting you through," I say, sitting down on the couch and pulling him down next to me. "I'm so sorry, Ben. If it weren't for me, you would never have gotten tangled up in all this."

"Seriously . . . ," Ben says. "I can't believe you were in my *mind*. That's messed up."

"It was the only way," Finn says. "Rudy wasn't coming out without a fight."

"That was an experience," I say. "Leave it to you to have a museum for a brain."

Ben rolls his head from side to side. "Man, does it feel good to have him gone. He was like a horcrux or something."

"A what?" Finn asks, sitting in the chair across from us.

"Later," I say, turning back to Ben. "You really feel okay? No lingering effects?"

"All my memories are intact," he assures me. "Including the time you fell in the mud behind the gym and you still had mud in your ear the next day."

I open my mouth, then close it again. "Nice. And I was going to offer you some breakfast."

"I already ate." He stretches back on the couch. "And now that my head is clear, I can remember what I really went to

Wickley's for yesterday. The museum called my dad—the mirrors are in and we can pick them up."

"Why would we need to?" I ask. "Rudy's gone. And Eversor's cut off."

"Cut off, yes," Finn says. "But no less dangerous for it. She may not yet realize that Rudy's out of the picture."

"So she may be sticking to the game plan?"

"Precisely. Until she's been made to see the light, I think we need to stick to our game plan as well."

"It's not a big deal," Ben says. "I can have them returned."

"But I want to see them," I tell him.

"Then let Ben hold them for a time," Finn says. "At least until we know that Eversor's gotten the message."

"He's probably right," Ben says. "Better safe than sorry."

"What's this?" I ask in an exaggerated tone. "Civil conversation?"

"He's much more agreeable without a godlike creature meddling about in his mind," Finn says. "Have you noticed?"

"And that gives me unfettered access to my near-encyclopedic knowledge of medieval and twentieth-century weaponry," Ben says, giving Finn a forced smile.

I guess I spoke too soon. Obviously, they're not ready to join hands and sing "Kumbaya" yet. And I can't delay what I need to do any longer.

"Finn, don't you have someplace to be?"

He looks at me quizzically. "What?"

"You were going to walk down to Mugsy's for coffee, weren't you?"

"I drink tea," he reminds me. I give him a glare because he's not getting the point.

"I know that. Go get some." My eyes dart to Ben, then back to Finn. "Please."

His lips press together into a thin line, and he gives me a nod before he stands up. "Very well," he says. "I'll return shortly."

He strides to the door and walks out, shutting it behind him. I'm still staring at the door when I hear Ben take in a slow breath.

"So," he says.

"So," I echo. "I'm sorry. About last night. About it all. I never wanted you dealing with this stuff."

He shakes his head. "I don't blame you, St. Clair. I'm just glad the worst is over."

I think about Finn's warning about Eversor. "Let's hope so."

"So is he going to be sticking around for a while? Or is he finally taking off once we figure out what Eversor is doing?"

"I don't know." I say it, and I realize it's true. Finn's goal has been Eversor from the moment he got here. Once she's out of the picture for good—what then? Something tightens my throat, and the words have a hard time coming. "I'm not sure if he's staying," I manage to say.

Ben is looking at me, and the silence hangs between us.

"He's winning, isn't he?"

Ben's voice is soft, and I feel the sadness in it like a hand squeezing my chest.

"This isn't a contest, Ben. You are who you are to me, just like he is who he is."

"I can see what the thought of him leaving does to you," he says. "And no matter how good it is between us, it's all on the back burner the minute he shows up."

We stare at each other and I force myself to hold his gaze when I really want to run away.

"I'm sorry," I whisper. And I am. Because he's right. "I don't know what to say."

"You don't have to say anything. It's just the way it is for you, right? The only time I get a shot is if I'm in a world without him around." His hand is resting on his knee, and he curls it into a fist. I sit up straighter and he blows out a huff of air at my look of wide-eyed alarm.

"I'm not fixing to off the guy," he says. "Although that particular thought has been cropping up over and over again lately."

"That wasn't you, that was Rudy," I tell him. I move over on the couch so I can slide my arm around him. "You've been put through a lot. I've put you through it. I should never have—"

He shakes his head as he sticks a finger to my lips. "Stop it. You told me from the get-go that you'd give it a try. And I suppose you did. You tried to warn me away and I wouldn't go. So I guess I've only got myself to blame."

I pull his fingers off my mouth and hold his hand in mine. "Don't say that. I'm sorry. I'm so sorry, Ben."

The tears are coming now, and I bury my face in his neck. I feel him shake his head. "It's okay, St. Clair. Some things just aren't meant to be, right? Maybe there's a whole universe of somebody elses out there for me." He gives a little laugh, and it only makes me cry harder.

"Stop. I mean it," he says. "You'll get me crying, too, and I really make a lot of noise."

Now it's my turn to laugh, but that doesn't stop the tears. I rub my face on my sleeve and look at him through bleary eyes. "Ben—can we—are we still friends? *Can* we be friends?"

"I don't know."

I suppose I deserve that. But the thought of losing Ben's friendship is a hard price to pay for my choices, even if I know they're the right ones. He stands up, and I slowly get to my feet.

"So . . . tomorrow," Ben says. "The museum's open from noon to four."

"I really do think I should go along," I say, walking Ben to the door. "If it turns out the mirrors aren't from this guy Tizoc, we can send them back, but I think it's worth finding out before you go to the extra trouble."

"It'll save me having to bring them to you," he muses.

"I can always come to your house. I don't mind."

"I'd rather not, okay?" He rubs his hand on the back of his neck. "I need some time. I'm not saying we can't ever be friends. I just—I don't think we can hang together like we used to for a while."

"I understand." I swipe at my eyes, determined I'm going to keep it together.

"I think I just need some space. We've got all of Christmas break to get through. Give me time to think."

I give him a shaky nod. "Okay."

We look at each other, and then he gives me an awkward nod. "Thanks for freeing me from megalomaniacal mental manipulation."

"Nice alliteration," I say, forcing a smile. "See you tomorrow."

"See ya."

He turns and walks down the stairs, and I watch him go, feeling like I'm a hundred years old but a thousand pounds lighter.

"What is it that you're working on?" Finn asks.

We haven't spoken much since he got back from Mugsy's. He's not stupid—he can see the redness in my eyes, and it's clear Ben and I didn't have a great conversation. I expected him to start prying the second he got through the door, but he's been strangely quiet, choosing instead to flip through the TV channels while I sit here at the table, sort of working on a story.

I say *sort of* because I keep getting distracted by memories and moments—the way he looked that first day on his ship when I met him, and again at the ball. Our dance on his ship yesterday and the way it felt to turn and sway in his arms. The way his lips tasted when they touched mine . . .

"Jessa?"

"Sorry," I mumble, tapping my pen on my journal. "It's a story. A memory."

"Of . . . ?"

I flush. "Of you."

"Really?" He seems intrigued. "Care to share?"

My internal war must show on my face. "If it makes you uncomfortable . . . ," he says.

"No, it's okay. You can read." I get to my feet and walk over to the couch to sit next to him. Then I slide the notebook across to his lap, and he settles in, his fingers tracing the words I've laid on the page.

It was a warm day, and her bonnet was stiflingly hot. Her gloves had caused her hands to sweat, and she wanted nothing more than to tear off every bit of restrictive clothing and run free.

She glanced around, as if afraid someone had heard her thoughts, but that was silly. There was no one around. The cove below the lighthouse was private property, belonging to her family. There might be the occasional passerby walking the coastline, but it was a rarity, to be sure.

Still, she gave one last look behind her down the beach before she moved deeper into the cove. In the shadow of the rocks, she removed her gloves, shoes, and stockings, then took off her bonnet and let loose her hair. She hiked up her skirts and gripped them in her fist, eager to feel the delicious chill of the water on her overheated skin.

She gave an audible sigh as the surf swirled around her toes, then sighed again as she lifted her heavy hair in the breeze, letting it fly about her face as it fell. She laughed at the feel of it, at the joy of being here under the high overhang of the cliff walls, hidden from the view of her mother, who would surely be undone to see her daughter behaving like this.

"Don't wade in too far," a voice called from behind her, and she whirled, forgetting her skirts and letting them drop into the water.

He was sitting on a rock in the shade of the overhang, and her eyes hadn't found him at first, coming from the bright light of the open beach. Now that they'd adjusted, she could see him clearly, one bare foot up on the rock and the other dangling carelessly off the side. His arm sat across his knee, and in his hand was a half-eaten apple. He was shirtless, and his breeches had been rolled to his knees.

He turned his face into the wind, and the breeze ruffled his dark hair, giving her a clear view of his profile. She realized she'd stopped breathing.

This would never do. For heaven's sake—it wasn't as if she'd never seen a man's chest before. The men in the fields and down at the dock went about shirtless all the time.

None of them looked like him, though. No one could look like him.

He turned his face back to her and gave her an apologetic look.

"Did I startle you, love?"

"This is a private beach," she replied, trying to sound firm, but failing as his eyes stayed locked with hers. "What are you doing here?"

"It's a devilish hot day," he said with a shrug. "This is the only shade on the beach. It's a good thing you didn't arrive ten minutes sooner—you'd surely have had your delicate sensibilities offended."

She felt her spine stiffen. "I'm not delicate."

"No," he said, studying her a moment. "I can see that you're not."

"You have a name?"

"Captain Finn Gallagher," he said, getting up from his seat. He swept her a courtly bow.

"Have we met, Captain Gallagher?" She stared at him, trying to place him, for he seemed familiar somehow, despite his lack of a shirt.

"Now that," he said, pointing his apple at her, "is a question, and a good one." He took one last bite of the fruit before pitching it off into the sand.

"You have an accent," she said. "Irish?"

"Aye. I've taken up a new route—my ship is the fastest solar schooner in port."

"The tall one? With the tree painted on the mainsail?"

"That's the one," he said, grinning. She stared at the dimple that appeared on one side, just above the curve of his lip.

"It's a fine ship." She turned her head to look out to sea. "I would imagine you've had many adventures, with a ship like that."

"I have," he agreed, leaving the rock and stepping to the edge of the beach, where he offered a hand to assist her out of the water. "I've had a fair few without it as well. Would you like to hear about them?"

She couldn't stop the excitement that leapt into her eyes. "I would. I want to hear them all." She reached her hand out as she drew closer, and he grasped it gently, placing a light kiss on the backs of her fingers. He didn't let it go.

"My name is Jessamyn," she said, a little breathlessly. "But my friends call me—"

"Jessa," he finished. And something inside her shifted at the familiarity of her name on his lips.

"You were so damned beautiful that day," Finn says. "Not that you're anything less any other day, mind you." He traces the words on the paper. "But, oh, with the wind in your hair, and your skirts sodden and dragging at you as we walked the beach . . ."

"I—she—had a rash on her legs for a week after that," I say, pulling up her memory. "It was worth it, though."

He smiles. "Aye, it was at that. How do you come to have that memory?"

"The night of the ball—that last night I saw you—I was in the coach, riding to the party. I got bored and I was thinking of you and wondering how we met. This memory came back to me."

I realize I'm discussing the last night of his Jessa's life, and I don't go on any further. I look away instead.

"You were thinking of me?" he asks.

I feel myself flush. "Well, you and I did have an interesting first meeting."

He chuckles and reaches over, pushing my hair back so he can see my face better, tucking a strand behind my ear.

"Aye, that we did."

The front door opens and suddenly we're interrupted by Danny singing "I'll Make a Man Out of You" from *Mulan* very loudly. Finn gives me an amused grin as I absently start mouthing the words and I shut my mouth and make an embarrassed face.

"Sorry," I say. "Habit. He watches that movie all the time."

"It's a rousing good tune," he says, getting to his feet. "How are you, Danny?"

"We're having meatballs for dinner," he replies as he heads into the family room. "Mom said so."

"Okay," I say, getting to my feet and pulling Finn along into the kitchen. "You want to stay for meatballs?" I ask him.

"Shouldn't you ask your mother?"

"She won't mind. It's only meatballs." I open a cupboard door and grab a drinking glass. "Want some iced tea?"

He makes a face as I pour myself a glass. "Why the devil d'you drink it iced? It's bloody cold outside."

"So you want a cup of hot tea?"

"I'll take whatever you have that passes for tea," he says begrudgingly. "I keep a tin of good, Irish tea on my ship that's replenished on a regular basis. But here . . ." He shudders. "Perhaps I should take it iced. Might improve the taste."

"It's better iced." I offer him my glass. "Try."

He takes another reluctant sip and I laugh at the face he makes just as the front door opens.

"Jessa?" my mom's voice calls out. "Are you home?"

"I'm in the kitchen," I call back. I hear her close the door as Danny asks her about meatballs, and she walks into the kitchen, stopping short at the sight of Finn.

"Oh," she says, dropping her purse and a stack of mail on the kitchen counter. "You're not alone."

"Is something wrong?" I ask.

"I got an e-mail from Mrs. Lampert at the school today," she says, stuffing her car keys into her purse. "You were supposed to pick up that scholarship application three days ago. She was going to mail it home, but if it's not postmarked by tomorrow, you'll be disqualified."

"It's not a big deal—"

"Not a big deal? Jessa, what has gotten into you?" She looks at Finn while she asks that, but then turns her eyes back to me.

"I can probably download it off their website," I tell her. "You're blowing this out of proportion."

"Am I? It seems like you've been scattered this last week. I know Christmas break has started, but you can't be throwing it all away like this."

"Throwing it all away?" I can't believe she's getting nuts about this.

"You need to develop some perspective," she says, not willing to let this go. "You've got scholarship and college applications to be thinking about. You can't afford to drop the ball now."

"*I* need to develop perspective?" I counter with a laugh. "I didn't start World War Three here!"

Finn sets the glass of tea down on the counter. "Jessa, perhaps what your mother is trying to say is—"

"Stay out of this, Finn," I warn him. "She's trying to say she thinks you're a bad influence, that's what she's trying to say."

"I didn't say that," Mom grits out. "But I do think you've been a little unfocused since Finn showed up again." She turns to look at him. "If you're really watching out for her, you'll encourage her to stay on track. She's got six months of high school left and she's an honor student."

"And you don't want that put in jeopardy," Finn finishes. "I understand."

"I am not in jeopardy!" I say in exasperation. "For creep's sake!"

"Why are you shouting?" Danny calls out from the other room.

"It's okay, Danny," Mom says. "Everything's fine."

"Is it my fault?" he asks.

Mom sighs. "It's not your fault, Danny," she calls back.

"Whose fault is it?"

I slam my glass down on the counter. "It's mine," I say loudly.

I walk over and grab our coats off the back of the chair. "Come on, Finn. Let's get you some decent tea."

I don't look back as he follows me out the door. He's wise enough to let me get a few blocks down before he tries to talk to me.

"Jessa, at the risk of sounding trite," he says, "she's only looking out for you."

I put a hand up. "Don't."

"I'm only saying—"

"You don't know how it is with her," I gripe. "No matter what I do, no matter how great my grades are, she's always convinced I'm one failed paper away from ending up on the streets or digging ditches for a living. Nothing's ever good enough."

"That's because she's your mother," he says. "It's her job to want the best for you, aggravating though it may be."

"She has no idea what it's like for me!" I fume. "You try to write a paper or work on calculus with *Mulan* blasting in the background. You try to finish a big project when you have to pack up every other weekend and move to another house! And then I was stepping through mirrors and dodging maniacs who are out to kill me! Like I didn't have enough to deal with!"

He reaches out, grasping my shoulders with his hands. "And you've borne it all with a tremendous amount of grace. But don't fault your mother for being concerned when you aren't *yourself*."

"You don't understand."

"I do. But I think you're inflating things a bit."

"Inflating!" I pull away from him, raising my arms and slapping them down at my sides in frustration. "Look, you don't have a mother like that, so you can't really understand—"

"No, I don't have a mother like that," he snaps, and I can see the hurt in his eyes. "I grew up without any mother at all, but I believe I can still offer some insight."

My face reddens with chagrin. "I forget what it's been like for you," I say by way of apology. "Don't you ever get to have a complete family?"

He smiles slightly. "Here and there. But never for very long. There always seems to be something to pull me away or pull them away somehow. The only real constant in the vast majority of the realities I've seen is you. So I presume you're as close as I get."

There it is again, that swelling warmth inside of me that no one else can seem to tap into. I don't like the idea of him being alone. He's been alone too long. And if I'm the one who makes him a little less that way, I'm glad.

"Sorry," I mumble. "It's just . . . sometimes my mom rubs me the wrong way."

"I can see that," he says. "And just where the devil are we walking? I'd like to get out of the cold."

"Wickley's," I say. "They have four different varieties of European tea. There should be something that you'll like."

"And then we're going back home." It isn't a question, and he's right. It's not like I can stay out forever.

"Yes, we're going home," I sigh. "I'm not a completely ungrateful bitch."

He stops and turns to hold me gently by the shoulders. "I would never think that of you, love," he says. "I'm only telling you these things because I know that you love your family as much as they love you. You always have, in every incarnation I've encountered. It's as much a part of you as my devilish good looks are a part of me."

He gives me a cocky grin and I reluctantly smile back. "I know it's natural for her to be worried . . . under the circumstances," I admit. "I just feel like she should cut me some slack, considering. I'm a pretty good kid."

"You're an amazing human being. You're buying me some decent tea, and for that alone, you should be enshrined."

"And now you're going to tell me to go home and apologize, right?"

"No. I'm going to tell you to go home and eat some meatballs. But text your mother first to tell her where you are so she doesn't think I've kidnapped you for lascivious purposes."

"*Lascivious.* That's another archaic word." I smirk as I reach for my phone.

"It's only archaic if its purpose is forgotten," he says, sliding his hand down my arm and twining his fingers with mine. "I'll be happy to add it back into your personal vocabulary."

I raise my brows. "Finn."

"Very well, then. If that's off the agenda, why don't we find something fun to do after dinner?"

"Such as?"

He gives me that gorgeous, crooked grin. "How about another adventure?"

27

A Little Touch of Magic

"SO WHAT SHOULD I EXPECT?" I ASK AS I STEP AWAY from the glass door we're in front of.

Finn won't tell me a thing about who we are over there or where we're going, so I have no idea who's switching with us. I only hope they can drive, because Mom gave me the car. Finn arranged this earlier today while he was getting tea, and I'm just along for the ride.

Now we're standing in a hallway at Rambling Acres, a retirement home in Greaverville, not Ardenville.

"What are we doing here, anyway?" I ask.

"We're here to put on a show," Finn says, smiling.

I stare at him in dismay. "I'm not singing, am I?"

He chuckles and squeezes my hand. "No. No singing."

"Well, that's a relief."

"I'm an entertainer. You help out as my assistant," he says.

"And I'm your assistant. Okay." I search back through my memories for pointers as he goes on.

"I'm a magician and hypnotist—that's the act and what we'll be performing today."

My mouth opens and closes like a fish's. "Hypnosis?" I can't help it, I laugh out loud. "Are you serious?"

"You don't think I have showmanship skills?"

"I know that you do. I just can't see you swinging a watch in front of a bunch of zombie-eyed people."

"I'll have you know I'm in high demand," he says. "Come on; let's grab some tea before we get started. They have refreshments at the back of the room."

We make our way into the auditorium, where volunteers are setting up the refreshment table. A few people dot the seats in the middle, but we're still ten minutes from the start time.

"I hope we get a bigger crowd," I say.

"They'll be here," Finn says. "I've always been able to fill the house."

He hands me a cup of coffee as he drops a tea bag into a cup of hot water for himself and we make our way backstage to wait.

"How did you get started with something like this?" I ask.

He blows on his tea to cool it for a moment before he answers. "In this particular reality, I had to make my way at a very young age," he says. "I learned card tricks from a street hustler in New York City at the age of twelve, and I found a corner of my own to work after school. That branched out to other sleight-of-hand tricks, and, soon enough, I had a following. Eventually I got an offer to play a legitimate venue, and then another. Along the way, I met a hypnotist who hired me as an opening act. I became his partner. When he retired, I started my own act, and while touring about last summer, I met you. The rest is history."

Yes, it is. Him and me, together, of course. This Jessa plans on leaving with him right after graduation to take the act on the road full-time. And my mom is fine with that! I let out a laugh as the memory surfaces.

"What's funny?" Finn asks, finishing off his tea.

"I'm not even going to college here! And my mom is remarried to a guy who plays in a *band*?" I'm shaking my head as the memories come through.

"Ah, that would be Jason," Finn says with a nod. "Your mother is quite bohemian over here. She paints."

She *paints*? I let that memory flood in, along with a few others. Jason is nearly ten years younger than my mom, and along with Danny we all live in a big renovated warehouse so they can both have studio space. Danny works as a roadie for Jason's band.

"You're not using hypnosis on me now, right?" I ask him, just to clarify. "I'm really remembering my mom this way?"

"She's devilish fun and terribly whimsical," he says. "She and I get along quite famously."

He reaches for his top hat and his tuxedo jacket with tails, and my lips start to twitch, holding back a grin—until I slip out of my long coat and see my sparkling purple leotard with a tulle pouf attached to my butt. It's high cut at the thighs and low cut in the front, and with the four-inch heels I'm wearing, I look like a showgirl.

"It's time," he says, giving me a slow perusal from my rhinestone-clipped hair to my fishnet-clad toes.

"You brought me here just so I could see that my mom has it in her to be a little wild, didn't you?" I ask.

"I brought you here just to see you in that outfit," he responds with a grin.

The volunteer coordinator at the retirement home is announcing us, and a moment later we step out on stage to a full house, and Finn gives a brandishing wave of his hand as our banner unfurls from the catwalk overhead.

GALLAGHER'S GRAND ILLUSIONS, it proclaims in large, sparkling letters.

"Good evening, ladies and gentlemen!" Finn calls out. "For my first trick, my lovely assistant, Jessa, will take a personal item from someone and place it in this magic box." He pulls me forward by the hand. "Jessa, if you please. . . ."

I quickly search my memories to remember how this trick works.

One gentleman offers his hearing aid, but I smile and tell him I don't want him to miss a bit of the program. Another woman in a bright red sweater at the back lifts her hand slightly, but she's too far back.

"How about you?" I ask a gentleman in the middle of the third row who fits the bill perfectly. "May we borrow your wristwatch, Mr. . . . ?"

"Jenkins," he says. "John Jenkins. And this is an expensive watch." He glares up at me as I step over a few feet and nudge my way in to him.

"No harm will come to your timepiece, I assure you," Finn says grandly. "It's all in the spirit of fun, am I right, everyone?"

A few lackluster claps sound, and one of the aides encourages Mr. Jenkins.

"I don't want a scratch on it," he warns me as he puts it in my hand.

"Not to worry," Finn assures him as I hold the watch close and nudge and bump down the row to return to the stage. I give Finn a nod and he takes the watch from my hand and holds it over the box.

"Now, everyone, watch the magic box," he says, tilting it out to the audience so that they can clearly see inside it. "Are we all agreed that it's empty?"

Again, a lethargic response from the group, many of whom are looking over at the table that holds the refreshments.

"Very well, then," Finn soldiers on. He drops the watch in, then holds the box out and I tap on it once with a magic wand from a nearby table. He opens the door on the box, and, of course, the watch is gone.

"Great," says John from his seat. "Now bring it back."

"'Fraid I can't do that, mate," Finn says, opening the empty box again with a sly grin. "It appears good and lost. Perhaps it's rematerialized in the room somewhere. Let's all have a look around, shall we?"

Finn steps down off the stage, making a great show of looking under people's chairs and even asking a few to move their feet, as I do on the opposite side of the room. He eventually works his way back to John.

"Well now, John," he says, clapping a hand on the man's shoulder. "I've never had this happen before. I'm terribly sorry. I'll give you the name and number of my insurance agent, and he'll cover the replacement."

"Damn right he will!" John blusters.

"Do you have a pen?" Finn asks, patting his lapels. "I seem to have misplaced mine."

John reaches into the breast pocket of his shirt and pulls out his watch. His mouth forms a perfect O and then he finally cracks a smile. "Well, I'll be darned," he says. "I didn't even feel you slip it in there!"

The room breaks out in applause, and Finn silences them with a flourish of his hand. "I'm not done yet!" he says, reaching out for John's watch and holding it before John's face, tilting it ever so slightly back and forth. He clasps John's shoulder firmly and leans down, making direct eye contact.

"How's that chair feeling, John?" he asks, in a low, soothing tone. "It looks awfully comfortable. The kind of chair you can just sink into."

"Yeah . . . it's pretty good," John agrees.

"And that ceiling fan up there," Finn goes on. "Spinning and sending all that cool, fresh air down here. Breathe that in, John. Isn't it nice?"

John's eyes focus on the fan, and he nods slowly as Finn continues to speak to him in a calm and nearly monotone voice. It happens in just a few seconds—Finn has him hypnotized. John stands up, turns a circle, and walks to the stage at Finn's suggestion. Then he proceeds to tell us all that he's the reincarnation of King Arthur and he owns a dragon, before Finn brings him out of it.

I'd call it nonsense if my memories weren't telling me Finn manages to do this at all his shows. He's got a real gift for it, and people eat it up.

We spend another thirty minutes with Finn hypnotizing various audience members, and it pulls raucous laughter when he convinces three older ladies that they are actually hens. They strut and flutter their arms, clucking loudly as the whole room roars. We've got the crowd in the palm of our hands, and I am loving it.

"Now for the fun part," Finn says as he escorts me back to the stage. I take my place beside him, and before I can ask what's next, he pulls my hand behind me, snapping it into a pair of handcuffs, along with my other hand.

"Finn!" My surprise is genuine and draws more laughter from the crowd.

"Don't worry, darling," he reassures me, to their delight. "I only want to keep you immobile while I throw the daggers at you." They laugh again as I give him a look that plainly asks if he's out of his mind.

He leads me over to a very large bull's-eye target and stands me so my head is right in front of it.

"This is the tricky part," he says under his breath as he positions me. I feel him press a tiny piece of what feels like wire into my hand, moving his body in front of mine to block the audience's view. "I'll draw it out a bit longer," he tells me quietly, "but I need you to perform your signature trick. On five."

On five? What is that supposed to mean? Finn turns away to give the crowd the lowdown on our next trick. I am to break out of my cuffs and stop him before he murders me.

For a moment I have an oddly uncomfortable flashback, and then I search my memories frantically. The wire in my fingers is familiar now, and I begin feeling around behind my back for the keyhole and the delicate spring inside.

Finn finishes regaling the audience, picks up his daggers, and turns back to me.

"Smile, my love," he says. "There's been many a woman thrilled to be my target!"

The women in the audience just love that, laughing and clapping, and a few of the older ladies even hoot and catcall him. He gives them a saucy wink, and it's all I can do to concentrate on the task at hand.

Which becomes impossible when the first dagger whizzes by my right ear and embeds itself in the wooden target with a *whump*. I start visibly, and Finn gets another laugh when he asks me how much coffee I've had. Knives two and three seem to come with alarming precision and even more alarming frequency. I have to get this done by knife five, and the tumblers inside the cuffs still aren't cooperating. My hands are sweaty, and that's making it even more difficult.

I give Finn a panicked look, and he gives the audience a shrug. "She's not herself today," he says. "Normally she enjoys this sort of *pointed* attention."

They laugh again, and he throws another knife. They didn't get the emphasis he put on that first phrase, but I did. *She's not herself today.* My eyes lock with his and I get what he's trying to tell me. I know how to do this. I just need to relax and trust that I do.

There. With a click, the cuffs are off, and I move them to my left hand. My eyes go wide as I remember why I need to do that, and Finn shoots me an encouraging smile as he picks up the last knife.

"Steady . . . steady . . . ," he says, taking aim.

I give him a shaky nod, and I take a deep breath. The knife flies straight for me, and my right hand snaps out, arresting it in midair. I can feel the difference in the weight, and I step to the side, holding the knife in position so the audience can clearly see that it would have hit the center of the target. I dangle the cuffs in my other hand, smiling widely.

Finn comes up to take the knife from my hand, then pulls the remaining daggers from the target. No one sees him switch the rubber dagger for the real one in his upstage hand, placing the dummy in his pocket. He turns back to the wooden prop table with his hands full of daggers, slamming them point-down so they all stand up.

The room roars with applause, and I take a bow, grinning madly. Wow! We really are good together!

"You're a natural," Finn says, winking at me.

"I'm a circus performer, you know," I say under my breath. "Haven't been her yet, but now I can't wait to try!"

"That's my girl," he says, and I'm not even going to try to hide how much I like the sound of that.

"We make a great team," I tell him as our audience files out.

"We managed to put on a good show," Finn agrees. "The Senior Citizens' Alliance was quite thrilled by our performance. Gallagher's Grand Illusions continues to flourish." He makes a show of straightening his bow tie. "I heard several of the ladies ask to have us back."

I study his face from his slightly tousled hair to his perfectly angled jaw.

"What a surprise," I say blandly.

Finn rubs his chin thoughtfully. "D'you think Dreamers can be hypnotized? I need to repay one for dropping me in a lake, as I recall. . . ."

28

The Question of Us

"WHAT THE DEVIL AM I WEARING?" FINN ASKS ONCE WE transfer back, coming through in my bedroom. My eyes widen as I take him in.

"It's an old concert T-shirt of mine," I tell him. "And it's obviously too small for you."

"Obviously," he agrees. "I can barely move my arms. Why would I . . . ah. I have it now," he says as the memory comes through. "We were helping Danny clean up after dinner."

"And you thought it would be funny to tickle me as I reached for a bowl," I say, remembering as well. "You ended up wearing a whole lot of marinara, so I offered you the shirt."

I'm trying really hard not to stare at the way the tight shirt is clinging to his chest, but I'm not doing too well with that.

"Like what you see?" he teases.

"It's not a glittery leotard and fishnets."

"Haven't hit a world yet where that might come true," he says. "But you never know. . . ."

I grin as I open my dresser drawer and find him a large T-shirt left over from a Spanish Club car wash last year, and then I turn my back so he can change. I'm not going to be caught ogling again.

We make our way downstairs, and Danny is in front of the Xbox, as usual. He tears his eyes from the TV to look at me.

"Hi, Jessa. You're back now?"

Finn looks startled and I give a shrug. "He knows," I say. "He always seems to know." I smile at my brother. "Yeah, Danny. I'm back."

"Okay," he says, facing forward again. "Why don't you stay instead of swapping?" he asks. "You could be twins."

"It doesn't work that way," I tell him.

"You guys should get together sometime," he says, turning to look back at his game.

"Yeah, we should." I look around. "Where's Mom?"

"She says we're out of bread but we're only out of her bread. The brown bread. We have bread," he assures me. Mom eats wheat bread, which Danny can't stand.

"So she's at the store?" He nods an affirmative, keeping his eyes on the TV. "Tell her Finn went home and I went up to bed, okay?"

"Okay. Good night, Finn."

"Good night, Danny," he answers. He gives me a questioning look as I lead him over to the front door and step outside with him, pulling it shut.

"Stay with me tonight," I whisper.

He reaches out to take my hand. "Eversor won't come near

you, love. I promise. And soon enough she'll realize that she has no power anymore."

"I know. Meet you at the back door."

"I look forward to it," he says, and his eyes are gleaming in the darkness.

I do need to work on that scholarship application and on a writing project, and I seem to write better with him around. I feel better telling myself that's my motivation.

Once we sneak back upstairs, I set Finn up with Danny's portable DVD player that we take on car trips, a pair of headphones, and the entire Harry Potter series. He's engrossed, and I'm able to get some work done.

Soon it's nearly midnight, and I know we should probably both get some sleep, but somehow I'm nervous as hell about sharing a room with him. I know that doesn't make sense considering I platonically shared a bedroom with him just last night, and with his counterpart before. But then again, that Finn and I had no previous physical history at the time.

And while I wasn't the one who shared the four-poster bed on his ship, I got a wealth of memories all about it—and several other occasions as well when I was there. I'd like to say I got the memories by accident, but the truth is once the first of those memories was triggered, I thought about him—about us—a lot while I was there. And here.

"Jessa?"

I look up from my story and glance at the door, but he kept his voice low so Mom can't hear us. Her room is down the hall from mine, and she usually sleeps with the TV on, but I'm not taking any chances. She's just warming up to Finn—the last thing she needs is to find him in my bedroom at midnight.

"What are you working on now?" he asks, taking off his headphones and moving the DVD player off his lap.

"It's another story," I say. "Now that I'm writing again— crap!" I interrupt myself. "I need to change back to creative writing for next semester."

"Is this a story for class, then?"

"No. I'm thinking about entering it in a flash fiction scholarship contest."

I can already see the question forming, so I answer it before he can ask. "Flash fiction is a short story that's usually five hundred words or less. You have to tell a lot in very few words."

"And you could win a scholarship with that?"

"Yeah. It's for Westport College in Connecticut. They're a private school, and not very big, but their writing program is one of the best around. If I win the scholarship, it's almost a guarantee that I'll be offered admission, as long as I keep my grades up."

"That sounds like a fine idea," he says. "May I?" He gestures down to my journal, and my hand covers it reflexively.

"It's not very good yet. . . ."

"Rubbish." He reaches over and pulls the notebook onto his lap and leans back against the headboard next to me. I fidget with my pen and gnaw my lip as he reads, but after a moment I find myself studying his face again, the way the light plays along the line of his nose, the way his oh-so-long eyelashes fan out, the curve of his lips. I move back up to his eyes, and then flush hot red when I meet them dead on. His mouth quirks up into a smile.

"It's all right, love," he says. "I was staring at you the whole time you were writing."

"You've known my face longer than I've known yours," I remind him.

"Ah, but I don't know you, do I?" he says. "Not entirely. I get bits and pieces. Like this story."

"It's not about me."

"I can see that. It's about me. Or I should say, *your* Finn."

I start to tuck my hair nervously behind my ear, and he reaches out to help me. I feel the flush of my skin where his hand touches.

"This story is kind of a first for me," I confess. "I usually write from my memories—both here and other places. He—you—told me once about the tree. I just went from there."

"And with only that to go on, you've captured us well. All of us," he says. "That's quite the gift you have."

His comment lights me up inside. It feels so good to be writing again, and his return has reignited whatever it was that burned out of me. I'm absurdly grateful for it.

"Finn . . . do you ever talk to your other selves?"

"'Bout what?" he asks. "I know what I need to know while I'm there, as do they."

"I guess I question myself more. It's good to get other points of view."

He gives a soft chuckle. "I suppose that's one way to hear the advice you want to hear."

"It does seem kind of self-serving," I admit. "But it's nice to have a support system."

"Perhaps Mario can arrange a tea party for the lot of you,"

Finn says. "Danny should be invited, of course, since it was his idea."

"Of course," I agree with a smile. I have to ask: "Did it feel weird to you? Reading about your other self?"

"A bit," he says. "Like I'm a voyeur and victim at the same time."

"Yeah, I guess I know that feeling."

"We've both got the same walls to chip through, you know," he says, leaning back against my headboard again. "You're her and yet you're not. I'm not him, but he was so much of me. And are we drawn to each other out of familiarity? Or is it more?"

He folds the journal shut and places it on the bed beside him as he continues.

"And do you feel as guilty as I do?" he asks. "Because more than anything, I want to be holding you right now. I want to smell your hair and feel your weight against me and—"

He doesn't get a chance to finish before I crawl into his arms. He pulls me in sideways across his lap and I rest my head in the crook of his neck as he slides his arms around me, holding me close. Nothing has felt this good in entirely too long.

"You feel guilty, too?" I ask in a muffled voice as I breathe him in.

"Yes. Even though I know I'm gone in the head to think it. You are you and I am me wherever we are. We both know that. And no matter where we go, we're usually in each other's lives."

"It's like we can't help but be pushed together," I say. "Like we don't have a choice."

He pulls back to look at me, and his face is troubled. "That's not how it is at all," he says. "We always have a choice. If we didn't, we certainly wouldn't need Dreamers. And they wouldn't need us."

"But we'd still need each other." The words come out and I know that they're true. "I think . . . maybe they'd be okay with this, your Jessa and my Finn. You and me."

He goes very still.

"So there's a *you and me*? And what of Ben?"

"I looked in the mirror and told myself the truth. And he wasn't part of it. I owed him the honesty of letting him know that."

"I see." He lets out the breath he'd been holding and he doesn't even try to hide his smile. "Well, that's a load off. And as for your story . . ."

I wait nervously for whatever he's going to say.

"It's good," he says. "Bloody good. Don't question your gift, Jessa. And you've nothing to lose by sending it off. If you don't get this scholarship, you keep on trying. You're one of the brightest, most persistent people I know, love. You'll get there."

"Thanks."

"Let's get some sleep, love," he says, reaching across me and pulling the edge of my comforter over me. He scoots down, pulling the other pillow over to prop his head up, and I resettle myself on him. For a long time, the only sound is his steady breathing, and mine.

"Finn?"

"Hmm?"

"Are we just fill-ins for who the other person wishes we could be? Or something else?"

"Does it matter?"

I lean back to look up at him, and his hand brushes my face. "What I'm saying is that none of that makes a difference, does it?" he continues. "I cannot help but see her when I look at you, and I suspect I'm very like the Finn you knew and loved. But you and I have a relationship beyond that—*this* you and *this* me. We've forged that all by ourselves, and it's made from melded parts of what we had before. You cannot possibly try to escape it or put that in the context of a normal relationship. What we have here is entirely unique."

"I guess it is. I'm just not sure where we go from here."

"Neither do I, love." He leans in and gives me a lethal grin that begins with that dimple and ends at those gorgeous green eyes. "We call that 'an adventure.'"

I'm smiling as his lips meet mine, and I want to lose myself in the feel of him pressed against me and the magic of his lips as they move on mine, but I'm just not sure who it is he wants me to be. Or who I want him to be. I only know he feels right, and I wonder if that's enough.

I pull away, and I think I hear him sigh, but he pulls my head down to his chest.

"Get some sleep, love. Tomorrow we start over, you and I."

29

Fate

I WAKE SLOWLY, IN STAGES. MY CHEEK IS WARM AGAINST his chest, and somehow, my hand has slid under his shirt during the night, lying flat against his skin. Finn's arm is around me, and his hand is resting right on my hip. I snuggle in with a sigh, and I'm starting to like this entirely too much until I realize I can hear my text tone going off. Loudly.

Crap! I scramble to find my phone, and I pull up the screen.

"Who is it?" Finn asks, rubbing his eyes groggily.

"Shhh!" I put a finger to my lips and tilt my head toward the door. The daylight is streaming in the window and I can hear my mom in the hallway.

"It's Ben," I whisper, checking the text. "I'm supposed to meet him at the museum to get the mirrors."

Finn sits up. "The mirrors?" he whispers. "I thought we agreed you were staying put?"

"Shhh!" I shush him again, and not a minute too soon.

"Jessa?" Mom's voice calls through the door. "You okay?"

"Yeah," I call back. "I'm on the phone with Ben."

"Oh. Okay. Danny and I are getting ready to leave—we've got that bus trip to Albany today with the retirement home."

"Have fun," I tell her. "Hey, if I drive you to Haven House, can I have the car?"

"We're riding there with Mary Ann. Keys are on the hook in the kitchen."

"Thanks!"

Finn starts to say something, but I hold up a finger, making him wait until we hear the front door close.

I turn back to Finn. "You were saying?"

"I was saying that we had an agreement. Let Ben fetch the mirrors."

"I want to see them."

"We don't even need the bloody mirrors," he says, shoving a hand through his hair in exasperation. "There's no need to be venturing that far from home."

"In case Eversor still hasn't gotten the message yet, you mean? Come on, she has to have slept by now—especially if she thinks she's meeting her true love on the overnight." I think back to the way she looked in the museum in New York, and I can't help but feel awful for her. "I hope she gets some help, now that she's free from Rudy. She was really sick."

"Don't tell me you pity the she-demon," Finn says incredulously. "After all she's done to the both of us."

"She was tortured, Finn. Just like Ben was—but worse. Imagine having that sicko playing around in your head."

"I had him for a while, remember?" Finn makes a grim face. "I was just an unwitting pawn, but I'm finding it hard to feel any sympathy for her."

"I'm only going to Manortown," I press on. "That's like . . . not even five miles. And besides, I want to see these things. Think about it, Finn—these mirrors may have belonged to a Traveler who was Aztec. Can you imagine? The things he's seen? The history unfolding? The stories he could tell?"

Finn lets out a loud, gusty sigh. "You *had* to be a writer," he grumbles, rolling off the bed. "Very well, then. Let's get the damned mirrors and be done with it."

"You can stay here," I tell him. "I'll be back in twenty minutes, tops."

Finn says nothing. He just arches a brow and stares at me.

"All right, all right." I wave a hand in his direction as I start digging through my dresser for some jeans. "We meet Ben in half an hour. We can grab some muffins at Mugsy's on the way."

The Lower Hudson River Museum turns out to be about the size of a large house, situated right on the river and just outside Manortown. I've only been here once with a class trip when I was in fifth grade, and all I remember about it is that I fed the birds Cheez-Its from my lunch when we were out in the parking lot.

The museum has abbreviated hours in the winter months, but we have time to make it before it closes. As we get out of the car, a flock of seagulls scatters from whatever it was they were picking at in the parking lot. The sound of the river carries over their calls, and Finn stops to look at it, drawing in a deep breath.

"Ah, this is just the tonic I need," he says, stretching his arms behind his head and leaning back. "It's good to be near the water again."

"I told you the town was on the banks of the river."

"It's lovely." He stands and stares a moment longer, and I watch the wind lift his hair.

"You miss it, don't you? Your ship?"

"Aye. I do."

"I wasn't there long," I say. "But it was a really cool ship. It must be an interesting life, waking up in the morning on a ship, traveling all over."

"You'd love it. She's the fastest solar schooner on the water. She's a marvel." He smiles a genuine smile. "I should take you out on her sometime."

I zip my coat up tighter against the chill coming off the water. "That'd be nice."

"Just you and me and the open sea." His eyes are closed and he's smiling as he imagines it. "We can fly with the wind or roll with the waves. I'll take you out on the water someday, love, I promise you."

"I'll hold you to that," I say, smiling back. "But can we go inside now? It's like ten degrees out here."

"There's nothing wrong with enjoying the view," Finn says, taking a deep breath of the fresh air. "You need to take in the moment."

"The view is the same through the windows," I remind him. "I'd like a warmer moment."

We head through the door and just make it inside as Ben emerges from a back room, talking over his shoulder to someone who must work for the museum.

"Well, the Greavers were big in these parts," she says as she steps through the door behind him.

"I'm embarrassed to say I didn't know half of what you've got," Ben tells her. "I can't believe you have daguerreotypes of the original Lewis and Clark diaries."

"Ben?" I stare at the two of them in shock—not that I'm shocked to see Ben discussing daguerreotypes with a museum employee, but with this *particular* museum employee, I'm a little surprised. And more than a little thrilled. Unfortunately, Ben looks less than thrilled to see Finn with me.

"Jessa . . . Finn." He gives Finn the barest nod. "This is Olivia."

"Nice to meet you," I say, sticking my hand out and grinning like an idiot, I'm sure. "Is Ben talking your ear off? He's a bit of a history buff."

"So am I," she says with a shrug. "I never knew Ben's dad was on the board here."

I take my eyes off Olivia long enough for it all to click. "Wait— do you two know each other?"

"Her brother plays soccer for Manortown," Ben says. "We met at a game."

My eyes pop wide. "*She's* the soccer girl? The one you were supposed to meet for coffee the day your truck broke down?"

Olivia looks up at Ben. "It really did break down?"

"Why would I lie about that?" he asks.

"I thought you had second thoughts, you know . . . since my brother's team is the enemy."

"No . . ." Ben makes a confused face. "I really wanted to go. But then after that you had a boyfriend, so . . ."

"I made him up," she says with an embarrassed smile. "I thought you stood me up, and I didn't want to look pathetic. Like I'm somebody who spends her free time at museums or something." She laughs at her own joke, and I laugh, too. Because that is such an Olivia thing to do.

"Hate to interrupt a lovely reunion," Finn says. "But we do have a reason to be here."

"Oh. Right. Got 'em right here." Ben lifts up a small box. "They're not much to look at. Two of them are more like pieces than full mirrors."

Olivia steps up behind him. "They're in pretty good shape, considering the age," she says.

Ben sets the box down on a nearby table and I carefully lift the first piece of obsidian from between the layers of tissue paper and bubble wrap in the box. It's about six inches long, and it still doesn't look like a mirror to me. I set it gently aside and reach my fingers in again. They curl around a smaller shard and I let out a gasp. I can feel the power radiating off it, pulling at me, like it's demanding that I use it.

I turn startled eyes to Finn. "This is it," I say. "It was definitely his."

I hand it over, and Finn's eyes widen as he touches it.

"That's really something," he says.

"We have it all documented," Olivia says, eyeing us curiously. "Ben has the paperwork. You can keep the items for six months, and then they have to be shipped back—at your expense, of course."

"We'll take good care of them," Ben says. "I promise."

"I know you will," Olivia says, packing the mirrors safely back into the box. She hands it to Ben.

"Hey," I ask. "Do they need other volunteers here, do you know?"

Olivia shrugs. "We have plenty of stuff to do around here. And it's kinda boring when you have to work alone."

"Do you have an application form or anything?"

"You really want to spend your afternoons here?" she asks.

I look over at Ben, then back to Olivia. "My friends tell me I need to get out more," I say.

Olivia steps behind the front desk and returns with a pen and a pad of paper. "Just leave your name and number," she says. "I'll make sure the docent sees it when he's in on Monday. Or you could just stop in."

"Will you be here Monday?" I ask Olivia. "You could give me a tour before I talk to anyone so I can get familiar with the place."

She gestures behind her to the small room with the display cases. "That'll take about ten minutes," she laughs. "But I promise to make it riveting."

I can't help but laugh, too. Oh, it's so good to see Liv! "I wouldn't miss it," I tell her. "See ya."

Finn gives her a nod. "A pleasure meeting you," he tells her.

Ben shifts from one foot to the other. "I better go," he says. "Thanks for the loan."

"No problem," Olivia says. "Good to see you again."

"You, too." He strides out after us, and once we get outside, the smile drops from his lips. He hands me the box.

"Let's get this all done and over with so I can get on with my life," he says as he climbs into his truck.

"Thanks, Ben," I say, stepping back so he can close the door. He turns the key in the ignition, but nothing happens. He tries again, and again, and the engine won't even turn over.

"Dammit!" Ben says. "Did I leave the dome light on?" He checks the light switch, but it's in the off position. "If one of the doors didn't close tight, sometimes the cab light stays on."

"You weren't in there that long, mate," Finn points out. "That's hardly time for a battery to die."

Ben pops the hood and climbs down out of the truck to look under it. I stand there watching the seagulls while the two of them poke around under the hood. I decide to copy Finn and enjoy my moment, taking a deep breath of fresh air off the water—which I promptly let out in a huff of panic as the box is wrenched out from under my arm, and the barrel of a gun is stuck hard into my side.

"Hello, Miss Jessa," an all-too-familiar voice says. "Thank you for this."

30

Adrift

I CAN FEEL THE BARREL OF THE GUN JAMMED AGAINST my rib cage. Why doesn't she just pull the trigger? End it? End me? Eversor answers me as if she could hear my thoughts, leaning in to speak quietly in my ear.

"Not here, Miss Jessa. I will still live in this world once you are gone, yes? So you see, I must have no messes to clean up. No questions."

She looks over at Finn and Ben, who have frozen in place and are staring back.

"You are looking for the distributor cap. I took it." She says it almost cheerfully. "I'll put it back later when I move your truck. But for now, we all go for a ride together."

"They're not going anywhere with you," I say, trying to turn. She only rams the gun into my side harder, and I can't help the gasp of pain it draws from my lips.

"Where are we going?" Finn asks evenly. He's not looking at me—his focus is entirely on Eversor.

"She can't shoot all of us," I tell them. "I'm not going through this again. I'm not taking you with me."

"This is my fault," Ben says. "She knew we were going to be here because they've been monitoring me. I should have remembered that."

"I can shoot all three of you now, and deal with the mess," Eversor says, smiling through gritted teeth. "Wouldn't you prefer a few more moments together before you say good-bye? Now, step over to your car, Jessa, and Ben will get behind the wheel."

"You want me to drive?" Ben asks.

"Isn't that what I just said?" Eversor snaps. I guess the friendly act is already wearing thin. She's aware that we're starting to look odd, positioned the way we are. Someone's bound to notice if we don't get out of here soon.

"Why don't you let me drive," Finn suggests. "I'm a far better driver."

"*What?*" Ben gives him a look. "What the hell are you talking about?"

Finn raises his eyebrows, and I realize he's stalling. "I'm only telling the truth, mate. She's going to kill us, but you'll kill us faster."

"Where do you get off—"

"Enough!" Eversor recognizes the stall as well and once again rams the gun into my ribs, and I make a sharp sound in response. Finn is looking at me now, and his eyes are blazing with helpless anger.

"Over to the car, please. Finn, you will be in front with him. But first . . ."

She takes a quick look around and then tosses something to Ben. "Put this over his head and help him into the car."

It's a pillowcase, in a dark navy blue. Ben starts to walk with Finn to the car, but Eversor stops him, pulling the gun from my ribs to gesture at him.

"No! Cover him now, please." She hands me one, too. "Over your head as well, Miss Jessa," she instructs. "I don't want either of you seeing yourself in a window along the way."

I give Finn one more look before I do what she asks, and I feel myself being led to the car. She pushes me into the seat and keeps on pushing, forcing me to slide across as she gets in beside me. I hear Finn's door, then Ben's close.

"Drive," she says to Ben. "Out onto the highway."

I hear the ignition, and then we pull out and onto the road. We travel in silence except for the occasional command given by an increasingly more nervous Eversor. Now may be my only chance to reason with her.

"Ms. Eversor, you have to listen to me." My voice is muffled under the pillowcase, but I know she hears me. "What you're doing—it's going to destroy us all if you keep it up."

"Is that what Mario tells you?" She sounds amused. "He's afraid to lose the control he thinks he has. It is a fallacy. The only way to preserve control is to simplify. Rudy will preserve the origin, through me."

"Rudy's gone." Finn's voice is brutally sharp. "Mario has imprisoned him for good. Haven't you wondered why he's deserted you?"

"You lie! He's . . . busy! There is much to do to prepare for the convergence!"

"They found him in my dreams," Ben says. "And that was a seriously dick move, by the way."

"Mario imprisoned him and you're all alone," Finn taunts.

"Be quiet!" she snaps. "I must think. I must think on this."

"Listen, I can pull off the road—" Ben offers, but she only shouts at him to be quiet as well. A few minutes later, she's directing him to turn, and then turn again. Soon we pull to a stop and park.

"Stay in the car until we get you out. And do not move or I will shoot your friend," she hisses at me. "Out!" she says to Ben, I presume. I hear his door open, then shut, and then another door opens and I'm being pulled out the way I came in. Once I'm out and away from the car, she takes my pillowcase off, but I know before she does exactly where we are. I can feel the breeze off the water and hear the gulls calling out overhead.

We're in front of a medium-size fishing boat at the very end of the marina. With it being the middle of the day in December, there's almost no one here.

"Onto the ship," she says, and then she directs us to stop once we reach the deck.

"So this is where you've been living?" I ask.

"It's not much," she says, wrinkling her nose distastefully. "But it serves its purpose. No one thought to look for me here, and buying the boat was easy enough." She keeps the gun trained on me and looks over at Finn and Ben.

"How fast does this ship go?" Finn asks, casually leaning a hand on the deck railing, right next to a tall box that has a scattering of assorted tools resting on it, including a very large and heavy wrench.

"Fast enough," Eversor says. "Once I take her out to sea, I'll do what needs to be done." She's talking to herself more than to us, looking off into the distance, and I see Finn's fingers slide closer down the rail.

She turns her head to look at him again, but before I can think of a distraction, Ben steps between Eversor and Finn.

"You won't get away with this," he says, getting right in her face. She backs up, waving the gun at him.

"Step away!" she threatens. "All of you! You can go peacefully in the cool water, or you can die slowly and in agony," she says in a hard voice. "Blood washes right off the deck. Your choice."

I look over at the box with the tools, but the wrench is still in its place.

"Turn around," she commands, and she hands me a length of rope to tie Ben's hands behind his back with, then she forces me to tie Finn's hands as well. I wonder how she's planning on tying me up without putting the gun down, but I get a pair of handcuffs.

"Please," I say as she snaps each cuff in place. "You have to listen to me. I have no reason to lie to you. We can get you the help you need."

"Oh, Jessa," she says, smiling as her hand comes out to lightly stroke my cheek. "Such promise you have. It is unfortunate that your potential must remain unknown. I am sorry for this." She looks at Ben and Finn. "But it must be done. Rudy is right—we must save what can be saved."

"You've no reason to sacrifice yourself for his mad scheme," Finn bites out. "And without Rudy to protect you, it's only a matter of hours before the other Dreamers find out what you've done."

"He's right," I say. "You don't have to do this. These drugs you're taking are dangerous."

"But they *work*," she says, in a tone of near-reverence. "Finally, I'm more than a visitor to the dreamscape. I *belong* there. I belong with him." Her eyes harden. "And what better way to prove my love than to finish his great work?"

"Finish?" My jaw drops open. "You want to start the convergence? Still? Can't you see he was playing you?"

"Walk." She pushes the gun into my back again. "Down," she says.

She herds us all toward a short set of stairs that lead down to a small cabin and shoves us inside, and then she opens a compartment in the wall, retrieving a life vest and something in a large canvas bag, which I'm guessing is a life raft.

"Once the convergence is complete, I'll sink the boat," she says. "It will be quick—I'll make a hole near the bow. Do not worry—you won't suffer. With you all in the cabin at the bottom of the river, there will be no bodies to find. I am sorry."

She's saying it even as she closes the door, locking us into our tomb. I beat against it, throwing my shoulder at it again and again.

I can see Finn struggling with his bonds, and I begin looking frantically around the cabin, using my nose to move a pile of papers and reaching down with my fingertips to open drawers.

"What are you looking for?" Ben asks. "I don't see any mirrors."

"Neither do I," I say. "I need a paper clip."

"A paper clip?" Ben asks.

The engine roars to life and we're all thrown back as the boat races across the water, bouncing along the waves with serious speed.

I push myself back up to my feet, and Finn is right behind me. "Here you go, love," he says, pressing a bent-open paper clip into my hand. I force myself to calm down so I can remember, and a few moments later, the handcuffs spring free.

"How'd you learn to do that?" Ben asks.

"Later." I make short work of getting his hands free, then I loosen the knot on Finn's, but I let out a groan as I stare in dismay at the door.

"It's a U-lock," I say, tossing the paper clip down. "This is useless on a U-lock."

"How do you know that?" Ben is swimming in confusion. "So we're back to square one if we can't pick the lock."

"Then it's a good thing I managed to nick this," Finn says. I turn to look back at him, and he's twirling a screwdriver in his fingers.

"That's too big to pick the lock with and not big enough to beat a hole in this door," Ben says. "You should have grabbed the damn wrench."

"I vote for using the screwdriver to remove the doorknob, if it's all the same to you," Finn says, pushing past me.

"Hurry, Finn!" I say, holding onto the edge of a countertop as the boat bounces hard on another wave. The boat is showing no signs of slowing, and this is taking entirely too long.

"What's the problem?" Ben asks.

"The screws are rusted," Finn growls, and the screwdriver slips, scoring the skin off the back of the hand he has on the knob. "Dammit!"

He starts in again, just as the engine cuts out, and we're slowing now, bobbing lightly.

"You've got to hurry," I urge him.

"I am, I am!" he answers. "Just a few more turns on this one—there!" The screw falls off, hitting the floor with a metallic *clink*. He goes to work on the second one as I strain to hear something, anything . . . even though I know the universe will end in complete silence.

"Finn . . . ," I urge.

"He's almost got it," Ben says, bending over him. "It's fixing to fall. . . ."

The second screw hits the floor, and now he's got his hand inside the opening, fiddling with the mechanism.

"Just a little . . . farther . . . ," he says as he pushes his hand farther in, flexing his fingers to pull on the locking mechanism. "That's got it! Give it a push!" he says, and Ben slams a shoulder into it, sending the door flying.

"Ow!" Finn says, and then he lowers his voice to an angry whisper. "You damn well tore my fingers off."

"You said to give it a push!" Ben whispers back furiously.

"You're a veritable juggernaut of destruction!" Finn says.

"Guys—" I interrupt. "It's really quiet."

Finn motions me to get behind him, and Ben pulls me back and steps in front of me as well. We cautiously climb the stairs, conscious of every creak and groan. There's a lot more wind out here on the open water, and I hope it's enough to cover the noise we're making. Finn gets up to the deck and motions us to follow, and we edge as quietly as possible along the side of the ship toward the main cabin.

"That's far enough," Eversor says from behind us. We put our hands up and turn slowly to face her. The hand that's holding the gun is shaking—she's shaking all over. Her eyes are filled with tears and her nose is running as well. She's taken her coat off and I can see now that she's lost even more weight since I last saw her, to the point that she's nearly skeletal.

"Did you think I didn't hear you?" She laughs and she keeps on laughing, too long, until it evolves into a wail that makes the hair on the back of my neck stand on end. "So alone . . . ," she sobs. "So alone. Emptiness and *nothingness*." Her eyes meet mine. "All because of you."

She raises the gun, and it wobbles wildly in her hand as she points it straight at me, but before she can fire, Ben knocks me out of the way and Finn dives straight at her. They're wrestling, slamming into the railing, and she's got the strength only madness can lend her. I see Finn's head jerk back as she slams him into the wall of the wheelhouse, and then his hand closes over hers on the gun. For a moment I'm not sure what I'm seeing; it looks like he's trying to point the gun at her head.

"Finn! No!"

And then I realize he's doing the opposite—he's trying to pull the gun away, but she's laughing, then sobbing as she yanks the gun hard to her temple and pulls the trigger. She falls backward into the water, and Ben and I rush to the rail to grab Finn before he falls in after her.

Finn recoils, stumbling and falling to the deck, and I scramble over to him.

"I'm all right," he gasps.

"Is she . . . ?" I look over at Ben, and his face tells me what I need to know.

"She's dead," he says, looking over the rail.

"I knew we hadn't seen the last of her," Finn says with a grimace. "But I wasn't expecting this level of delusion."

"Oh my God, oh my God . . . ," I repeat as Finn helps me to my feet. "Where are we?" I ask, glancing out at the water. I can see the shore off in the distance, but I have no idea what that translates to in miles. We seem to be the only boat out here at the moment, though, and that's a good thing.

"I know where we are," Ben says, pointing off toward the shore. "That's Founder's Hall Clock Tower over there. That means the marina is down that way, around that bend in the river."

I stagger over to the wall of the boat cabin and lean against it. And I finally look at the water, at Eversor's floating body.

This is the woman who killed someone dear to me. The woman who killed me, again and again, in so many horrific ways. The woman who was nearly responsible for the destruction of millions of lives. I should feel vindicated. I should feel like justice has been served, even though I know her one death will hardly atone for all she's done.

I feel none of that. I just feel sorry for her.

She loved a man who was literally nothing more than a dream, and for that love, she gave it all. The deck was stacked against her from the beginning.

I look through the wheelhouse window at Finn as he starts up the motor on the ship, guiding it into a turn. The afternoon sunlight glints off his dark hair, catching the planes of his face. He's in his element here, and the wind ruffles his hair as the ship flies across the water.

Ben puts an arm about my shoulders, leading me away from the cabin.

"You okay?"

"I will be. I'm just glad it's over. It's finally over."

"Just stay here," Ben says. "And hold on to this." He hands me the box with the mirrors.

I numbly take the box, and I watch the water churn behind us until Ben comes back up the stairs.

"I found this in the cabin, along with Finn's watch," he says, holding out my compact mirror. "He's fixing to pull us into the marina in just a minute. . . ."

I give him a shaky nod. Finn slows the boat, inching it back into its berth. He cuts the engine and Ben jumps down onto the dock to secure the mooring line.

"We'll run you back to the museum," Finn says to Ben. "You'll need to collect your truck."

Ben makes a disgusted sound. "It's going to need a distributor cap. She took it, remember? Might as well drop me home."

"We need to call the police." My voice is shaking, just like the rest of me.

"And tell them Eversor tried to kidnap us?"

"You think they'll believe that?" I ask.

"You said that they believe her to be enamored of me," Finn says. "And she's a known drug addict who recently robbed a local business. I would imagine it's not too much of a stretch to play her as a scorned and unbalanced woman. We just need to be sure our stories match. Perhaps it's best if we don't split up just yet."

"We're less likely to screw up the story if we're all on the same page," Ben agrees reluctantly.

We all look over our shoulders because Ben had to raise his voice in order to say that. There's a steady roar behind us, and as I turn to look, I'm startled to see that the marina parking lot is full of convoy trucks and soldiers, lots of soldiers. They're all geared up, and I stare wide-eyed as a tank rumbles down the road.

"What the hell is going on?" I ask.

Ben smacks his head. "Oh yeah! I forgot. It's the third Thursday of the month. Recruitment day."

"Recruitment day?" I look at him like he's crazy. "I have no idea what you're talking about."

"The new quotas," he reminds me. "We got the papers in the mail last week. They even held that special assembly at school about it, remember?"

"Ben, I have never seen these soldiers before in my life," I tell him.

Finn shakes his head slowly in disbelief. "I've seen them," he says. "And it's best if they don't see me."

31

Law & Order

"WHAT'S GOING ON?" I ASK WITH MOUNTING DREAD. "What's happening?"

"I don't know," Finn answers, "but I've seen them before." He pulls me around behind the ship's wheelhouse, and I reach out and pull Ben in beside me.

"You've both seen these soldiers?" I ask.

"Not those particular soldiers, but that army," Finn says grimly. "The New Republic of Canada. Only they weren't *here*."

The cold feeling in the pit of my stomach has now spread to all my extremities, freezing the breath in my lungs and stopping my heart for a beat.

Finn turns to look at Ben. "How much of this morning do you remember?" he asks him.

"All of it," Ben answers. "Eversor, the boat, the announcements on TV about the annexation . . ."

I'm afraid to ask. "The annexation?"

"We're part of the New Republic of Canada now, remember?"

Ben says. "We had to fill out all those forms to register in school last week. And I saw the army coming into town last night on the drive home. Am I the only one who remembers this?"

"Hate to break it to you, mate, but . . . yes," Finn says. "You're the only one who remembers because the army wasn't part of this reality yesterday."

"Splintering," I say, holding my hand to my mouth as if I can keep the word from being real. "She's started the convergence."

"Doubtful." Finn pats himself. "I'm still here."

"How is Ben remembering things from a week ago that we don't know?" I ask.

"Yeah," Ben says. "How do you explain that?"

"It appears that the lines between realities are getting fuzzy. He's got a merged memory. A new reality with both histories incorporated into it. Our abilities must enable us to see the differences in the reality streams."

"I need to get home," I say, peering around the corner. "How do we get through them to the car?"

"They're not going to do anything, St. Clair," Ben says. "We're both under eighteen. We're not required service until after we graduate."

"Wouldn't the same hold for you over here?" I ask Finn.

"I wouldn't chance it," he says. "Besides, I'm eighteen now. And I'm not in school here until next semester."

"Then let me and Ben get the car and you head down the dock to the far end." I point off down the pier. "There's a service road that way that goes out to the highway. I'll meet you there."

"I don't know, St. Clair," Ben says, looking apprehensive. "If they catch you helping a runner . . ."

"I'm going to get my car," I tell him. "And you keep your mouth shut if they ask you about Finn."

Ben gives me a look but he does what I ask.

"You stay low and don't let them see you," I say to Finn. He gives me an encouraging nod.

"Not to worry," he says. "I've evaded them before. I'll see you in a moment."

He slinks off along the gangplank and disappears down the dock, moving fast. I motion to Ben with my hand and together we start walking toward the parking lot.

"Halt!" a soldier calls out as we near them.

Ben throws his hands up and I put my left hand in the air, but the right is still holding the mirrors.

"Put the box down!" the soldier shouts, and two more men run over to back him up. One of them lets out a shrill whistle, and a moment later, a woman in camouflage with command insignia steps out of a nearby armored vehicle and walks over to us.

"State your names and business," she warns Ben and me, and we look at each other in panic.

"I'm Jessa—St. Clair."

"Ben Hastings."

"What are you doing here?" she snaps. "And what's in the box?"

"It's got m-mirrors," I stammer. "Aztec mirrors from the museum. We got them on loan."

"The paperwork is all in there," Ben says.

"And what were you doing here at the marina?" the commander asks.

"I wanted to see the sunset on the water," I improvise with an embarrassed laugh. "But we didn't realize how cold it was down by the water."

"We're freezing," Ben says, playing into it. "We were just fixing to head home."

The soldier snaps her fingers at one of the men, and he moves forward, kicking the box away from me. He nudges the lid open with his gun, then squats down, pulling out the papers.

"I don't see any mirrors," he says. "Just some rocks."

"They're obsidian," Ben says. "The Aztecs used polished obsidian since they didn't have reflective metals."

"That so?" the commander says. She looks at the soldier again. "The paperwork?"

"It's reading legit," he says. "Ben Hastings has these objects on loan for six months."

"It's for a school project," I tell her. I force myself not to look over to where Finn might be. "It's really cold out here," I say, and I don't have to fake my chattering teeth. "Can we please go?"

"What school?" she asks.

"Ardenville," Ben answers her. "We're seniors."

"So you'll be joining the citizen-soldier brigade after school," she says. "Did you get the information pamphlet?"

Ben nods. "They handed them out last week in school. We both signed up."

"Good. We need every hand we can get to keep our towns safe." She gestures down to the box. "Now grab your stuff and go home. We're using this lot as a staging and transport area for the next six hours—it's off-limits to civilians."

"We understand," I say, scooping up the box. "Sorry we trespassed."

"It was an accident," Ben echoes.

"Once you're sworn in to the citizen-soldiers, being in an unauthorized area will go very badly for you," the commander warns.

"We won't do it again," I promise her. "Thank you."

"See that it doesn't," she calls after us as we walk toward my car at the opposite end of the lot.

Ben climbs into the passenger seat and we slowly pull out, waving at the soldiers as we go. I get onto the highway, carefully keeping my speed under the limit as more armored vehicles pass us on their way to the parking lot. A half mile down the road, I see the junction for the service road, and I slow the car and pull over.

Finn darts out from behind a tree and jumps into the backseat.

"Go!" he says urgently.

I pull out carefully, staying at the speed limit the whole way home. There are soldiers everywhere through town, some just milling around, some knocking on doors. I can't believe this is happening. What does it mean?

I barely get the car in the driveway when Danny runs out the door.

"Jessa! Did you see the tanks! And the trucks?"

I look at him in confusion as we all walk into the house. "You guys are back from Albany already?" I ask him.

"Albany?" Mom looks up from the kitchen table, where she's cutting a huge pile of coupons and sliding them into transparent sheet holders in a very full binder. My mom never uses coupons. Ever. "We didn't go to Albany today. We ran to Bagley's for some lunch—"

I raise my brows. "Bagley's?"

"Coffee shop?" Ben supplies. "We go there all the time?"

"Mom—" I reach out and grab her shoulder. "Have the soldiers been here?"

"The soldiers?" She smiles and shakes her head. "Not yet, but, honey, it's not a big deal. You're still underage, and I have Danny's disability paperwork. They're just collecting information, that's all."

I let out a sigh of relief.

"Jessa, what's wrong?" she asks, looking me up and down. "Have you been crying?"

I glance at both Finn and Ben, and I need a moment to pull myself together before I get into this and we call the police.

"I need to hit the bathroom," I lie. "Then I'll tell you about the day we've had."

She raises her eyebrows and looks pointedly at Finn and Ben. "O . . . kay," I hear her say warily as I close the bathroom door behind me.

I glance at myself in the mirror again and stare at my pale features in the reflection, and to me, it seems written all over my face that I just watched someone die. Again.

Then the reflection changes, and I see her. I recognize the room behind her, the pictures of the dolphins on the wall and the scuba gear in the corner. I realize at once from her face that something is terribly, terribly wrong.

She gives the slightest shake of her head, and her eyes fill with tears.

Help us.

She mouths the words, and a moment later she's gone.

She's vanished right before my eyes.

32

Torn

I STARE AT MY OWN REFLECTION, AND I FEEL A SENSE OF dread deep in my stomach that won't let go.

Help us, she'd said. Not help *me*.

Help *us*.

I press my fingers to the glass, but nothing happens.

Because nothing is there.

"Jessa?" Mom's voice carries through the door. "Are you okay?"

It takes me a moment to find my voice. "I'm just—I'm not feeling well." I open the bathroom door, and Finn has moved into the kitchen. He's looking at me closely—he's not fooled by my tone of voice at all. I move up next to him.

"We need to talk to Mario. Now," I say in a low voice. "I guess I'm hitting the NyQuil again."

"You need NyQuil, honey?"

Mom gets up from the table and moves past me to the bathroom, where she starts rummaging through the medicine cabinet.

"What the bloody hell is going on?" Finn asks quietly. He takes my hand, squeezing it gently. "What did you see?"

"I—I'm not sure." I turn wide, frightened eyes to his. "She's gone. The me that swims with dolphins. She's just . . . gone."

"She's missing?" he asks.

"No." My head is spinning, and I'm trying to put this feeling into words. "It's all gone. Her. Her reality. I can't . . . I can't feel it anymore." I step over to the microwave and put my hand to the glass door, concentrating, seeing her room in my mind's eye, but nothing happens.

"How does an *entire* reality disappear?" I whisper. *"How?"*

"It's spreading. It is a convergence." Finn says the word, but I shake my head wildly.

"No. No, that can't be what happened." I wrap my fingers around Finn's hand. "You're here. You're still here. If Eversor started the convergence, you'd be gone."

"Then what the hell is going on?" he asks.

I'm rubbing my chest because I swear I feel the ache of my loss—her loss. "I can't believe she's gone."

"You don't know that for sure," Finn says. "We need to talk to Mario."

Mom hands me the bottle of NyQuil, and I'm tossing back a dose when we hear a pounding on the front door.

"Door!" Danny calls out. I push past Ben and Finn to get to the door, and when I open it, I'm met with the sight of soldiers in full camouflage on my front porch.

"Can I help you?" I ask warily.

One of them has a clipboard, and he flips through a stack of papers that are clipped into it until he finds what he's looking for.

"St. Clair?" the soldier asks.

"What's going on?" I ask.

"Your name, please?" the soldier asks, clicking his ballpoint pen.

"Jessa St. Clair."

"What's going on? Jessa?" My mom pushes past me to stand in the doorway. She seems just as confused as me.

"Are you Jacqueline St. Clair?" the soldier asks.

"Yes."

"By order of the guard of the New Republic of Canada, we have orders for Daniel St. Clair and Jessa St. Clair."

"Orders?" my mother says in alarm. She takes the papers the soldier is pushing at her and reads them, shaking her head.

"Wait—why are you here?" I ask.

"This is a mistake," Mom says.

The soldier uses his pen to point at the papers in my mother's hands.

"Jessa St. Clair, age seventeen, is to report for part-time training for the citizen-soldier brigade, Ardenville chapter, beginning Monday. All the details are on her conscription sheet. Daniel is to come with me."

"Danny isn't a soldier," my mom says in disbelief. "This can't be right."

"Those are service orders, ma'am," the soldier says. "Daniel is being collected today for transport to the processing center at Hannacroix Creek."

"Collected?" I say, looking at my mom, and we're both confused. And frightened. "What does that mean? What is going on?"

My eyes widen as I look past him and see the first tank, then the second as they rumble down the street. I can feel the vibration under my feet as they go by.

"He's been reclassified to a WD," the soldier says, pointing again at the tablet. "Working disabled. Anyone over the age of eighteen classified as WD gets relocated to a work camp after processing. He'll be assigned productive tasks suited to his abilities. We're on a tight schedule, so just pack the necessities. You can ship him anything else after his indoctrination period ends at Hannacroix Creek."

"You're going to take him away?" my mother asks in confused horror. "Where?"

"His assignment location will be determined during processing. Now, if you'll get him ready, ma'am, we'll be leaving in fifteen minutes."

"Please! He has autism," I say, reaching out for the soldier's arm. "You can't take him away from his family."

"Autism, Down syndrome, deaf, blind . . . they all got to work," he snaps as he slides the clipboard back under his arm. "They're productive members of society," he says. "Guidelines for allowable personal items are on the back of the conscription sheet, and directions to the training center in town for Jessa are on the back of her sheet as well." He gives me a nod. "Fifteen minutes."

And with that, he and the other two soldiers he was with head down the street to the next house. And the next. I am staring, wide-eyed and openmouthed, in a numb kind of horror as my mother weeps silently next to me.

I feel a hand settle on my shoulder.

"Are they soldiers?"

I don't even turn to look at him. I don't think I can.

"Yes, Danny. They're soldiers."

"Do you think I can ride in the jeep? Jeeps have a stick shift."

I can't answer him. I just put my arms around him and hold him tight. My mother has made her way to the couch, where she's holding a throw pillow and rocking soundlessly, tears streaming down her face. She doesn't even notice Finn as he steps into the room and motions me to meet him in the kitchen. Danny goes to sit with Mom on the couch and she wraps her arms around him, rocking with him now.

"They're taking him away, Finn," I say, shaking my head frantically. "They can't do this! They can't!"

"They can, and they will, Jessa," he says grimly. "You need to get his things."

My mom pushes up off the couch. "Danny," she says, and I can see her jaw trembling as she tries to pull herself together. "You're going on a trip. A vacation."

"We're going on vacation?" His eyes light up as he stands up next to her.

"You pick out things you want to take with you. Like your movies and books," she says. "And I'm going to go pack your clothes, okay?"

"Are you sad?" he asks. "Or is it okay now?"

She wipes her cheeks with the backs of her hands. "It's okay. It's all going to be okay. But we have to hurry because the soldiers are giving you a ride and we don't want to miss them."

He scoops up his favorite backpack from the front room and starts putting things into it as my mom pushes past me blindly. She pauses at the foot of the stairs.

"Can you go check the laundry room for his baseball shirt?" she asks me. "You know the one he likes, with the red stripes?"

"Mom?" I can't speak, and she pulls me in to her, hugging me fiercely. "Go," she whispers. "We don't have a lot of time, and that's his favorite shirt. . . ." Her voice breaks and she runs upstairs.

I'm holding on to the banister because I really don't think I can keep standing.

"I can't believe they brought the tanks into your neighborhood," Ben says, staring out the front window. "They'd never get them across the bridge over the creek if they head down my street."

He's making no sense. "You don't live near the creek," I remind him.

Ben snaps his fingers in front of my face. "Wake up, St. Clair. My backyard floods three times a year from that creek."

I turn to look at Finn. "He doesn't live near the creek."

"He does now," Finn says.

I put my face in my hands. "This can't be happening. They're signing me up to be a soldier. And they're taking Danny away. Hanna—Hanna something."

"Hannacroix Creek?" Ben asks. "That's also where they take the deserters. It's not a very nice place."

"Oh God." I put my head in my hands. "This isn't supposed to happen. What has she done?"

"Wait—you're saying none of this should be happening?" Ben says.

"That's what we've been trying to tell you," I remind him. "None of this is right." My eyes well up and I swipe at them. "I can't let them take my brother, Ben."

"Service is mandatory, remember?" Ben says.

I lock eyes with Finn and repeat it. "I can't let them take my brother."

"We could run," Finn says grimly.

"That might be an op—"

I don't get to finish my sentence, because there's a knock at the front door. The soldiers are back.

My eyes meet my mom's and she shoves the last of Danny's things into his suitcase—the one with the Star Wars decals on it. She takes him by the shoulders and tilts his chin so that he's making eye contact, just like she used to do when he was younger.

"Danny," she says, smoothing his hair back, "you're going to go with the soldiers, okay? They're going to take you on a vacation, and then they've got a job they need you to work on."

"But I work with you," he says, confused. "I work with you and I work at the library."

"I know. I know," she says, touching his cheek and smoothing his hair again. "But now you need to go to a new job, and they'll show you just how to do it. They'll make sure you have a place to stay and show you where the cafeteria is there, okay?"

"But am I still going to go to the library?" he asks. "That's not a job. It's volunteer."

The knock comes on the door again and we all look, including Danny.

"I work with you," he insists again, and my mother cracks. She turns away so he won't see her lose it, and reaches down, picking up his suitcase. Then she walks to the door.

"Come on, Danny." She can barely speak, and it's hard to

make out her words. "You listen to what they say, and you do it, okay? You work the way they tell you to. And I'll come see you just as soon as I can."

She opens the door and the soldier gives her a glare.

"It's about time," he barks. "We're behind schedule! Let's move!"

He passes Danny's bag off to another soldier, and I remember I was supposed to get his shirt. I run to the laundry room, dig through the hamper, and find it. I race back out and a very bewildered Danny is walking behind my mother, who has him by the hand. He turns to me and I can see the apprehension in his eyes.

"Are you going, Jessa?" he asks. "'Cause I don't want to go by myself."

"No, Danny," I manage to say. "I'm not going this time."

His eyes widen. "I don't want to go. I want to stay here. I work with Mom," he insists. He stops, digging his heels in, pulling my mother back by the hand.

"I work with Mom," he says again. "And at the library. They need me." His voice is rising with agitation, and the soldier turns to see what's going on.

"What's the holdup?" he shouts. "Get that man on board!"

Two soldiers peel off from the group milling around by the open-topped transport truck, shouldering their weapons and heading toward us.

"Mom!" I shout, but she sees them.

"Please!" She steps forward, raising her hands to stall them. "Can't you come back for him? I need some time. He doesn't do well with change, and fifteen minutes isn't—"

"We're leaving!" the soldier barks. "Now!"

The soldiers take Danny by the arms and he begins screaming.

"Mom! Mom! I work with you! I work with you! I don't want to go by myself!"

He's kicking now, trying to pull away, and my mom is screaming at him to stop, to calm down, telling him over and over it'll be all right, but he's not hearing. He's crying now, great, heaving sobs as they pull him along. He's shoved from behind up the steps and into the truck, where he falls, with a shriek, rolling into a ball.

My mom runs forward and I'm right behind her with wings on my feet as we rush to the truck. I can hear the engine revving and I'm reminded that I'm holding his shirt.

"Mom!" I wave it at her, and she yanks it from my hands.

"Danny!" she screams, and he pushes himself up, rubbing hard at his eyes.

"Mom! Jessa!" He sees us and he reaches out, straining toward us. Hands from inside the truck behind him pull him back, but we can still hear him calling for us.

"I have his shirt!" my mom is screaming as the truck pulls away. "I have his shirt! You can't take him! I have his shirt!" She runs, waving the shirt in the sky like a flag, as if the waving of it will slow them, stop them. She keeps running until her legs give out, and I watch, frozen, as she crumples to the ground, burying her face in the shirt as the last of Danny's screams echo down the street.

The soldier shakes his head, making a notation on his clipboard, ticking off just another name on a list. Just another number on a roll sheet.

My legs carry me to him as the anger burns through me. I am vibrating with the force of it as I grab him by the arm, stopping him from making yet one more tick mark on that damn clip-board.

"How can you *do* this?" I lash out. "Taking someone from the only home he's ever known? Not even letting him say good-bye?"

He gives me a long-suffering look as he shakes my hand off. "I have my orders," he says. "And you're out of line, citizen-soldier."

"You bring him back!"

"Stand down," he warns. "Don't make me arrest you—your mother looks like she can't take much more today."

"No!" I shout back. "Danny is a special case! There have to be exceptions!"

"No exceptions." The soldier tries to go around me, and I move to step in front of him, but the other soldiers are too fast and block me.

"Get your mother out of the street before we run her down," the soldier threatens. "We're moving! We got four more stops in this town, and I'd like to finish them off before dinner!"

I run out to help my mom to the sidewalk, and with our arms wrapped around each other, we watch the last of the soldiers pull away.

We move into the house, and Mom won't let go of Danny's shirt. She crumples down onto the couch, and I fall with her as we cry and hold and rock each other. Ben and Finn watch silently from across the room, and eventually I realize I need to get a grip. This isn't helping Danny. And right now, I'm the only one—the only one in the whole damn universe—who can help Danny.

"Are you okay?" I ask my mom as I pull away. "Do you need anything?"

She shakes her head. "Are *you* all right?" she asks. "D-did they hurt you?"

"I'm okay."

She nods and clutches Danny's shirt tighter as she gets to her feet. I follow her into the kitchen as she pulls a paper towel from the holder and blows her nose, then she looks over at me. "Did you take the NyQuil?"

"Yeah," I tell her. "I've got a pretty bad cold. My head feels congested and I'm achy."

She reaches out and touches my arm.

"I don't think they'll delay your enlistment for just a head cold, Jessa."

"I know."

"The literature they gave us last week was pretty clear about that." She takes in a shaky breath. "It didn't say a thing about work camps, though, did it?" The tears are tracking down her face and she steps back over to the paper towels, ripping off a fresh one and cramming it against her eyes.

"We'll figure it out," I tell her. "We'll get him back."

"I don't think we have a choice, Jessa," she says, blowing her nose again. "But I think—maybe I should go see Representative Richardson. He comes to the senior center to visit his mother, and we've talked. Maybe he can help. He's always liked Danny." She looks up at me. "Where did they say he was going again?"

"Hannacroix Creek," Ben says. "But that's probably just for processing."

"Maybe I can get in to see Danny," she says, more to herself than to us. "I mean, even if it's for just a few hours. I could take him his shirt, at least."

"Maybe," I answer. "It's worth a try."

She grabs her car keys off the counter. "I'll be back in a while," she says, leaning in and hugging me tight. "Stay in the house, please." She runs her hand across my hair and hugs me tight, and for a very long time. "It'll all be okay, Jessa. It'll be okay."

I wonder if she says it twice so she can convince herself. She heads out the door, still holding Danny's shirt.

33

Splintered

I LEAN BACK AGAINST THE COUNTERTOP, RUBBING MY hands over my face.

"I've got to fix this, and I need to talk to Mario to figure out how," I say. "I need to get to sleep, and fast. We don't have a lot of time."

"You can sleep?" Ben asks. "Now?"

"I have to try," I tell him. "Anyway, I'm dead on my feet."

"Please don't use that word," Finn says quietly. "You came entirely too close to it today already. Let's get you lying down."

I wave him off, choosing to curl up on the couch, clutching a pillow. I try to clear my mind from the events of the day, but it's just not going to happen. It's all whirling around me—Danny's face, Eversor's death, my counterpart's disappearance. It's too much. Despite my bone-numbing fatigue, I start to feel like it's an exercise in futility as I close my eyes and begin slowly counting each breath in and out, in and out. . . .

Mario is already in the classroom when I walk in.

"We have a problem," I say.

"Yes," he agrees grimly. "And unfortunately, it all makes sense now."

"Is she really gone? The me who swims with the dolphins?"

He doesn't have to answer; I can see it in his eyes. "It's just as Finn suspects," he tells me. "A convergence has already begun."

I look at him in alarm. "How? And how is Finn still here, if that's so?"

"I said *a* convergence—something close to what we were expecting, but not as it was before—and that's the distinction," Mario explains. "As I told you before, splintering occurs naturally, on a random basis. We've always been able to maintain and repair these with strategic corrections, things that heal the stream."

He gestures to the whiteboard, where a series of lines appear, fanning out like the spokes of a wheel from a central point.

"We occasionally see fragmentation in the later streams that have split interminable times from various realities." His finger traces the lines in front of him. "Two realities shear off toward each other, and we see a collision. Events will begin to intersect. But a fragmentation shouldn't be reaching the origin in anything other than a very mild form."

"Such as?"

"Occasional déjà vu. Like I said—it's a very rare thing that can be avoided by strategic readjustments."

"Can you do that now?" I ask.

"It's too late for that. Rudy and Eversor were trying to start the convergence based on what they knew of its last occurrence. Picture yourself standing in the safety of the origin, almost like the eye of a hurricane," he continues. "We assumed—like last time—that the convergence would eradicate everything outside of your protected area."

"And that's not what happened?" I ask.

"No. Eversor wasn't strong enough. Even with the aid of the Traveler's mirror it wasn't enough to do what they'd planned. My guess is whatever drug she took couldn't keep her in a stable hallucinatory state. But that doesn't mean she didn't have an effect. What she did was start a chain reaction."

He gestures to the whiteboard behind him again, and it suddenly shows a dozen lines all traveling in one direction until one of them shatters, colliding with another, and another, showing a wave of splinters that begin to grow exponentially, splitting off and crossing over one another, merging and diverging in chaotic ways.

"This is overload," he says, running a hand over his face. "Too many splinters—a tidal wave of them, and it's building exponentially. We're having a hard time controlling it." His eyes aren't quite able to meet mine. "We've got Travelers out in force, making corrections, but we can't keep up with it. And we're losing them almost as fast as we send them."

"What does that mean for us? I can stop it, right?" I ask frantically. "You said I'm the one who can stop it."

"Not like this. The wave is now monstrous in its proportions. It's grown far beyond anything we can control."

"Tell me what to do!" I plead. "Tell me what I need to do!"

His eyes close for a moment and he lets out a breath. "Wake up. Say your good-byes. Then come back here and we'll do what we can to keep your reality from sustaining too much damage. It's the best we can do, Jessa. I'm sorry."

I run for the red door, feeling like the universe is falling down around me, and I wrench it open. I come awake with a start on the couch, sitting up and gasping, feeling the crushing weight of every one of Mario's words.

"What's happened?" Finn asks, hovering over me. "Has Mario got a solution?"

"No." It comes out as a whisper. "He says it's too strong to stop. It's going to keep building, and we can't stop it." I raise my eyes to look at him, and they flood with tears. "I can't stop it."

"But aren't you the chosen one or whatever?" Ben asks. "If you can stop the annexation, get Danny back—I mean, if none of this is really supposed to be happening—"

"It's not." I swing my legs down so I can sit upright. "But there are too many realities colliding. Mario says they're like a wave of dominoes, falling into one another." I use my hands, mimicking the way they'd fall. "It's only a matter of time until it swamps us."

"And I disappear," Finn adds tensely as he begins to pace back and forth across the living room.

"One little shard of obsidian," Ben marvels. "And this is the result."

"It might as well have been a boxful of shards," Finn says with disgust. "At least it would be over quickly."

A sliver of a thought begins to wedge itself into my brain, pulling at my memory. "The double mirror," I say to myself. "Two mirrors. Double the power."

"What's that?" Finn asks.

"Ben told me that ancient oracles sometimes used mirrors held over pools of water," I tell him. "They created a portal to the gods by looking at the reflection reflected again into the pool. A double mirror."

"You think that might work?" Ben asks. "But you said the other Aztec mirror wasn't anything special."

"It's not. I only need one on this side."

"Come again?"

Now I'm up and pacing opposite Finn. "What if I use the Aztec mirror to transfer to the dreamscape and use a mirror in the dreamscape as well? Mario can pull one up—he can find anything in there. If I'm looking from one into the other—I can link them. Make the wave feed back on itself."

"You mean, create a counterwave?" Finn interjects.

"Exactly."

"Not sure I'm following you, love. You can't bring that mirror into the dreamscape, and a dreamscape mirror won't register in the real world. You'd have to be in both places at once."

"Which involves drugging yourself up so you can do that," Ben points out.

"And where am I going to get those kind of heavy drugs—and fast?" I shudder, remembering how Eversor looked toward the end. "Mario said it wasn't stable enough doing it that way, anyway."

"Well, it's not like you're one of the oracles, with a temple full of volcanic steam to send you off to La-La land," Ben says.

"I can't do what Eversor did," I say firmly. "How the hell are we going to get me into a sustained hallucinatory state?"

"There are other drugs," Ben says. "Maybe safer ones. Lower dosages. Can you ask Mario?"

"He wouldn't have that knowledge. And we don't have time

to try to get a doctor's appointment or even break into somewhere. The universe is already changing around us."

I turn fearful eyes to Finn, because he could quite literally vanish at any moment.

"I won't gamble you that way," he says firmly as he continues to pace again. "We'll have to find something that won't put you at risk."

"Sleep deprivation might work," Ben says. "It's been a military tactic for hundreds of years. Sleep deprivation can bring on paranoia, hallucinations, psychosis. . . ."

"Still not going to be fast enough," I say, shaking my head.

"Well, unless you can wave a magic wand or something, I don't see how we're going to beat this," says Ben.

"Jessa." Finn stops his pacing, freezing in place.

"What?"

"I know what we're going to do."

34

The Plan

"SO THIS IS THE PLAN?" BEN ASKS, LOOKING AT US BOTH like we're crazy. *"Hypnosis?"*

I shut the door to my room just in case Mom gets home sooner than I think she will, and I sit down on the bed as I try to lay it out for Ben.

"Finn's going to hypnotize me, and while I'm under, he's going to give me a trigger word—something he can say that will make me open my eyes and go to the mirror."

"Then I'll give her another command to travel," Finn explains.

"Since I'm hypnotized, I can be both here and in the dream-scape at the same time—and it'll be stable. Then I'll simultaneously start a transfer in both places. If it all goes right, the second I make the transfers, it'll create a counterwave."

"Like lighting a fire line to stop an oncoming fire," Ben says, nodding slowly. "Make it consume itself."

"If it goes right." I cross my fingers, silly as it is. We need all the help we can get.

"How am I going to know if it worked?" he asks, still looking at us uneasily.

"I'll still be here," Finn says. "I'm not from around here, remember? If the universe goes, I go with it."

"No pressure, right?" I say sarcastically. "Now we just have to hope I can be hypnotized. First, we need to pick some command words." I look over at Finn. "When I need to open my eyes, you're going to say 'open sesame,' and when I walk to this mirror"—I prop the Aztec mirror up against the mirror on my dresser—"that's your signal that I'm ready to transfer in the dreamscape. You're going to say 'bon voyage'—that'll direct me to transfer out and then back here again."

"Do we all understand the plan?" Finn asks. "Jessa will be traveling simultaneously both here and in the dreamscape, creating a counterwave and saving the universe. And then we all go get some coffee. Or tea."

"How long will it take?" I ask Finn.

"Guess I should get comfortable," Ben says, kicking off his shoes. "We could be here for hours, right?"

"Not that long. If all goes well, this should be nearly instantaneous," Finn says. "Over in a heartbeat."

"And if it doesn't go well?" Ben asks.

Finn makes a grim face. "It'll still be over in a heartbeat. Mine."

Ben sucks in a breath. "Well. Okay, then. Let's get this party started." He grabs a couple of pillows and stacks them up against my headboard, and I start to lie back against them.

"Wait—am I sitting? Or lying down?" I ask.

Finn fishes something out of his coat pocket before he takes his coat off and hangs it on the doorknob.

"Lie back, but only semi-reclined," he says. "You'll need to be able to easily see this." He holds up one of my mom's scented candles that he must have grabbed from downstairs, as well as the clicker she uses to light them.

"A candle? What about your pocket watch?"

"It's not as good for this. A candle flame can be quite mesmerizing. It has just enough movement to keep you interested, but not enough that your eyes might wander and distract you." He pulls over the chair from my desk and sits down on it, then lights the candle.

"What scent is that?" I ask, wrinkling my nose.

"Ocean breeze," Finn replies dryly. "But it smells more like an aged aunt."

"I'm not so sure I like the idea of him controlling your mind," Ben says dubiously. He looks at Finn. "No offense."

"None taken—but only because I'm not controlling her mind. That's not how hypnosis works. Hypnosis is actually *self*-hypnosis. I'm only here as a guide, directing her into a trance state—much like when you slip into a daydream and someone has to snap you out of it. Jessa can't be made to do anything she wouldn't want to do. That's why it's especially hilarious to an entertainer when a group under hypnosis acts like a pack of wild monkeys or says something untoward. They're not doing anything they don't want to do, I assure you."

"Well, I definitely want to do this," I say, settling myself in and getting as comfortable as possible.

"That makes it easier," Finn answers.

"I'll debrief Mario on the plan once I get there," I say, taking in a deep breath and letting it out slowly. "I'm ready."

"Now," says Finn. "Listen to my voice, love, and look at the candle flame. You can blink when you need to; the object is to keep your focus upon it as you listen to my words. All right?"

I nod. "Okay."

"Let's start by having you relax your muscles, beginning at your toes and working your way up. Flex and release. Flex and release."

My breathing begins to deepen as I keep my eyes on the flame and do as he asks, squeezing my toes, my calf muscles, and working my way up, slowly tensing and releasing. The flame is dancing in front of me, flickering and definitely mesmerizing. Finn's voice is a soothing lilt as I begin to drift.

"You can feel a heavy, relaxed feeling coming over you like a warm blanket," he says. "And as I continue to speak, that heavy, relaxed feeling will grow stronger . . . and stronger . . . until it carries you into a deep, peaceful state of relaxation. . . ."

His voice drops to more of a hum, like I can hear that he's saying words but I'm not sure exactly which words. I vaguely wonder if I've slipped back into Danny's dream as the flickering candlelight varies in color and pattern and . . .

I am looking at a very surprised Mario.

"Jessa?" He hurries over to me. "You're all right?"

"I think I know how to stop the convergence wave," I say, getting right to the point.

He glances up at the whiteboard and it springs to life, showing me all sorts of mayhem—zoo animals running through shopping malls and my school now being held in a warehouse surrounded by barbed wire, wars and strange-looking cities, and places of complete devastation.

"I was actually worried I wouldn't be able to reach you in time," he says. "We don't have much of it left."

"Listen to me," I say. "I'm here because Finn has me hypnotized."

Mario's eyes widen, and then they narrow as he looks at me more closely. "That's *brilliant!*" he says, reaching out a finger and running it along my arm. His finger slides right through me, like I'm a ghost. Only half there. "Are you registering this? In reality?"

I concentrate for a moment, and part of me is pulled back, feeling my body breathe, feeling Finn, silent now. His hand is touching mine.

"Yes," I say. "I can feel both places. I don't know how long I can hold this, though. But we've got a plan."

"I'm listening." Mario is looking at me intensely. "I gather it involves Finn?"

He no sooner says the name than I feel Finn beside me here.

"What are you doing here?" I demand. "You're supposed to be in charge back in the real world."

"Ben knows the command to make you transfer," Finn says. "I'm here to help."

"How did you fall asleep so fast?"

"I didn't want to wait for the medicine, so I let Ben hit me."

"He knocked you out?"

"He's been itching to have at me for days now. I gave him his chance. Took the bugger two tries before it worked," he grumbles. He reaches down for my hand, but his fingers slide right through.

"Sorry," he says. "Forgot you're not entirely with us."

"The plan?" Mario prompts. He's got a sense of urgency in his voice, so I cut right to it.

"We're going to do what the oracles used to do and use two mirrors to make a stronger portal. I'll use two mirrors to transfer simultaneously—the Aztec mirror in the real world, and a mirror here in the dreamscape. If I can keep my focus in both places, it might counter the wave and make it feed back on itself."

Mario stares at the whiteboard, his lips moving silently as his mind tries to calculate the probability of it. He shakes his head.

"I don't know, Jessa," he says. "I can't forecast this—there are too many variables now."

"I've got to try," I say.

"What do we have to lose, really?" Finn asks.

"You're right." Mario's voice is grim. "We're running out of time."

I nod to Finn. "Open the door."

Mario races over, and then gestures to Finn. "I'll get you the mirror in the dreamscape," he says. "Head immediately to your left—you'll be in a curio shop. There's a large mirror on a wheeled base. Use that."

"Right," Finn says. He gives me a nod and steps through as Mario opens the red door.

"I'll force the door to remain open," Mario says as the dream-scape shimmers to life in front of me through the door. I stand in the doorway and watch as Finn brings the mirror over, standing on the other side of the doorway with it.

"Ready?" he asks, tilting it so I can see myself perfectly. The people in the curio shop behind him are milling about, seemingly unaware of what is taking place.

"And this is how we save a universe," I say, reaching through the doorway to put my fingers to the glass. I can feel my conscious self as well, the smooth surface of the Aztec mirror cold against my fingertips, I feel the power pulsing through both sides, and then on Ben's command filtering through from the waking world, I step through in both places—it doesn't matter where. I just connect and go. I feel myself sucked into the in-between, pulled tight between reality and dreams, and whirling all around me are the flotsam and jetsam of hundreds of shattered realities, beating their way in, trying to take root. I push them away, slapping at the waves—the soldiers, the places that don't belong, the redirected streams and the rewritten histories.

I can feel my conscious body panting with the exertion of it, but I also feel my strength, pushing it all back, sweeping away the loose ends until all that remains is what *should* remain. It seems to take hours, and I am shaking with fatigue, but as I transfer back and stumble into the room, I realize it's been only the length of a heartbeat.

"Well?" Finn asks in disbelief. "Is it done? That seemed rather . . . anticlimactic."

"For you, maybe," I reply, sucking in a lungful of air and flexing my arms to wring out the last bits of overexertion. "I feel like I just cleaned house—for the entire world."

Finn steps back through the door, leaving the mirror standing behind him. "You wouldn't even know we just saved the bloody universe," he says with a smile.

"That's because you didn't," Mario says quietly, and he's looking at a whiteboard full of splintering chaos.

35

The End of the Story

"NO." I SHAKE MY HEAD VIOLENTLY. "WE'VE STILL GOT the mirror. Just tell me what to do and I can do it."

"It's no use," Mario says, and the calmness in his voice is infuriating. "Jessa, when you used the dual mirror, the portal created a shield around the origin, but it didn't extend much beyond it."

"So my reality is back to normal?"

"It should be."

"But not the rest," I say flatly. "I can't save the rest."

"You simply don't have the kind of power to arrest this motion."

"That can't be," Finn says. "We're talking about countless lives—"

"We're talking about *your* life," Mario says, not unkindly. "And that lends desperation to your actions. But no matter how desperately you try—or Jessa tries—she simply doesn't have the power to contain all of this. No one does."

"But the prophecy!" I say. "You said I could stop it."

"I've told you before," he answers quietly, "it was a forecast, not a prophecy. The forecast was made on the assumption that you were a direct descendant—and therefore better equipped to deal with this situation, and that we would have learned enough in the passing centuries to guide you properly. We didn't anticipate *this* level of convergence."

"So you were *wrong.*" My words lash out, dripping with venom, with my own personal fury.

"Yes, I was wrong." Mario's voice is weary and heavy with sorrow. "It's too far gone, Jessa."

"You told me I could save them," I say, and the complete uselessness of that word overwhelms me.

Finn moves closer, his fingers trying to twine around mine, but passing right through instead.

"And so you did, love," he says. "You've saved your family. Your world."

He's calm, steady. His eyes carry the pain for both of us, and I feel like I'm being ripped into pieces. Like the wave has already hit and leveled me.

"I don't want a life without you in it," I whisper.

He shakes his head emphatically. "Don't say that. You'll have a life. You'll have a wonderful life."

I turn to look at Mario. "Will I remember him? When everything else goes away? Will I keep these memories?"

"Some, perhaps," he says. "Not all."

The thought tears into me like a twisting, burning knife, and I turn back to Finn. "I can't . . ."

He looks at me with those green, green eyes, and I am lost.

"You'll remember me, love," he promises. "And you'll go on to college, you'll write your books." He tries to crack a smile, but it's only a painful imitation. "Put me in a story. You told me once that's how you live forever, isn't it?"

I nod, but I'm blinded by tears. "I love you, Finn."

"Ah, Jessa," he murmurs. "When it all comes together, I'll be here. Somehow, I'll be here with you. I swear it. I'll love you to the end of it all and beyond."

I think of all the many lives I've known and those I will now never know. My families. My friends. My lovers and my selves. I owe them better. They deserve their lives as much as I do. All the Jessas that I could have been.

You guys should get together sometime, Danny said once. I've learned so much about myself, taken so much strength and knowledge from every bit of who I am, wherever I am. But it was all for nothing. In the end, Danny is one of the only people I can save. Danny, my family, my world, and myself.

And if I'm lucky enough to remember, I can write about the selves I'll never meet again or be again. I can write about the man I love, and I know I'll never feel this again. I cannot imagine putting a pen to paper and letting this kind of anguish pour out on the pages. Finn steps closer, and I wish I could feel his arms around me.

I glance over at the door to the dreamscape, and the tickle of a thought floats in my mind. Like a line of dialogue or a scene description waiting to form the rest of the story. . . . It teases my brain, and in my conscious reality, I feel my fingers tighten around the mirror.

You guys should get together sometime.

Mario was right. Danny never misses the important details.

"Finn?" I ask.

"Yes, love?"

"This isn't how this story is going to end."

"Jessa . . ." Mario's voice carries a question, but I hold up a hand, stopping him.

"I've got an idea."

"What are you doing?" he asks warily. "We don't have much time."

"This will only take a few minutes." I step over to the red door again, and simultaneously, in the waking world, I feel myself standing in front of my bedroom mirror. "I know what I'm doing, Mario."

"Jessa, whatever you're thinking of doing—" Mario begins.

"You said yourself I wasn't strong enough to save them all."

"You're not," he says gently. "No matter how much you want to be."

"But *we* are," I say. "All of us. Together."

"You want to . . . use your other selves? How?"

"As long as I'm hypnotized, anyone who transfers to my reality will be under, too—correct?"

"Yes." His eyes widen as the possibilities begin to flesh out in his brain. "Yes—they'll be in both places at once. And you won't transfer over because—"

"Because I'm not really entirely in one place or the other."

Mario is shaking his head uneasily. "Jessa, we can't know if this will work. It may be the equivalent of spreading yourself too thin. It could tear you apart. Nothing like this has ever been done."

"We're out of time," I say fiercely. "And it's going to work." I look at Finn—*my Finn*. No matter where he is, he is who he is, and so am I. And we—all of us—are going to keep these amazing lives we lead.

I concentrate, feeling my body in the conscious world. I lift my fingers there, I can feel it, and I touch them to the mirror glass.

"Hurry," I say to the reflection in both places. "We've got work to do."

Here in the classroom, I reach through the doorway into the dreamscape, and my hand closes around another. Another Jessa steps through from the other side, wearing our favorite leotard and leggings.

"Hey," dancer me says. "Who's next?"

We both reach through, and out steps another me, glittering head to toe in sparkling gold and red sequins this time. And another, this one in faded jeans and a plaid shirt. We all give one another a nod, turning as one and reaching through for more.

"Keep 'em coming," I urge, and another Jessa steps through, signing hello as she gets out of the way to make room for the next, who's wearing ski gear, and the one after her, who has short hair and a nose piercing. I see Mario at the doorway now, and with a flourish of his hand, a group of Jessas appears, then dozens, tens to hundreds to thousands, and the room grows to fit us all. An infinite number of Jessas in their realities and throughout the dreamscape, all held in this moment. I feel every one of them as we reach and connect, growing stronger with each addition, taking in their power, their strength, their resilience.

I can feel the splintering wave as it moves through us from

our various realities, pulling at us, trying to scatter us, but like a chain, link by link, we hold fingertip to fingertip, then hand to hand, tightening, circling and surrounding the wave, reaching out and pulling in fragments as we go. We enclose it, like it's a fire and we're cutting off its air, leaving it no fuel to burn or destroy. But it doesn't go down easy.

I can feel some of it slip through, disintegrating before we tighten ranks again, pulling in. I hear Mario shouting over the sound of the vortex, directing us.

"Jessa with the ponytail—over there! That one! Now, Jessa with the tattoo—trace this stream—no, not that way—over here! You! With the house in the valley—grab that one—send it over here!" His eyes lock with mine. "Jessa—keep it together!"

I tighten my grip on their hands, bearing down hard as he continues calling out directions to the multitudes of Jessas, helping them chase down diverging streams, circling them back in, pulling them like gossamer flyaways, reeling them all back into the reality stream, pulling the flying fragments and melding them together.

My body shakes with the effort in the conscious world; I taste the blood of my lip where I've bitten into it. I feel the pain screaming through me, pulling sounds from my throat and from the lips of all of us, before everything spirals at a furiously dizzying pace, wrenching us this way and that, until, with a scream of fury, the wave peaks and falls.

In the real world, my body sinks to the floor, and I hear both Ben and Finn call my name before a blinding light and a deafening crack render me senseless.

36

Coming Down

MY VISION SLOWLY CLEARS, AND IN A SEA OF JESSAS, I find the face I'm looking for.

"Finn!"

"I'm here, love." He's grinning widely. "You've done it." He looks over his shoulder at all the many, many me's. "All of you."

Some of us are already transferring back, and several are just popping out indiscriminately as Mario waves them off. A few of us are high-fiving or talking among ourselves, laughing and comparing hair and clothing and scars.

Mario is standing at the red door as the long line of Jessas moves past me to him and then back to the waking world and their own realities. He's congratulating all of us, and we're all hugging and laughing and patting one another on the back as we pass through. I see a familiar face—more familiar than the rest, anyway—waiting for me near the door.

"Hey," she says. "You going to keep dancing?"

"Yeah, I am."

"I wrote my first fan fiction," she tells me with an embarrassed shrug. "It's probably not too good, but I'd love it if you'd read it."

"Definitely!"

"See ya," she says, and she steps through.

Mario turns to me with a wide smile. "You did it, Jessa!"

"*We* did it," I correct him. "And does that mean the universe is saved?"

He waves a hand and the whiteboard behind him flickers to life, showing me people in parks or sitting down to dinner, deserts and mountains and football games and crowds jostling down city streets.

"You've all managed to save quite a bit," he says. "Though what remains has been condensed somewhat."

"*Condensed?*" I don't like the sound of that.

"Some of the reality streams were lost before you attempted to save them," Mario reminds me gently. "Those cannot be recovered completely. And when all of the Jessas moved to control the splintering, there was *some* convergence, eliminating most of the fractures by combining certain realities—specifically, the ones without any Jessas."

I feel like I've been hit in the chest. "So . . . people were lost?"

"Not lost," he reassures me. "Redirected. Splintered realities were merged back into similar streams. I directed where we could to save and combine as much as possible. Think of it as a kind of . . . recycling."

I cover my face with my hands. "Please tell me there won't be any more tanks driving down Main Street in Ardenville."

Mario chuckles. "No, Jessa. Your life is very much like it was. The adjustments are spread across countless realities to lessen the impact." He smiles a very smug smile, like he's got a secret. "I think you'll be happy with the way it all came out."

Whew. I exhale in relief. "So now what?" I ask.

"Live your life," he says with a shrug. "Go to college. Write a novel or two. It's all up to you, after all."

"Will I still be traveling?"

"I'm still going to need you," he says. "And Finn."

"How do we keep this from happening again?" Finn asks.

Mario lets out a sigh. "We'll certainly be more vigilant on our end," he says truthfully. "But now that we know how to manage a convergence, I know to keep an eye on your descendants."

I reach for the doorknob so I can follow Finn out, but Mario's hand comes out to hold the door a moment.

"You're an amazing individual, Jessa St. Clair."

"We're all amazing individuals." I shrug. "There are a lot of Jessas to go around."

"Let's keep it that way," he says. "It makes the universe a far more interesting place." He gestures to the door. "See you tomorrow."

"See you tomorrow," I echo, then I wave to the remaining multitude of me's in the room. "See ya around!" I call out, and I hear them calling back as I open the door.

As I fade back into reality, I realize I'm lying down and my eyes are closed.

My fingers register a hand, sliding over mine, a thumb slowly and rhythmically rubbing the back of my hand. It's a good feeling, because it's Finn. I'd know that hand anywhere and the way it feels in mine. It's warm and wonderful and I can float here forever with Finn at my side.

If only I didn't have a shoe in my back.

My eyes flutter open at that discordant thought, and I hear Ben suck in a breath as he sits back in pure relief.

"She's okay!"

"I'm . . . not," I struggle to say.

"You're hurt?" Finn's face hovers over mine, his brow knit with concern. He chafes my hand gently between his. "You're going to be all right."

I try to sit up, but his hand comes to my shoulder, pressing me back down. "Easy now, love. Stay still."

I swat at his hand and make a sound as I roll to my side.

"I've got a . . . damn shoe under me," I huff.

Ben lets out an explosive laugh, and he pulls the offending footwear out from under my back. "I got it," he says. "Sorry—didn't realize I'd left them so close to the bed."

"Lie down now," Finn tells me again as he pushes me gently to my back once more.

"You scared the hell out of me!" Ben accuses. "You just . . . dropped! Like a sack of rocks!"

I look over at him. "So I guess I didn't crumple languidly to the carpet with the back of my hand to my forehead?"

"You landed on a shoe," Finn points out. "Perhaps you need lessons in the proper deportment of fainting ladies."

"Help me up," I demand, reaching for their hands. As I sit up, it all hits me like a ton of bricks.

"We did it!"

"You did it?" Ben is grinning from ear to ear.

"Aye, love, you did. All of you."

"Jessa?"

It's my mom's voice, and I leap to my feet, tripping over Ben's shoes again.

"Dammit!"

"Sorry!"

"Keep your voice down!" I hiss.

His second apology follows me as I tear down the stairs—limping a little because I twisted my ankle on Ben's shoe. Mom is standing in the doorway, and I throw my arms around her.

"Mom!"

She pulls away and looks at me carefully. "Are you okay?" she asks.

I nod. "You?"

She looks a little confused. "Honey, I just heard the news."

"From the soldiers?" I ask, feeling my stomach clench.

"Soldiers? Jessa, what are you talking about?"

I exhale in relief. "It's nothing. What are *you* talking about?"

"About that teacher," she says. Her hand comes out, pushing my hair off my face. "The one who took off last semester."

"Ms. Eversor?"

She nods. "That's the one. I ran into Officer Glauner at the grocery store—he was the one who was here asking questions about her last month, remember?"

"What about her?" I'm holding my breath—and trying not to look like I'm holding my breath.

"Her body was found in the river late last night. According to the police, she was an addict." Her face is sad, and I know mine is, too. "They're saying it was suicide, honey. I'm sorry I had to tell you."

I swallow hard, almost afraid to ask. "Where's Danny?"

"Danny!" she calls out over her shoulder. "How long does it take to get groceries?"

"Coming!" he shouts, which is really unnecessary, since he's already stepping through the doorway. I can't help myself; I throw my arms around him, too. He drops the grocery bags and hugs me back, hard. Good old Danny. He doesn't ask questions. He just gives you what you need.

I stagger back a bit under the exuberance of his hug.

"Ow! Ow!" I say, picking up my foot and rubbing my ankle.

"Did you kick your head again?" Danny asks.

I sink into the nearest chair, laughing entirely too hard, but I can't seem to stop.

There's no place like home.

Epilogue

"THEY HAVE THE COOKIES THREE FOR A DOLLAR NINETY-nine," Ben is saying to Danny. "But you've already had some."

"Danny, no more," I say as I take my seat. "If you eat too many cookies, Mom will smack me with a frying pan."

"No, she won't," he says. "She doesn't hit." He gives me a pointed look.

"Oh for . . . I didn't hit Finn! He was *teasing* you." I look at Finn in exasperation, and he gives me an unrepentant grin. Danny couldn't help but notice the bruise over Finn's eye from where Ben clocked him earlier, but Finn found it amusing to tell Danny I punched him.

"You shouldn't hit, Jessa! You shouldn't hit, *Jessa Emeline St. Clair!*"

"You heard him, Emeline," Finn says blandly.

"I am never going to be free of that," I grumble.

"This frosting is amazing," Ben says, digging his finger into it. "So . . . you're working at the museum, St. Clair?" He gives me a grin. "Really?"

"One day a week," I say with a shrug. "Maybe I'll pick up some new story ideas. You should give the place a try—they can use the help."

He drags his finger through the frosting again. "Maybe I will," he says.

"You can tell all the patrons about your extensive travels in Mexico."

Ben shoots me a long-suffering look, but before he can fashion a suitable retort, Danny stands up.

"It's time to go, Ben," Danny says. "You said I could ride in the truck and it's time to go now."

"He's got a shift at the library this afternoon," I explain. "Better get him back."

"I'm on it," Ben says. He points a finger at me. "Don't be punching anybody while we're gone."

"You be nice!" Danny admonishes me as he swipes up the last cookie and heads for the door, with Ben laughing and following.

"See ya!" He waves back over his shoulder as he goes.

I set down my empty coffee cup with a sigh.

"All right there, love?" Finn asks.

"I'm debating whether or not I want another cup of coffee," I say. "You want anything?"

"I'm finishing this. It's been entirely too long since I've had a proper scone," he says, biting into his treat with relish.

"Too bad you never got a chance to try glitter mousse."

"Is it only served on certain days?"

"It's only served in certain *realities*." I smile at the memory, and instead of a shaft of pain, I'm feeling something strangely like contentment, both at the memory and the thought of introducing this Finn to a bowl of glowing deliciousness.

"I'm going to go get that coffee before we go," I say, reaching for my purse.

Finn stays my hand. "My turn to pay," he says, pulling out his wallet.

"Where did you get money?"

"I'm not without means," he says in an offended voice. "Mario made sure I'm accommodated, and that includes this lovely new wallet."

He opens it up, and inside is cash. A lot of cash. And a driver's license with his name and address on it.

"So that's Mario's surprise," I say. "You're now officially a part of this reality."

"Oh, you don't know the half of it," he assures me. "Do you mind a short detour on the way home?"

"Sure." I shrug. "I don't have to get the car back till bedtime."

He's got a devilish twinkle in his eye. "Then let's use every bit of that time, shall we? Do you mind if I drive?"

"You know how?"

"I do. And I have just the place to spend the day." He holds out his hand, and I take it.

We head out to the parking lot and I hand him the keys, and we make idle small talk about next semester as he drives. Eventually, we pull off Main Street and onto the highway, then off again onto a smaller, narrower road.

"The marina?" I ask, recognizing the area.

"It's chilly, but we're bundled up well," he points out as he pulls into the parking lot. "I thought a walk down the pier might be just the thing. All that fresh air, you know."

He helps me out of the car, holding my hand as we walk. He's having a hard time keeping his decidedly sneaky grin off his face, too. What is he up to?

In less than five minutes, I have my answer. There she is, bobbing at the end of the pier. Her gangplank is down, the tree painted on the mainmast is rippling with the breeze, and I can read her name clearly as we get closer.

~ THE TRAVELING LADY ~

My eyes meet his and I am thrilled for him, grinning a crazy grin that he answers with one of his own.

"Mario thought I could do with a permanent address, since I'll be staying."

We're still grinning at each other. His joy is contagious, and I laugh as he takes my hand and pulls me up the gangplank.

"I'm going down below to check things over," he tells me. "Why don't you sit at the bow and enjoy the view?"

I tighten my coat around me to ward against the breeze coming off the water.

"All right," I say, getting up on my toes to give him a quick kiss. "But don't be too long."

He pulls me in closer, kissing me longer, his hands shifting over my back as the kiss deepens and becomes so much more. I feel like

I can't get close enough, and my hands are fisted in his hair as our tongues touch and slide and caress. He finally releases me with a reluctant groan. "You, my gorgeous girl, are in great danger of being carried off by a pirate."

I hold his gaze, and I know my eyes are just as bright as his. "And . . . ?"

He lets out a gusty sigh. "And you're not going to distract me. I promised you a sailing, and a sailing you shall have. We have all the time in the world now, love. I'm in no hurry."

"You can do that without a crew?"

"I can't take us out far, but I can manage well enough. The ship practically runs herself, but I'm sure you'll be an able hand with a bit of instruction."

"Okay." I kiss him again and I turn to head toward the bow, but he stops me.

"Just a moment," he says. "You'll need this." He scoops up my messenger bag from where I'd set it down and pulls out my journal. I take it, feeling the familiar smoothness of the leather cover in my hands.

"You know me so well," I say.

"I do. Now off with you. Take a seat at the bow and open that book. You've got stories to tell."

I can't help but laugh. "You can say that again."

"We're going to make more, you and I. Many, many more."

"I'm counting on it."

I stroll toward the bow, feeling the ship rise and dip gently beneath me, drinking in the fresh air and the waning winter sun on my face. Contentment fills me up until I feel I might burst with it.

"What do you say, love?" He gives me a wink. "Are you ready for our next adventure?"

I turn my face to the water, and I open my journal, putting pen to paper as my mind skips over the endless possibilities on the horizon.

Acknowledgments

As before, I'm going to start by thanking my editor, Holly West, and the rest of the Swoon staff—particularly Lauren, Emily, and Kelsey. You've all been so persistently good at what you do that it's made me better at what I do. A *lot* better. Holly, you deserve an enormous amount of credit for this book. I took this story on a ride down so many different roads before you pulled out your magic compass and helped me find the way. Thank you.

Massive thanks to all my family and friends for buying my book, talking about my book, posting pictures of my book on social media, and telling all your friends to read my book. Having a built-in marketing division that works for free is always a big plus. You're good people, the lot of you.

To my children, who learned to recognize my raised hand as a sign that Mom's on a roll and can't have her thought train derailed right now—thank you for putting up with me always holding a laptop. You let me bounce ideas off you, you turned down the TV when I asked, and you petted my head whenever I mashed it into the keyboard in frustration. This book was the third child you've had to accommodate, and you've done it with an incredible amount of grace. I love you both to my last breath and beyond. You're amazing, and I still can't believe you're mine.

Lastly, I'd like to thank my cats. Even though you drink out of my tea mug, even though you walk across the keyboard while I'm trying to write, having you next to me through this adventure has been a comfort. I promise I'll write you both into my next book if you'll just stop barfing on the carpet.

FEELING BOOKISH?

Turn the page for some

Swoonworthy EXTRAS

The Elephant in the Room

"YOUR TURN," OLIVIA SAYS, PUSHING THE BOWL TOWARD me. It's Saturday afternoon at the Lower Hudson River Museum, and there isn't a soul in the building other than us, so I reach out and pluck what I think is the perfect piece of popcorn for this challenge. Not too oddly shaped and very nearly kernel-free.

"No fair going for the brains," she says, staying my hand. "That makes it too easy."

"The brains?"

"Because some pieces of popcorn look like brains," Ben interjects from his spot at the end of the counter. "Like pale alien brains. But still cruciferous."

"And they have a nearly round shape and the best weight for throwing," Olivia says, reaching for a piece of popcorn. "So we really should add points for level of difficulty if we choose an oblong piece or something."

"Rather than a brains piece," I say solemnly.

"Exactly."

I look at Ben, and then I look at Olivia. Then I look at Ben again. "You two are mental. Popcorn is popcorn, and you're just mad because I'm really good at this and you're not."

Ben slides down the counter and reaches over it, cramming a handful of popcorn in his mouth. "Don't be talking smack," he warns. "I hold the record as of last night. Sixty-two."

"Sixty-two!" I look at him in disbelief. "Nobody can catch sixty-two pieces of popcorn in their mouth in a row."

"He can." Olivia jabs a thumb in Ben's direction as she reaches for a handful.

I raise my eyebrows skeptically. "You're taking his word on that?"

"I saw it." She shrugs. "Seriously impressive. God knows there wasn't anything else to do while they traipsed around that alien planet, fighting off the giant pink baboons."

I stop my hand before it can reach for the popcorn again. "Wait—what? Pink baboons?"

"*Primatus*," Ben says around a mouthful of popcorn. "Bad flick with vampire space baboons. Saw it last night."

"Oh?" I look from Ben to Olivia, who suddenly seems to be very interested in her manicure. "Liv didn't mention that's where she was last night."

"You said you didn't mind if I bagged out of my shift," she defends.

"I thought you were doing homework. And I thought we were going to see that movie."

"We are. We totally are," she reassures me. "I just—I thought I'd prescreen with Ben so I could highlight the best parts for you. And it's not like the museum is crazy busy on a Friday night."

"Or any night," Ben agrees. "Although today's Cub Scout troop was a real hoot."

"Oh, you did not just say that." Olivia points a finger at him in warning. "Don't be bringing your cowboy talk into our nice, genteel northeastern museum."

"Thought you liked my cowboy talk," he says, and for a moment, I appear to have faded into the paneled woodwork of the wall behind me. They finally realize they floated off in their own little bubble—they've been doing that a lot lately—and Ben steps back from the counter. Olivia rubs her hands together nervously.

"I gotta get this grease off my fingers," she says. "We're supposed to be cataloging old magazines today. Wouldn't want to ruin them."

She makes a beeline for the restrooms around the corner, and Ben watches her go. I watch Ben watching her go.

"So." I'm fighting to keep the grin off my face. I have been watching this thing between them germinate for nearly three months now, and I'm loving it.

"So," Ben answers, and he's looking everywhere but me. Finally, I give an exasperated sigh.

"It's okay, you know. I'm not mad about the movie. Well, maybe a little because I wanted to see that flick, but I get it if you two wanted to go together. Alone, I mean."

"It was just a movie," he says, moving to the end of the counter and making a great show of restacking the brochures and pamphlets we have there. "No big deal."

"And you stopped by today just like you do every Saturday because it's no big deal?" I can't help the smile now. But he's still not looking at me.

"I've always liked museums. And my dad's on the board here. . . ."

I can't help it. I throw my hands up and an exasperated *whoosh* of air leaves my lungs.

"Honest to God, Ben! Just say it! You like her! It's okay!"

He freezes in place, caught, and he knows it. He glances nervously toward the hallway, as if Olivia's going to suddenly appear with a giant net and a spear to finish him off.

"Am I being too flirty or something?"

"No, you're being an idiot. I know you like her because I know you. And how you are. When you like someone."

Now it's my turn to not meet his eyes. It's been months since we broke up, and we're still friends, but we haven't hung out like we used to until lately—and always with Olivia. I can see he's trading on his friendship with me to get to her and I am 100 percent fine with that.

"I should just back off," he says. "This is weird, isn't it? It's just weird."

"No!" I shout it a bit too loudly, so I lean out to look around the corner, too. Then I stand up to come around the counter. I grab him by the shoulders.

"Ben. She likes you. She really likes you."

"I like her, too, but it's just weird. I mean, she's your best friend and I'm your ex and also your friend and it's just . . . I don't know. We sort of talked about it last night and it's a thing."

"A thing?"

"It's a thing we have to get around, I mean. You know . . . a thing."

My eyes widen in disbelief. "Are you saying *I'm* the elephant in the room?"

He shrugs. "If the saggy, gray skin fits . . ."

"You're telling me that the only thing keeping you two from moving forward is *me*? Like you both think I'd have a problem with it?"

He rubs his neck and looks at me uncertainly. "You don't? Seriously?"

"I may take to my bed with a fit of the vapors," I say, smacking him on the chest. "You are such an idiot."

He glances at the hallway again. "You think we make a good couple?"

"I *know* you make a good couple," I say. Then I glance at the decorative mirror on the wall in the foyer. "Just about everywhere."

His eyes widen with realization. "Really?"

"Really. I told you I've met Liv in other realities. I know what I'm talking about."

"And you couldn't tell me this before?"

"I didn't want to force it on you. I am keenly aware that our choices make up the sum of our lives. You both deserved to choose each other."

"Thanks, St. Clair." He reaches out to chuck me on the arm.

"Don't mention it. But you're moving slow as molasses uphill in wintertime. Which is a great phrase I learned from you, by the way. Describes you perfectly."

"So I should ask her to go out with me?" he asks. "I mean, eventually?"

"Monogram it on a tea towel. Brand it on your forehead. Just do it." I reach over and grab the stack of pamphlets again. "And stop touching the brochures with your greasy popcorn fingers."

"Seriously?" Olivia rounds the corner, shaking her head. "How many did he wreck?"

"Just the top ones," I say, tossing them in the garbage can. "Go wash your hands before you damage something valuable," I tell him, pointing in the direction of the bathrooms.

"Yes, ma'am." He gives me a sarcastic salute.

"You do know how to use modern plumbing, right?" Olivia teases. "I know it's fairly new to your country."

"No *agua* necessary," he says, reaching out and wiping his greasy fingers on my face.

"Yech!" I jump back, and Olivia makes a clucking noise with her tongue as Ben laughs and lopes off around the corner.

Olivia and I both wait for him to go, and finally she folds her arms and gives me a look.

"Thanks for putting in a word for me."

"You caught that, huh?" I slide into the seat next to her, still rubbing my greasy face. "How much did you hear?"

"From molasses. Uphill in the wintertime."

"It's just frustrating to watch you two circling each other."

"Don't sweat it. I'm gonna ask him out tonight."

I give her an admiring look. "Go, Liv!"

"Why should I have to sit around and wait? You're okay with it, right?"

"I'm more than okay. As long as you realize that if you two ever break up, I'm keeping you."

"If we ever break up, you're helping me bury the body."

I grab a handful of popcorn with a smile. "This is fixing to be one hell of a friendship."

A Coffee Date

between author L. E. Delano and her editor, Holly West
Getting to Know You (A Little More)

Holly West (HW): What book is on your nightstand now?
L. E. DeLano (LD): *The Hate U Give* by Angie Thomas. And oh man, is this a good book. So rich and vibrant and amazing.

HW: What's your favorite word?
LD: *Wonder.* I want to live my life in a perpetual state of it. I want to seek it and find it in everything.

HW: If you could travel in time, where would you go and what would you do?
LD: I'd just want to live a day in the life with some tribal Celt or Neolithic indigenous person. I was at Stonehenge for the first time this year—paid extra to have the private tour and stand among the stones—and oh, the timelessness of it. I wanted to know about the men who hammered away at that stone and the women who fed them and the lessons they taught their children. I want their stories!

HW: Do you have any strange or funny habits? Did you when you were a kid?
LD: My children could write a tome on this, I'm sure. My weirdest one is probably that I talk to myself and always have. A lot. Even in public. It's just the way I reason through things.

HW: Jessa goes to lots of amazing alternate universes and sees a lot of different versions of herself. If you could fall through a mirror into a different version of *your* life, what would you want to experience?

LD: I'd probably be the me who took a fellow castmate up on her offer to share her apartment in New York, so I could follow my dream and do theater. Then again, if I'd done that, I may not be sitting here talking about my books today. But it would be fun to know what "might have been."

The Swoon Reads Experience (Continues!)

HW: What's your favorite thing about being a Swoon Reads author so far?

LD: The sense of community, for sure! The readers, the editors, my fellow Swoon authors—there's just so much love and support. It really is wonderful.

HW: How has the Swoon Reads community impacted your experiences as an author?

LD: I have had the best experience, hands down. I know I wasn't just chosen on some arbitrary whim, I was read and hashed over and selected because enough people saw something worth reading.

HW: Did *Traveler* being published change your life?

LD: Most definitely. Now and forever, I am a published author. And I put out a book I can be really proud of. No more dreaming about it, wishing for it, talking about "someday"—I did it. There is no way I can put that feeling into words.

HW: Do you have any advice for aspiring authors on the site?
LD: Put up your best work, then when the dust settles, realize that your best work is an evolving thing. Feedback is a valuable tool, and not just yours—read the comments on all the books. Readers know what they like and they aren't hesitant to let you know that.

The Writing Life

HW: What were some of your main inspirations for *Dreamer*?
LD: The original idea for the series was inspired by a childhood encounter with *Through the Looking-Glass*, but *Dreamer* has a theme song. "With a Little Help from My Friends" by the Beatles. I wanted this book to be about Jessa really coming into her own, and in her case, learning to trust herself—and her selves.

HW: Second books are notoriously difficult. What was the hardest part about writing *Dreamer*?
LD: Everything. Honest to God, everything. We'd done such major editing on *Traveler* that *Dreamer* was nothing like I'd originally imagined it to be. I had to write it almost from scratch, in terms of where I'd planned to take the plot. I went down a lot of wrong streets before I found my way with it.

HW: What's your process? Are you an outliner or do you just start at the beginning and make it up as you go?
LD: I'm a "pantser" for the most part. I start out with a rough outline and just get writing. Somewhere around midpoint, I

stop and write the ending, then I work backward to make every-thing fit.

HW: What do you want readers to remember about your books?
LD: Adventure! Of course, I want them to remember the romance, but a good romance should be an adventure, don't you think?

ONE MISTAKEN IDENTITY LEADS TO OUT-OF-THIS-WORLD TROUBLE.

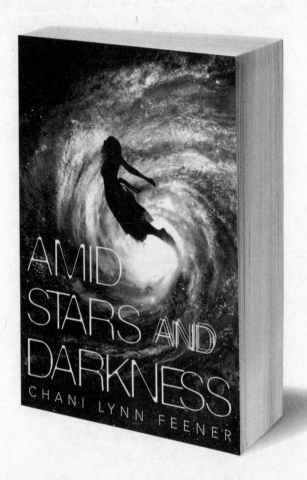

An ordinary teenage girl is kidnapped by an alien bodyguard and forced to pretend to be a princess to stop an intergalactic war.

RUCKUS AND PETTUS led Delaney off the ship and down a long hallway that attached to the castle. They moved quickly, giving her only enough time to catch glimpses of the place as they wound their way through the vast halls.

The smell was strange, foreign, a bit like mothballs and evergreen, and she trailed after Ruckus quietly, checking out the guards they passed from the corners of her eyes. And they passed many.

At each entry and exit point, there were always at least two guards. They stood tall, shoulders back, sort of like the ones she'd seen guarding the queen of England in all the pictures. Except they didn't have poofy hats, and she found she sort of wished they did. It would certainly ease some of the tension.

Their uniforms were similar to Ruckus's in that they wore charcoal military pants tucked into boots. The buttoned-up jackets were different, however, skintight and the color of moss, with heavy gold accents strewn about. She'd expected to see more of the silver weapon Pettus had used back in the alley against the Tars, but if they had any weapons on them, they were well hidden.

Everyone dropped their chins to their chests in a bow when she passed, but the move was mechanical, like toy soldiers, and it creeped her out.

They finally stopped at a set of tall golden doors, and Ruckus reached for the handle.

"Wait here," he told her and Pettus, opening it just enough for him to slip through without exposing the inside of the room.

"He needs to brief them," Pettus explained quietly. "It's best that he does that alone first."

Right, because it was doubtful they'd react well to the news a human had been brought in their daughter's stead.

Delaney kept silent, partly because she was unable to think of anything to say, and partly because she was afraid that if she did, she'd lose it. The more details she paid attention to in this castle, the more it sunk in that she was no longer on Earth. The walls were a material that'd been made to appear like wood but wasn't. She could see the metallic sheen of it from where she stood a few feet away.

Everything was done in earthy and metallic tones; even the lighting had a gold sheen to it.

The sudden opening of the door had her jumping, and she bit her bottom lip in embarrassment when she was met with Ruckus. His facial expression was tight, and he merely nodded at her and angled his head over his shoulder.

Taking a deep breath, she braced herself and then stepped beneath the archway.

The room was an office, with a fireplace to the right of

the double doors and a small, round black table to the far right, big enough to seat five. At the center, positioned between two large bay windows that overlooked the sprawling yard, was a desk three times the size of any she'd seen before. Her gaze immediately landed on a tall man seated behind it; he had the same inky hair as Olena. A woman stood closely by his side, hands clasped before her.

There were no computers that she was used to, but a glass screen sat propped at an angle in front of where the man was sitting. She couldn't make out what he was watching, and there was no sound, but movement on the other side of the glass clued her in that it was a video of sorts.

Ruckus came up to her then, lightly touching her elbow as he held his other hand out toward the pair. "May I introduce the Basileus Magnus Ond, and the Basilissa Tilda Ond."

Delaney wasn't sure what to do, so she tried a bow, grateful for Ruckus's steadying grip on her arm when she almost wobbled. She wasn't sure how much longer she could stand there, pretending everything was fine, and hoped this conversation would end quickly.

She hoped they'd put her directly on a ship headed back home.

"Ander Ruckus tells us your name is Delaney." The Basileus's voice was sharp, though she got the feeling he was attempting—poorly—not to intimidate her.

"Delaney Grace, sir." Was it appropriate to call him sir? He didn't correct her.

Both he and the Basilissa took a moment to openly inspect her. There wasn't much to look at, of course, seeing as how she appeared exactly as their daughter did on the outside, but she held still and waited for them to finish.

"The Sutter did this?" The Basilissa, Tilda, pursed her lips in either disgust or confusion. Delaney couldn't tell which.

"It was his device," Ruckus said carefully, "but it was stolen by the Lissa, who used it without Sutter Gibus's knowledge."

"And Trystan doesn't seem to know?"

"If he did," the Basileus said with a grunt, "he would have declared war by now. No, she must have fooled him."

His stare was making her even more uncomfortable, and Delaney barely resisted the urge to clear her throat pointedly. Instead she held her head high and tried to make her voice as calm and respectful as possible.

"I'd just like to go home," she told them.

"This is not an ideal situation," the Basileus said then, "and I assure you we will be taking steps to right the wrong my daughter has done us all. However"—he folded his hands across the surface of his desk slowly—"it has also come to my attention that we have no real knowledge of where she is. As you know, Earth is a big planet. Therefore—"

She felt the blood draining from her face before he'd even finished his sentence.

"We simply cannot allow you to leave."

Check out more books chosen for publication by readers like you.

L. E. DeLano is a blogger and autism advocate under her alternate moniker, Ellie DeLano. She comes equipped with a "useless" theater degree that has opened doors for her in numerous ways. Though mostly raised in New Mexico, she now calls Pennsylvania home. When she's not writing, which is almost never, she's binge-watching Netflix and trying her best not to be an unwitting pawn in her cats' quests for world domination. She is the author of *Traveler* and its sequel, *Dreamer*.

ledelano.com